"Do you think we can we still be real friends?"

His answer was a stare that made her stomach flip. "What if told you that I don't want to fake break up?"

"Oh, Flynn," she quipped, trying to lighten his mood, because did he realize what he was saying here? "Everyone knows fake long-distance relationships are tough."

"No, Iris, I mean I want to end this stupid charade right now."

"Flynn, we can't break up yet. We're having dinner with your ex-wife and we still have kayaking with my boss tomorrow and..." Her words trailed off as he stepped closer.

Iris froze, her pulse ratcheting up, rocketing into overdrive. Flynn stood before her, strong arms settling on either side of her. His face was only inches from hers. There was no mistaking he was going to kiss her and Iris knew that if he did, this time, he'd claim her heart forever.

Dear Reader,

Growing up in a big family is awesome. Growing up in a big family is awful. Being the youngest is the worst. Being the youngest is the best. Speaking from experience, I can assure you all of the above statements are true. Perspective. It's a powerful and wonderful thing. It can also be hard and challenging. I'm often amazed at how drastically different my childhood memories are from my sisters and brothers.

Iris James is the youngest in her family, too. Born premature, she had medical problems that made it impossible for her to keep up with her active, athletic siblings. She made up for it in other ways, but it left her a bit removed from the family dynamic. To make matters worse, she grew up in Rankins, a small town in Alaska—a place her entire family adores and embraces almost to the point of worship. Iris doesn't. Full of painful and awkward childhood memories, she doesn't like much about the place, except for her old friend Flynn Ramsey. Flynn she likes a little too much.

Now a doctor, Flynn wants only to practice medicine in Rankins, prove to Iris that her dislike of her hometown is unwarranted and show her that he's the right man for her. It's just a simple matter of changing her perspective. Which shouldn't be too difficult, right?

Thanks so much for reading!

Carol

HEARTWARMING

In the Doctor's Arms

—

Carol Ross

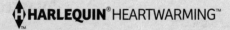

Recycling programs
for this product may
not exist in your area.

ISBN-13: 978-1-335-51059-4

In the Doctor's Arms

Copyright © 2019 by Carol Ross

Printed in U.S.A.

Carol Ross lives in the Pacific Northwest with her husband and two dogs. She is a graduate of Washington State University. When not writing, or thinking about writing, she enjoys reading, running, hiking, skiing, traveling and making plans for the next adventure to subject her sometimes reluctant but always fun-loving family to. Carol can be contacted at carolrossauthor.com and via Facebook at Facebook.com/carolrossauthor, Twitter, @_carolross, and Instagram, @carolross__.

Books by Carol Ross

Harlequin Heartwarming

Summer at the Shore
Christmas at the Cove

Seasons of Alaska

Bachelor Remedy
A Heartwarming Thanksgiving
"Autumn at Jasper Lake"
A Family Like Hannah's
If Not for a Bee
A Case for Forgiveness
Mountains Apart

Return of the Blackwell Brothers

The Rancher's Twins

Visit the Author Profile page
at Harlequin.com for more titles.

For Jill, Julie & Tammy.

My fellow founding members of the TJCJ Club. You are my people. Thank you for making my childhood, my memories and my perspective so much fun.

PS: I'm also glad we survived.

CHAPTER ONE

"BERING JUST CALLED. We've got a four-party transport showing up in fifteen."

"Is it an emergency?" Iris James grimaced and glanced up at her brother Tag standing in the doorway of her office. Tag was the owner of Copper Crossing Air Transport, the business where Iris was temporarily employed. In addition to conveying goods, animals and people of just about any shape and size all over the state of Alaska, Copper Crossing was contracted with the hospital in Rankins to handle emergency medical transport. Tag's fiancée, Ally Mowak, was the hospital liaison in charge of arranging trauma flights. Iris should have heard from Ally by now if that was the case.

"Nope. No rush. It's for some friends of his. He's sending you the passenger manifest right now." Their cousin Bering James owned James Guide & Outfitter Service, a company that provided a variety of excursions to remote wilderness locales. Bering utilized Tag's services to transport clients.

"Must be some friends," Iris said, curious now. It was the first week of July, and their cousin was booked solid through the summer months and well into fall. It didn't matter how wealthy, famous or important, Bering treated all clients with equal respect and consideration. But he always left a little room in his schedule for family and close friends.

"Yep. Very special. He's guiding this one himself. It's a group from Seattle, a girls' trip."

"A girls' trip? Doesn't anyone go to the spa around here?" she joked. "Or take in a movie or a show?" Of course, there wasn't a spa within miles and miles of Rankins, Alaska. Or a movie theater for that matter. She missed Washington, DC. With any luck, she'd be back there soon, with a "good riddance" to Rankins. This place might be her hometown, but it was far from her ideal.

Tag chuckled. "Ally and I go to the movies."

Iris gave him a playful glare. "Not everyone has their own fleet of planes to pick up and fly their fiancée to a movie whenever the mood strikes."

"I know. You should get one. It's very cool."

Iris had to agree. It was pretty cool. She loved

airplanes and she enjoyed working around them and for her brother. Okay, so there were a select few things she'd miss about the town—her family, her job, her friend Flynn Ramsey. Well, she'd sort of miss Flynn. Probably. But her feelings for Flynn were complex and best left hidden, deep in her emotional well. Inconveniently, Iris was a bridesmaid in Tag and Ally's upcoming wedding and Flynn was the man of honor. In typical small-town USA fashion, Flynn happened to be Ally's best friend. Thus, all this wedding business meant spending undue time with Flynn, where said emotional well kept getting deeper, those feelings more difficult to ignore.

Her email pinged with a message from Bering. "Got it," she said and hit Print.

Tag ducked back out and jogged across the tarmac toward the hangar, presumably to get the plane ready.

Iris took the paper from the printer tray and glanced at the four names listed—Anne Specter, Chloe Bennet, Kayleen Carlisle, and Summer Davis. What in the world would possess a group of women to spend a weekend fishing and hiking in the wilds of Alaska? Then again, why would anyone—man, woman, child, visiting space alien—knowingly fly directly away from the safety and comforts of everyday living and into the bush?

Unlike the other members of her large family, and pretty much the rest of the town, Iris didn't connect with most things quintessentially "Alaskan." Camping, fishing, clam-digging, hiking, hunting, kayaking? No, thank you. Electricity was invented so the entire human race didn't have to camp anymore. She didn't care for seafood. She abhorred blisters, was terrified of bears and avoided frigid water. And then there were the mosquitoes. Let's just say bug repellent was her signature scent by necessity. Add in her inherent lack of coordination and things got ugly.

All of this was a good reminder of how much she didn't fit in here. She never had.

It was bad enough to be the odd one out in her own family, where people loved her, but school had been its own special kind of torment. Skinny, awkward, homely, ugly, weird, nerd—yep, she'd been called all of those and worse. Ugh. Why was she thinking about this? She'd thought those days were behind her. And they were. Of course they were. For the most part.

Since going away to college seven years ago, her visits home had been infrequent—the longest one had lasted a week. She'd fly in, visit her mom and dad, brothers and sisters, while doing her best to avoid the general population of Rankins, and then fly back to school.

In the supply room, she stopped to check the passenger list for allergies or other health concerns. She did a double take as she noted the ages of the women—73, 77, 74, 79. Iris felt her heart sink. She hoped this wasn't one of those cases where one of the ladies was terminally ill and fulfilling a bucket-list thing. Was that why Tag had called them special?

Approximately twelve minutes later, Iris had all the normal items they handed out to passengers—water, snacks, airsick bags, earplugs, safety information. Even though Bering hadn't requested them of her, she had a few extras waiting in the wings, including a wheelchair and a walker in case anyone needed assistance boarding. She wondered if she should have secured some insulin or possibly a nitro pill. Since Bering had arranged the trip personally, surely he'd be aware of any medical issues. Still, flying in small planes was no joke. If these women weren't prepared, she'd make sure they were.

Iris headed outside to see a blue full-size pickup pulling into the far edge of the parking lot. It stopped in the area designated for "long-term" vehicle stays. Four people climbed out. Squinting toward the group, Iris watched them all nimbly move around to the back of the vehicle. One of them let down the tailgate, another hopped into the bed like a woman at least two decades younger than the manifest showed and began handing down packs and gear. Someone else jogged to the front passenger door, rummaged around and then returned to the rear of the vehicle. This couldn't be the right group, could it? Iris checked the paper wondering if the number *7* was supposed to be a *5* or even a *4*? Regardless, she reminded herself, she needed to do her job.

She hurried over to lend a hand, but the foursome was already headed in her direction, packs hoisted and draped over their shoulders. Talking, laughing, striding confidently forward, they radiated positive energy. Iris found herself smiling as they approached.

An athletic-looking woman wearing green cargo pants and a pink, long-sleeved Henley beneath a tan fishing vest greeted her. "Hey! You must be Iris." She wore a gray bucket hat decorated with an assortment of fishing flies.

"Yes, hi! You must be Bering's friends?"

"Yep, that's us. I'm Anne. Lovely to meet

you." Gesturing to her right, she introduced the rest of the group, all similarly outfitted. "This is Chloe, Kayleen and Summer."

As they chatted, Iris wondered if it would even be possible to feel like a bigger ninny that she did. By "special," her brother had clearly meant "awesome." He could have given her a heads-up. She threw up a silent thank-you that she hadn't actually brought out the walker. These women were all energetic, enthusiastic and prepared. Not to mention smart and funny.

Anne, she learned, was an English professor, Chloe a doctor, Kayleen a medical researcher and Summer a restaurateur. Chloe and Kayleen were both semiretired while Summer claimed to be "mostly" retired. Although, as the owner of six restaurants, Iris imagined that was an exaggeration. Anne proclaimed that she would work forever. After ten minutes in their company, Iris wanted to hang out with them forever. Albeit without the backpacking, fishing, bear-and-mosquito-laden activities.

"Bering said you're only here for the summer, Iris. What do you do?" Chloe asked.

"Well, I just got my PhD in economics. I'm hoping to get a job in my field soon. Not that I don't love working here for my brother."

"Academia?" Anne asked hopefully.

"Not at this point, although I do enjoy teaching. My dream job is to work at a think tank. I've sent my résumé to a few in the DC area." Iris didn't add that her sights were set ultimately on The Frieze Group, one of the most prestigious in the country. They weren't currently hiring but that hadn't stopped her from sending in her résumé. She'd even turned down a few offers from other firms in the preceding weeks, hoping to hear from the prized think tank. Her self-imposed deadline was Tag and Ally's rapidly approaching wedding. After that, she'd take the best offer that came her way.

Tag joined them.

"Ladies, welcome! I'm so excited to see you all again."

"Tag, hi!" Anne gushed and gave him a hug. The other women followed suit.

After a few minutes of catching up, Anne asked, "How's Hazel? Last post I saw she was in Nepal."

Iris smiled at the mention of her fellow triplet sister. Their brother Seth rounded out the trio and was currently traveling with Hazel. "You know Hazel?"

"Yes, that's how we met Bering. Five years ago, the four of us were climbing Kilimanjaro and Hazel was in our group. Talk turned to fly-fishing and she hooked us up with Bering. We've been back every year since."

Hazel, in direct opposition to Iris, was an avid adventurer. As a travel writer and blogger, she'd even managed to make it her profession.

"She's great," Iris said, answering the original enquiry. "She has been in Nepal with our brother Seth. They're due home tomorrow. I'm sure Hazel will have a post ready to launch." Hazel's blog had acquired a huge following.

"Fabulous! Can't wait to read it."

Iris enjoyed reading about her sister's adventures, too, even though she worried incessantly about her safety.

Tag said, "Bering told me you ladies have been backpacking in Denali?"

"We were," Anne answered. "Chloe had never hiked the Mount Eielson loop and none of us had done Kesugi Ridge Trail, so we conquered them both in addition to some of our old haunts. And since it's my birthday trip, we decided to squeeze in some fly-fishing at the end. We got lucky with the weather and finished Denali a little quicker than we anticipated, so I called Bering and here we are. Now we get two extra days fly-fishing."

"That's great," Tag said.

"So," Kayleen said, grinning at Tag, "you gonna let me land that plane of yours?"

Tag peered at her carefully and Iris could see that he was trying not to grin. "You did not," he said.

"Oh, yes I did."

"It's your own fault, Tag," Chloe said. "You threw it down. We all heard it."

Iris must have looked confused because Anne explained, "Last summer when we were here, Tag issued Kayleen a challenge. He told her if she got her pilot's license he'd let her land his plane."

"What?" Iris gaped at the woman.

Summer told the story. "We had some bad weather and the landing was a little rough, to say the least. We were all holding our collective breath. Tag got us on the ground with some bumps. After the plane came to a stop we were all quiet for a long moment, thanking our lucky stars and our skilled pilot. Finally, Kayleen says, 'Tag, what was up with that landing? Did you just get your license yesterday?' Well, of course, we all screamed with laughter." Summer flipped a thumb toward Tag. "But your brother here made the mistake of responding with 'Kayleen, you go get your license and next year I'll let you show me how to land this plane.'"

Chloe chimed in, "He didn't realize whom he was speaking to."

Iris gaped at Kayleen, her new idol. "So, just like that, you decided to get your pilot's license?" She added a finger snap. Iris wanted to also point out that Kayleen was in her seventies, but that would be obvious and possibly ageist, even though she didn't mean it that way. She felt nothing but mad respect for the woman. For all four of them.

"Well, none of us have time to wait, do we? Nailed my solo flight on my seventy-fourth birthday."

"We were all cheering from the runway," Summer said. "It was so exciting. Now we go flying almost every week."

"Wow," Iris said. "Congratulations."

"Thank you." Kayleen grinned. "It was pretty amazing."

"I can't imagine how thrilling that must have been. And…challenging."

Kayleen seemed to be studying her now, something that could only be described as mischief lighting her expression. "Don't let your brother fool you, it's not as tricky as it looks." Planting her hands on her hips, she turned toward Tag. "You should make the same offer to your sister." To Iris, she said, "What do you say, Iris? Are you up for it?"

"Oh, no. I'm not…" She was about to say "interested in flying," but that wasn't quite accurate. "I couldn't…" It had more to do with how that daredevil behavior wasn't in her makeup. Her siblings had gotten those genes. Although piloting wasn't exactly reckless, it was a learned skill. Still, it was a terrifying one, and Iris avoided anything terrifying when at all possible.

"Of course you can!" Kayleen exclaimed.

"Why not?" Summer demanded at the same time.

Iris grinned and shook her head, because in that moment she couldn't think of a reason that wouldn't make her sound like what she was—fearful.

Tag, hazel eyes flashing with a mix of encouragement and challenge, smiled at Iris. "If Iris gets her pilot license, I will give her an airplane."

"You heard the man," Kayleen said. "Get your butt in that pilot's seat. It's exactly where women like us belong."

Iris laughed, but the yearning she felt made

her heart hurt a little. "Well, ladies, we'll see," she answered cryptically, because if there was one thing Iris did excel at it was being cryptic.

CHAPTER TWO

"How you doing, Gabe?" Dr. Flynn Ramsey asked his six-year-old patient. It was his day off, but he'd made the trip in after receiving this urgent call.

"Oh-ay, I ink." The boy's answer was garbled due to the fact that his teeth were superglued together thanks to an experiment gone wrong with his brother, Finn. Gabe's head was under the faucet while the nurse, Anita, flushed his mouth with warm water and vegetable oil. Finn stood next to his brother, keeping one hand protectively on his knee.

They, along with their mom, Janie Hollings, were in the exam room of the newly renamed Ramsey Family Medical Clinic. Flynn's grandfather, Dr. "Doc" Ramsey, thought the double meaning so clever—the Ramsey family treating families. It was safe to say Doc might be a little proud to have his grandson working with him. The feeling was mutual.

Flynn interpreted Gabe's response as "Okay,

I think." He rephrased just to be sure. "You're doing all right?"

"Uh-huh." Gabe nodded.

Finn answered for his brother. "He says yes."

"Thank you, Finn." Flynn patted Gabe's shoulder. "Hang in there, kiddo, you're going to be just fine." Then he looked at Janie. Janie had been several years ahead of him in school, but Flynn knew her because she was a James, which made her Iris's cousin. "Good news, Mom, superglue isn't toxic in this small amount. The bad news is, it is waterproof. That's why it's a little tricky to get his teeth unstuck. But the glue will eventually loosen with the vegetable oil and warm water."

Janie heaved a relieved sigh. "Thank you, Dr. Ramsey. Aidan said it wasn't harmful, but I felt like I had to bring him in." Janie's husband, Aidan, was a scientist, currently out of town on a research project. Janie had been incredibly calm when they'd shown up this morning considering her six-year-old had glued his teeth together. Then again, as a mother of five children, including two teenaged boys, a set of twins and a new baby girl, that wasn't much of a surprise. Motherhood had a unique way of channeling anxiety into action.

Flynn turned toward the boys again. "So, no more experimenting, right, guys?"

"Right," Finn answered for both of them.

"Make sure an adult is around first," he added helpfully.

Jane gave her head a little shake. "Thanks, Dr. Ramsey, for instructing them on the finer points, when they know that they're not supposed to play with it in the first place."

"Oops," Flynn muttered, but he could see Janie's lips twitching with a smile.

"Also, boys, listen to your mother and don't use any glue without first asking for permission."

Janie rolled her eyes.

Flynn stifled his laugh. This was what he loved about practicing medicine in a small town; he'd never get bored with the variety of cases, and helping patients was often synonymous with helping friends.

"I think we've about got it," Anita said from her spot at the sink.

"They're free!" Gabe confirmed. "My teeth are free, but they feel weird and bumpy."

Flynn stepped toward him. "Pieces of that glue will probably stick around on your teeth for a bit, so be careful not to rub your tongue raw on any sharp edges. Let me take a look."

Flynn examined the boy's mouth and teeth, assured everyone that all was well and left the nurse to finish up.

In the hall, he pulled his phone out of his pocket. He needed to be out at Copper Crossing's airfield in a half hour for the flight to Anchorage. Nervous energy rose inside of him at the thought because this was the day. The day he was going to…do something. Something to let Iris know how he felt about her. Shopping for a bridesmaid dress today would provide the perfect opportunity for…for the as-yet-to-be-seized-upon moment. He blew out an anxious breath and texted Iris that he was on schedule and would be leaving the office soon.

Ally was like a little sister to him and he was honored to take on the role as head brides-person, or man of honor, as Iris liked to call it. He was taking his job seriously and at this point he was basically an amateur wedding expert. He'd already helped Ally find her gown and he'd spent a lot of time researching bridesmaid dresses, too. But he'd shamelessly admit that the added motivation of spending time with Iris made the job much more palatable.

Finding the door to his grandfather's office slightly ajar, Flynn tapped on the jamb and slowly pushed open the door. Seated behind a large oak desk, his grandfather, Ted "Doc" Ramsey, looked up from the mound of paperwork in front of him. Other than his cap of thick white hair, currently in need of a trim, no one would have ever guessed the man had passed his seventh decade.

He gave Flynn a smile and a wave. "Come on in."

"Just need to grab my stuff. I'm taking off."

"Going to Anchorage with Iris, right?"

His grin was wily, and Flynn felt affection well up inside of him. Flynn knew he wouldn't be half the person he was if it wasn't for this man, much less a physician finishing up his residency in family practice.

Navigating his way through a wildly unstable childhood with volatile parents at the helm, for Flynn, his grandparents had been the only constant. His grandmother had passed away while he was in ninth grade and his parents had allowed him to stay with his grandfather for the remaining years of high school. Spending time with Doc had grounded him and inspired his interest in medicine.

"I'm going to Anchorage with Iris, Ally and Tag, yes."

"Get your A game on, kiddo. And maybe a

little cologne, too, so you don't smell like antiseptic after working here this morning."

"You know, you could be a little less obvious in making your wishes clear."

"Yeah, well, I'm not sure that you could," Doc quipped.

Flynn tipped back his head and laughed. "Touché," he said.

It was true that his increasingly unsubtle attempts continued to fall flat where Iris was concerned.

"Since we're on the subject of your love life, I'd like a grandchild or two."

"It's not a subject I want to be on. Besides—" pointing a finger at himself, Flynn pretended to look offended "—*I* am your grandchild."

"Babies," Doc clarified with a chuckle. "I want some great-grandkids to spoil. Caleb is getting one."

Flynn narrowed his gaze and tried not to laugh. "You want me to have a baby because your best friend is getting one?" Caleb Cedar was an attorney. His grandson, Jonah, was also an attorney and Caleb's law partner. Jonah was married to Shay, Iris's oldest sister. After enduring several miscarriages, Jonah and Shay were expecting their first child. Everyone was pulling for them.

"Yep."

"You have no shame, you are aware of that, right?"

"Of course." Doc executed a perfectly contrived shrug of innocence. "Never claimed to have any. Although, I wouldn't want you to have a baby with just anyone. I want it noted that I never even mentioned babies when you were married to Sonya."

"Noted and appreciated." Doc hadn't needed to mention it—Sonya had mentioned it enough for everyone. The subject had heightened Flynn's misgivings and contributed to their breakup. Although Flynn had since realized they should never have married in the first place.

Nobody should get married while they're in medical school, especially to someone else also in medical school. Who was diametrically unsuited to you. With priorities that were the polar opposite of your own. He wasn't going to think about any of that now. The nightmare that was Sonya was now more than two years in the past. Although lately, said nightmare had been reappearing in the form of real-life texts and phone calls.

"Speaking of Jonah, he delivered some paperwork about the clinic when you're ready to have a look."

Flynn had a year and a half left of his residency at the local hospital. They'd worked out a deal where Flynn could work off his medical-school bills and eventually take over Doc's practice. Not only was the offer too good to refuse, but it was also a dream come true. Working with his grandfather and settling in Rankins had been his goal ever since he could remember.

"Definitely. As soon as the wedding is over, we'll sit down with him and review the details." If things went as planned, he and Iris would be working out some details, too.

"That's what I was thinking."

Flynn collected his jacket and bag before walking over and giving his grandfather's shoulder a squeeze. "I'll see you tomorrow."

He knew it was selfish, but he was glad Iris hadn't accepted a job offer yet. He may have screwed up when they were teenagers by not appreciating what was right before his eyes, but he was doing his best to rectify that now. He only hoped it wasn't too late. If he could get confirmation that she returned his feelings, he could make the case for her to stay in Rankins.

All he needed was a little more time.

"WHAT TEST?" TAG ASKED, looking over Iris's shoulder at the computer monitor on her desk. They were in the office at Copper Crossing waiting for Ally and Flynn to arrive so they could all fly to Anchorage.

Iris explained, "I need to start interviewing for my replacement. I've compiled a test that I'm going to administer to determine if applicants have certain specific traits necessary to do this job."

"Seriously?"

"Seriously. It'll weed out unqualified applicants and reduce superfluous interviews."

"Are you going to make me take this test and then fire me from my own company?" he said wryly.

"No, of course not," Iris reassured him with a breezy wave. "As the owner, you're grandfathered in," she joked. "You might be demoted, but not fired."

Tag peered at her again. "I'm not sure if that's funny or not."

She laughed. "Trust me, I know what I'm doing. This job isn't as easy as it looks. There's a lot of decision making that requires prioritizing and efficient time management. This is important work that you're doing here, brother."

Tag chuckled. "What am I going to do without you?"

"I have no idea. But it's possible you might need to hire two people to replace me." Iris was only partially teasing about that. She'd taken on a lot of Tag's duties as her own to free up more of his time for essential plane-related duties. She worried about the new employee handling the workload.

"Speaking of that, the schedule is all set for my honeymoon and everything, right?" Copper Crossing was scaling back transports in the coming weeks due to Tag's impending nuptials and the honeymoon to follow.

"Working on it. Stop worrying. Cricket and I have it handled." Cricket. Iris felt a stirring of excitement as an idea formed. A pilot, and also a member of the wedding party, Cricket Blackburn was one of Tag's best friends. He worked for Copper Crossing, piloting during the summer months. In the winter, he operated JB Heli-Ski with their sister Hannah. He gave flying lessons in his spare time and had offered to teach Iris many times. For the next month it would just be Iris and Cricket around here on light duty.

Before she could change her mind, Iris

tapped out a text: If that offer of flying lessons still stands I'd like to start ASAP. Top secret.

He responded immediately: You got it. We'll start tomorrow. These lips are sealed.

She grinned because she knew he had the same thought as she did about Tag being scarce for the next month or so. She also knew she could trust Cricket.

Ally came through the door. "Hey, guys."

Iris watched her brother light up with all the force of a meteor shower at the sight of his fiancée.

"Flynn's still coming with us, right?" Tag asked, slipping an arm around Ally's waist.

No matter how she tried to squelch her stomach flipping at the mention of Flynn's name, Iris always failed. The flip was both good and bad. Like a perfectly executed series of somersaults that left you exhilarated in the moment, yet battered and sore in the aftermath. It was a flip that only a decade-old unrequited crush could instigate. She and Flynn had been friendly in high school, but Iris wouldn't have called them friends per se. They'd been more like study buddies. They'd run in different circles, or they would have if Iris had a circle.

Flynn's circle, on the other hand, was huge and included her brother Seth. Flynn was athletic, popular and smart. Iris was smart, too, but awkward, and not popular. The smartness was how they'd connected, both of them taking advanced classes, where they'd amicably competed for top honors. A shared study hall had turned into regular after-school homework sessions. To Iris, Flynn had been the bright spot to an otherwise miserable high-school experience. She'd secretly and desperately crushed on him. To Flynn, she'd been an entertaining distraction, a way for him to discuss diverse subjects that his buddies weren't as interested in. Flynn had been nice to her, but he'd never been into her. He'd been too busy dating all the girls in his circle—the beautiful, popular ones. The ones who, adding salt to a perpetually raw wound, had contributed to Iris's misery.

Although Iris and Flynn hadn't kept in touch after high school, Seth remained friends with Flynn, so she'd hear about him occasionally. After nearly a decade without seeing him, she'd assumed her feelings had faded. Since she'd been back home they'd reconnected and gotten to know each other on a new level. Being with Flynn felt easy and fun and she'd officially consider what they had now a friendship. So instead of fading, her feelings had…changed. Grown, matured, mellowed even. And yet, remnants of that crush remained. Like broken glass, her heart seemed forever shattered, the damage going mostly unnoticed until nudged by the man himself.

"As far as I know," Ally said.

"Hold on, I heard a text come through a few minutes ago." Glancing down, she smiled when she saw a message from "Dr. Hottie McBrilliant," along with his adorably goofy selfie icon. He'd entered his own contact information into her phone when she'd returned to Rankins.

She read the message: Hey bff! Superexcited to go to Anchorage and pick out your bridesmaid dress. We should make our hair and nail appointments! What do you think about artichoke dip and fondue for the bachelorette party? On my way in 5. C U soon.

He'd added a string of emojis—hearts, a dress, a hand with painted nails, flowers, a kissy face, a wedge of cheese and, for some reason, a palm tree. Probably the closest thing he could find to an artichoke. Iris laughed out loud. Leave it to Flynn to boost her mood even as a fresh pack of butterflies awakened, and then somersaulted mercilessly, at the notion of spending the day with him. See? Complicated.

She could do this, she reminded herself—it

was just a day of shopping. Plus, Ally and Tag would be there to provide a buffer.

"Yep," Iris informed Tag, "he's on his way."

A FEW HOURS LATER, which included the relatively short flight from Rankins and a car ride from the private airfield where Tag landed his plane, Iris, Flynn, Tag and Ally were gathered on the sidewalk in Anchorage.

Tag kissed Ally and then headed off to conquer his own list of non-wedding-related errands. Iris and Flynn listened while Ally outlined the plans for the rest of the afternoon. "Tag is picking up the lamb's quarters and some other items, and I'm going to get the salmon. Then he's going to meet me at Maverick's Sporting Goods. You guys text when you're through and we'll meet up for dinner before the movie."

Iris took a second to absorb this information before gaping at her soon-to-be sister-in-law. "Wait a sec, you're not shopping with us?"

"I don't want to. That's why Flynn is here."

"Ally, seriously, it's your wedding. You don't want to pick out my bridesmaid dress? Or at least approve of it?"

"Is that bad? You know I hate shopping. I'm fine with whatever you choose."

"Salmon and lamb's quarters, huh?" Flynn repeated, seemingly unsurprised by Ally's statement, making Iris think he'd already known he was going to be stuck shopping with her all afternoon. The guy had been a trouper throughout this wedding ordeal.

"Yes," Ally answered Flynn.

Flynn said, "This is going to be some spread at your nuptials. Is your friend Coda still going to roast the salmon over an open fire in the Native tradition? I love that. Get plenty of it. I don't remember lamb being on the menu."

Ally grinned. "Yes, he is. And there will be plenty, but this isn't for the wedding. It's lamb's quarters, and it's for my grandfather."

Then Ally looked back at Iris. "Flynn is better at this dress stuff than I am. He picked out mine." With a quick wave, she was off.

Flynn frowned thoughtfully.

Iris chuckled at a clearly confused Flynn and then explained, "Smoked salmon for the quiche our mom is making for the rehearsal brunch. And lamb's quarters as in the medicinal plant, not the ruminant that you make into chops and consume."

"Ah." He nodded. "That makes so much more sense."

They started walking and Iris said, "Do you

have any idea how much I love that woman? Ally is the only bride I've ever met who does not care about her own wedding beyond who the groom is."

"I know. Better than the opposite, though, right?"

"What do you mean, like one of those bridezillas you see on TV who obsesses about everything?"

He laughed, but it was a weak one for Flynn. Iris looked up to find him staring straight ahead, a rare frown in place. After a beat, he seemed to realize she was watching. He smiled down at her, dimples lethally attractive as usual, but the normal spark in his eyes had dimmed.

Refocusing on their path, he said, "Yeah, or like obsessing about the wrong thing."

Iris wondered if he was talking about his own failed marriage. He never talked about it and she couldn't bring herself to ask.

They continued in silence until Flynn stopped walking. Iris realized they were standing outside a charming little boutique that specialized in formal wear—cocktail, bridesmaid, prom and party dresses.

Gaze focused intently on her now, he asked, "What about you? What kind of wedding do you want?"

"Me? Ha. No kind."

"Oh, come on," Flynn urged. "Don't tell me you didn't dream about your wedding when you were a little girl."

"Not really. The only thing I ever dreamed about was getting out of Alaska and going away to school." *And that I looked like Ashley Eller so that you'd notice more than my math homework.*

"You managed that in a big way, huh, Dr. James? But what about now? What kind of wedding would you want now that you're all grown up?"

Iris stared at him, relieved that the unmistakable twinkle was back in his luminous brown eyes, even if they were trained on her in that way that made her brain fog over. She did not want to have this conversation, and especially not with him. She was pretty sure their opinions wouldn't match up on this subject.

Stepping toward the shop door, she pushed it open. "If you don't plan on ever getting married, it's kind of pointless to think about the wedding." She tilted her head and gave him a wink. "Don't you think?" And with that, she sauntered inside the shop without bothering to wait for an answer.

IRIS DIDN'T WANT to get married? Flynn paused, allowing her words to bounce around inside his brain for a few seconds where they landed hard. Following her into the shop, he found her holding up a powder blue dress.

"What do you think of this?" she asked.

"Too plain. And the empire waist won't do anything for your figure. You need to show it off, not play it down. Do you really not want to get married?"

"Huh." Iris frowned, studying the garment. "You're right. And no, I really don't want to get married."

"Sure, I'm right. You heard Ally, I know about dresses. Why not? How can you not want to get married?"

"I have my reasons. What about this one?" She offered up a blush-pink dress with a snug tank-style top and a tulle skirt.

"It's a wedding not a ballet recital. What reasons?"

Her laughter rang out and Flynn took a second to enjoy the sound because making Iris laugh was one of his very favorite things.

"A ballet recital, that's funny."

Arguing with her was a close second. Also

interesting was this marriage conversation. How had this not come up before?

"Well, I would not want to convey that impression in any manner whatsoever." Grimacing, she slipped the dress back on the rack. "Someone might expect me to pirouette or something. What a disaster that would be..."

Holding up another, she asked, "This?"

Short, black and lacey, Flynn had half a mind to say yes just so he could see her in it. But he needed to score points here, and not by ogling her in unsuitable dresses.

"Um. Black doesn't really work outside in the afternoon, not for this wedding, anyway."

Her clear look of approval made all the research he'd done worthwhile.

He shrugged like it was no big deal. And because she clearly didn't want to talk about her own wedding, Flynn went to work picking out dresses for her to wear at someone else's.

"This is pretty," Iris said a few minutes later, showing him a moss green satin print.

"It is. It complements your skin tone and brings out the million shades of green in your eyes. And it would go great with Ally's dress. Let's try that on."

Iris met his gaze, her eyes soft and warm. "You are good at this."

"I've done my homework." Stepping close to her, he watched the pulse jump in her throat. Satisfaction rushed through him and settled in and around his heart. Moments like this, when he was positive she was attracted to him, were what kept him hoping.

She swallowed nervously. "You know what you are? You're—"

Best teasing smile in place, he attempted to fill in the blank. "Brilliant, handsome, funny... the man of your dreams?"

And that was the moment he knew he'd lost her. This is how it went. He advanced. She retreated. He just couldn't figure out why.

Eyes clouded over, she forced out a weak chuckle. "Ha. I was going to say metrosexual. I think that's what they're calling it these days, heterosexual men who are interested in fashion and art and culture."

"I'm confident enough in my masculinity to take that as a compliment. But I think I prefer the slightly more dated, yet sophisticated term, Renaissance man."

She laughed, a burst of pure joy this time. "It is a compliment, I promise. You're a good friend, Flynn. To Ally, and to me. I don't know what I would have done these past couple months without you. It's cool how we seemed to have picked up where we'd left off after so many years. Actually…" She cocked her head like she was pondering her next statement. "If I'm being honest, I like you even more now than I did in high school."

"Same," he answered in a low tone, his gaze capturing hers as a slow smile spread across his lips.

In fact, it was the unqualified understatement of his lifetime. Back then, he'd been naive and interested in girls for all the wrong reasons. He'd dated the ones who liked him for who they thought he was, a jock—quarterback of the football team, point guard on the basketball team, baseball shortstop, a solid member of the "in" crowd.

It had been important to him to fit in, to be liked. In other words, the opposite of Iris. He wished he could have been as strong and confident back then as she seemed to be. Maybe they would be together right now, and he wouldn't have made so many stupid mistakes to get to this point. The worst of which he was still paying for as even now the latest unanswered text from Sonya seemed to prod him from the depths of his pocket.

"Good," she said, breaking eye contact.

He agreed. "Why don't you want to get married?"

She sighed. "I don't see the point."

"You don't see the point in getting married?"

"Nope."

"Do you believe in love?"

"Absolutely."

"Then why not marriage?"

She began shuffling through another rack of dresses that clearly wouldn't fit her. "I believe in marriage. I just don't choose to partake in it myself. It's not for everyone. Not everything that's conventionally *societal* is meant for every individual within that society."

Flynn was watching her carefully, saw the flash of pain in her eyes. What was that about? Maybe he didn't want to get married, either. Except, that wasn't true. Even with a bad marriage in his past, he wanted to have a good one. Desperately. Like his grandparents had.

Gesturing at the pile of dresses he'd collected and draped over one arm, she asked, "Are those for me?"

He handed the dresses over and decided to let the marriage thing go. It was probably similar to her professed dislike of all things Alaska, a trait he believed had grown into more of a habit than a genuine feeling.

"Not that I couldn't wear the heck out of this little red number if I wanted to."

"I don't doubt it, Renaissance man."

"Now," he said, holding up the dresses, he'd collected. "There's a satin halter-style in this stack that is extremely promising. In fact, I'd be willing to bet it's the one."

CHAPTER THREE

THE FIRST THING Iris saw when she woke up the next morning was the bronze-colored bridesmaid dress shimmering on the back of her bedroom door, where she'd hung it after returning home from the shopping trip to Anchorage the night before.

Which made her think about Flynn.

She didn't want to think about Flynn. Not about the fact that he'd been spot-on about the dress—how well it would go with Ally's simple, understated wedding gown, or about how perfect it would be in the woodsy, intimate setting by the Faraway Inn, where the bride and groom would say their vows. And definitely not about how perfectly it would fit her. How had he known that?

She'd had one of those rare but coveted trying-on-clothes moments, where she'd known it was perfect before she'd even gotten it zipped up, much less looked in the mirror. Most of all, she didn't want to think about his reaction when she stepped out of the dressing room. Except, that she kind of did want to think about it. Why did she torture herself like this? Her face went as hot at the memory as it had in the moment.

His eyes had gone wide before quickly narrowing in on her and then slowly traveling up and down. And up again, where his gaze locked onto hers.

"Turn around," he'd urged.

She did. And she would swear she felt his eyes burning into the skin of her bare back and shoulders. He'd walked right up to her, close enough that she could feel that heat, close enough to hear his deep whisper… "Perfect." Then his hands were brushing against her bare skin, innocently adjusting the strap where it tied at the back of her neck.

The contact had sent a jolt of electricity through her, zapping the air right out of her lungs. She started, every nerve end tingling as she'd turned to face him, her heart a frantic bird trying to escape its ribbed cage.

Her gaze tangled with his and she struggled to make words.

"Iris," he'd whispered a little roughly like he'd temporarily lost his voice, too, and for a second she had thoughts…

Then he'd spoken the magic words. Magic, mood-spoiling words. "You are so gorgeous."

The ones she'd needed to hear. Because they were exactly the same words he'd uttered to Ashley Eller his senior year, when Iris overheard him ask her to the homecoming dance. Iris had been waiting for him in the chemistry lab when he and Ashley had stopped and stood outside the door. He'd prefaced his invitation to the cheerleader, who deserved the compliment by the way, even if that beauty was only skin-deep, with that very praise. "Ashley, you are so gorgeous." Like a switch being thrown, Iris experienced a stark realization in that moment—Flynn Ramsey was way out of her league. Like some sort of heartbreaking mini-epiphany, the words reminded her whom she was dealing with and they'd fortified her against falling any further.

Just like they had that day, hearing the words again jarred her back to her senses. They'd given her the strength to step away only seconds before she did something really stupid. Like launch herself into his arms.

With an airy "How sweet. This is definitely *the one*. Thank you, Flynn," she'd smiled and somehow managed a casual stroll back into the dressing room.

Where she'd proceeded to fall apart.

Trembling from head to toe, she'd leaned against the wall, trying to still the frenzied drumming of her heart. She'd stayed there until the saleswoman had tapped on the door and asked if she needed some assistance. *Yes*, she'd wanted to say, *I need Flynn Ramsey not to look at me like I'm beautiful and special and then say words to me that I know he tosses out to women like birdseed.* Iris refused to be one of the massive and hungry flock scrabbling around for his attention.

"No, thanks," she'd bravely lied. "Zipper was a little sticky. But I got it. Getting dressed now."

"Your boyfriend says you've made a decision. Can I take it up front for you?"

Boyfriend. She'd flinched as that old, too-familiar longing sliced into her.

"Oh, sure, thank you." She'd quickly stepped out of the dress and handed it out to her.

At the register, she'd found Flynn buying the dress. Which pushed her already frayed nerves past their limit.

"What are you doing?" she had snapped, tone edgy, palms still sweaty.

"Buying your bridesmaid dress."

"Flynn! No, you're not. Don't be ridiculous. You don't… I can buy my own dress."

Teasing half grin in place, and absolutely no indication that *he'd* just melted outside the dressing room while she'd been puddling inside, he'd reached out to grip her elbow lightly. "Iris, calm down. Tag gave me an envelope of cash and told me he'd leave me stranded on the runway without my pants and shoes if I didn't find a way to pay for it."

"Oh." That totally sounded like her brother. "All right, then. I'll take it up with him."

The rest of the day should have been weird and awkward. But it wasn't, at least not for Flynn, who reverted to his usual friendly, jokey self. After they shopped for accessories and picked up his tux, he'd chatted like normal during dinner and laughed through the movie as if the moment had never happened. Iris, on the other hand, had been a bundle of tattered, tender emotions. On the flight home, she'd opted to shut off her in-flight communications and pretend to nap.

And that was just the thing, she reminded herself—it probably hadn't happened that way for him. Even if he'd felt something, it wasn't the same. Funny, flirty, charming, fun-loving—that was Flynn. He had a way about him. Everyone loved him. It was one of the many things that made him both an excellent doctor and a likable guy. Even his stubbornness and that confidence that bordered on egotism were easy to overlook in light of his better qualities.

Most of the time.

Bottom line, she both loved and hated the way she felt when she was with him. She knew it wasn't his fault that he brought back her youthful insecurities. But the fact was that he did.

She blamed this town.

All the childhood teasing and taunts, and the ensuing anguish of her teenaged years, had scarred her a little too deeply. Even though all of that had changed when she went away to college. There, her disinterest in sports and the outdoors hadn't seemed like a big deal. Her intellect had boosted her confidence and helped her stand out.

College had been good for her. She'd moved forward, thought she'd moved beyond it. But being back home for this extended visit, seeing the people she grew up with, spending time with her family, with Flynn, was a constant struggle against regressing.

Bottom line—she couldn't go back. She wouldn't. So much for that maturing and mellowing-of-feelings baloney she'd been feeding herself.

What she needed was to get out of here. She needed Flynn, and all her assorted and awkward teenaged Rankins memories, out of sight and out of mind.

So why did the thought of that give her chest cramps, too?

Outside the open window, she heard car tires crunching along the gravel drive. The sounds of car doors closing, raised voices and laughter had her up and moving. A needed and welcome rush of anticipation followed because her sister Hazel's laughter was unmistakable. Fumbling in her haste, she pulled on a sweatshirt, slid her feet into a pair of slippers and hurried toward the source.

Hazel came through the door while she descended the stairs. Iris paused halfway down. Triplet senses alerted, Hazel's head came up as she dropped her backpack. "Trippa!"

"Trippa!" Iris said at the same time, using the nickname they'd called each other since childhood. Seth was Trip and she and Hazel were the Trippas.

They hugged at the bottom of the stairs, where Hazel said, "Your sweatshirt is on backward."

"I was in a hurry to get to you." Iris chuckled, an unexpected rash of emotions clogging her chest and making it burn.

"That makes it perfectly acceptable. I can't believe we're actually standing here on the same continent and I have my arms around you."

"Finally." Tears clouded Iris's eyes and she blinked them away. "I can't believe it, either."

They emailed and Skyped as often as possible when Hazel was traveling, which the last few years had been most of the time. Lately she'd been trekking to more and more remote areas and the opportunities to communicate had been infrequent. The past three months she'd been exploring everywhere from Mongolia to the Himalayas, including Tibet, Nepal and India.

Iris pulled away to study her sister, the one that she felt the closest to, and suddenly wished they were closer. "Welcome home. You look fantastic."

And she did. Green-brown eyes sparkling, skin glowing, Hazel always looked refreshed and revitalized after a trip.

"Thank you. You, too." Voice pitched with fake enthusiasm, she added, "I think Alaska agrees with you."

"Very funny," Iris said drily, but chuckled

because Hazel had a knack for making the ridiculous funny. "I've been dying for you and Seth to get home so we could hang out for a while before I have to leave."

"Does that mean you've accepted a job offer then?"

"Not yet. But soon."

"Although…" Hazel paused to study her with the curiosity they shared, a trait that made Hazel an avid adventurer and Iris a successful academic. "You do have kind of a glow about you. What's up?"

"Caffeine withdrawal," Iris joked. Not Flynn thoughts, that's for sure.

Seth came through the door. While he'd been tall and lanky all through his teens, his subsequent years of work as a commercial fisherman had added bulk. His chiseled man-build still surprised her.

Depositing his pack next to Hazel's, Seth pulled her in for a hug and said, "Hey, there's my other third."

"Missed you, too, Trip," she said. "How was Tibet?"

"Incredible," Seth said.

"Amazing," Hazel gushed at the same time. "We wish you would have been there. I'm heading to Peru after the wedding. Any chance you'd want to take a little extra time before you start your fancy new career and come with me?"

"Will you be sleeping with anything over your head thicker than a piece of nylon?"

"No, but—"

"And there's your answer."

Seth gave his head a little shake. "Honestly, Iris, sometimes I can't believe you grew up in the same house as the rest of us."

Iris knew he was only teasing and yet the words cut at her just a little. Covering the sore spot with a smile, she said drily, "Well, Seth, imagine how I feel."

HE SHOULD HAVE just kissed her.

Flynn stepped from the dock onto the boat and took his customary spot—port side, stern—and pretended to be interested in the conversation unfolding between Doc and his best friend, Caleb.

Caleb started the boat and headed out. His grandfather zipped his jacket.

"Should we head over to Caribou Head or get closer to Opal's mouth?" Caleb asked. Caribou Head was a small, rocky island so nicknamed because of the gnarly mass of driftwood that often accumulated on the top, making it resemble a pile of twisted caribou antlers. Opal was the river that emptied into the bay.

"Crab Johnson says the kings are biting near the mouth," Doc said, as Caleb steered the boat away from a red buoy that indicated a crab pot was anchored to the bottom there.

"Ha," Caleb spouted. "Crab's got the worst case of angler envy I've ever seen. He will lie six ways to Sunday to keep us from catching a fish bigger than his."

Doc howled with laughter. "Caribou Head it is. Let's try trolling with herring first."

Caleb picked up speed as they motored farther into the bay.

Flynn tugged on the neckline of his jacket. It was early summer, but the morning breeze in Alaska could be chilly, especially blowing across the open water. He'd be peeling off the layers as the morning wore on. Glancing back toward the shore, he thought about texting Iris. Both morning people, they often exchanged texts first thing. It was still pretty early, though, and they'd gotten home late.

That moment outside the dressing room, he'd been almost positive she'd wanted him to kiss her. Almost. But that was the problem. It was so difficult to tell with Iris. Their relationship was filled with teasing and fun and he couldn't be sure if the light in her eyes had to do with the dress or with him.

Unbelievable. He'd always read the cues so well. Of course, it helped that there'd never been a woman he was interested in that wasn't interested in return and told him so. It was a new, strange, frustrating phenomenon.

"Flynn, did Doc tell you that Crab said that king salmon he caught last week weighed sixty-two pounds?"

"You don't believe him?"

"I saw the photo. No way was that fish even fifty pounds. He was posing right next to that Don't Feed the Birds sign at the marina. Dimwit didn't even stop to think that everyone knows how tall that sign is. Unless that salmon had recently eaten about fifteen pounds of lead, it was no sixty-two pounds."

Flynn forced out a chuckle.

Doc said, "Remember that halibut you caught back in ninety-eight?"

Caleb shook his head. "I'd like to land another lunker like that before I die…"

Normally, Flynn found their chatter highly entertaining. Fishing with Doc and Caleb was hands-down one of his favorite activities. But right now, he couldn't stop thinking about Iris. Truth was, ever since she'd been back in town, she'd occupied nearly every spare second of his thoughts.

If he kissed her and she kissed him back, then that would change everything. But the problem was if she didn't kiss him back, that would also change everything. And worse, it could irreparably harm their friendship. Bottom line, he'd come to value her friendship too much to lose it now. He loved Ally, too, of course, but she was more like a little sister. He and Iris were just...

Perfect.

That was the word he'd uttered when he saw her in that dress. Words had jumbled and formed pathetically in his mind, each one more inadequate than the last. He'd mumbled something lame about her being gorgeous even though he knew the usual praise and flattery didn't work on her. Besides, the way he felt about her wasn't anything close to usual. He just didn't know how to convey it.

In his pocket, his phone chimed, indicating a text. It had to be Iris. He nearly slipped off his seat trying to dig it out of his pocket.

A twist of disappointment churned in his gut when her green-brown eyes and mischievous smile failed to light up his screen. Not recognizing the number, he hit "view" anyway.

Sometimes patients or fellow doctors contacted his personal cell number. He didn't mind. That was not the case today. Blood pressure rising with irritation, he read the message from his ex-wife.

Seriously, Flynn? You're blocking my calls now? Please put your personal feelings for me aside. I need to talk to you. It's important. Please call me.

Two "pleases" in one text. Sonya was pulling out all the stops. What other feelings would he have for her besides the personal kind? The woman had cheated on him and then waylaid his career. Flynn stuffed the phone back into his pocket. Which part of "never contact me again" did she not understand? More than two years since their divorce, a year since he'd last heard from her and now suddenly she'd called twice and texted him four times in the last month. The last one he'd answered and then made it clear that if she needed to contact him she could do so through his attorney.

The boat slowed and bobbed gently on the water. Flynn knew that was his cue to rig up. Fingers flying with the assuredness of someone who'd performed the task countless times, he attached the weight and flasher to his line. He then took a new 40-inch leader from his tackle box and deftly attached a cut-plug herring to the double hooks. *Why won't Sonya leave me alone? Why won't Iris let me get close?*

Turning to face the stern, he lifted the rigging over the rail and lowered it into the water. Caleb throttled up a bit to trolling speed, and they each let out enough line to reach the right depth. *Does Iris really not want to get married? Had she been joking, as we often did with each other?*

After about fifteen minutes of trolling and what seemed like an excessive amount of non-verbal communication between Doc and Caleb, Doc suddenly yelled, "Fish on!"

Flynn grabbed his pole and swiftly reeled in his line to prevent it from becoming tangled. He glanced at the other two, who were reeling just as fast as him.

When his flasher neared the surface of the water, he asked, "Who had a fish on?"

"Me and Caleb," Doc replied, as both men lifted their rods to show the herring still attached to their hooks. "Little fish."

"But definitely not you," Caleb said.

Confused, Flynn looked from one man to the other—neither of them had been fighting a salmon on their lines. "What are you—"

Doc clued him in. "You don't have a hook on that line, son."

"Or bait," Caleb added. He pointed at the herring.

"Uh," Flynn said, lifting his flasher out of the water. Nope, no leader attached. He glanced behind him to see his baited double-looped leader lying on the deck, right where he'd put it, and struggled to come up with some kind of an excuse for such an absentminded oversight. It was futile, he realized, as they were both staring at him now with way, way too much interest.

"The way I see it," Caleb said, taking his time adjusting the hat on his head. "And, Doc, I could use your expertise here, so please feel free to correct me if I'm wrong. But in my experience... Now granted, I'm not a ladies' man like our boy Flynn here, but I do all right. As such, I am personally aware of only one thing that will so severely throw an experienced angler off his fishing game when the kings are biting that he'll throw his line into the water without bait or hook."

Doc and Caleb exchanged glances and then guffawed loud enough for every fish within a seven-mile radius to hear.

While they were recovering, wiping their

eyes with their sleeves and shuffling around, Flynn said, "I'm never going to live this down, am I?"

They both sobered. Caleb stepped up next to Flynn. After a firm slap on the back, he answered, "Well, no, son, you're not. That would be asking way, way too much of us."

"Yeah." Flynn chuckled and shook his head. "You're probably right about that."

"Seriously, though, do you want to talk about it? We could help. Doc and I have a solid track record when it comes to matchmaking. Look at Jonah and Shay."

Jonah fished with them occasionally and Flynn would even say that he'd become a friend. He'd heard the story of how Caleb had disingenuously lured Jonah back home to Rankins with the intention of putting him in Shay's path.

"I've been watching, kiddo," Doc added. "Iris isn't your average everyday girl. She's special. You're going to have to—and pardon my dated vernacular but it's the only word that will do here—woo her."

Flynn looked from Doc to Caleb and back again. Flynn wasn't too proud to acknowledge that they'd both enjoyed long, happy marriages.

Their spouses had passed away but neither had any problem finding dates even to this day.

"Woo her?" Flynn repeated with a chuckle, rubbing a hand across the back of his suddenly itchy neck.

"Trust us. Doc and me, we've been around the romantic block at least a dozen times between us."

"Think of it this way," Doc chimed in. "It'll be a great story to tell my grandkids."

A combination of desperation, resignation and hope swirled like an eddy inside of him. The simple fact was that he was running out of moves. Short of coming right out and telling Iris how he felt, he didn't know how else to move their relationship out of the friend zone. What could it hurt?

"Okay. Fine. What have you boys got?"

CHAPTER FOUR

WHERE WAS THE norovirus when you really needed it?

"You're sure about this?" Iris asked Ally, lowering her bright pink beach bag to the floor in the living room next to Ally's tattered backpack. "It's not too late to book a spa trip. Ooh, or even a weekend in Vegas! I could get online right now and—"

Ally interrupted her with a laugh. "Iris, I'm positive. You know me, just the thought of being around that many people gives me hives."

Tag and Ally had decided to forgo the traditional bachelor and bachelorette parties in favor of a joint gathering at Jasper Lake. Their friends Ryder and Jessie lived on its isolated shore and had graciously offered to host. Everyone was brimming with excitement. Almost everyone. The thought of a day of "fun" on the lake gave *Iris* hives. Never mind the fact that it might literally give her hives. But this wasn't about her and she'd already considered every excuse in the book to get out of it, but hadn't been able to think of a single one that her family wouldn't smile at and ignore. Despite her deepest wish for a brief but debilitating virus, she'd awoken feeling healthy.

"Okay, if you're sure?"

"Positive. It's going to be great. I can't wait for you to meet Jessie and Ryder. I still can't believe you've never been to Jasper Lake. How is that possible?"

"You've never been to Jasper Lake?" Flynn asked, brow scrunchy and cute, as he and Seth strolled into the living room. Both men had backpacks slung over their shoulders.

"Uh, no."

"You'd be surprised at what Iris hasn't done around here," Seth commented in a droll tone.

Iris scowled at her brother. This was true, but she didn't need him pointing it out in front of Flynn.

Rescuing her from the conversation, Tag strode in from the kitchen, travel mug in hand, backpack clinging to him like a friendly koala bear. Life with her family, she thought wryly—a never-ending backpack convention. Iris couldn't wait to get back to the city, where people carried designer handbags, briefcases or messenger bags and spent their free time partaking in sensible indoor pest-free activities like visiting museums, going to art galleries and attending concerts. Even the parks in DC felt safer, populated and patrolled by staff. The only wildlife encounters you had to worry about were pigeons stealing your lunch.

"Oh, good, you're here," Tag said, the comment obviously directed at Flynn. Frowning, Tag looked around. "Where's Hazel?"

Iris answered, "She's already outside loading the extra lounge chairs into the pickup."

"Excellent. That'll save us time." Tag checked his watch and pointed toward the door. "Let's go."

The six of them were riding out to Jasper Lake together. Assuming the role of Fun Captain, Tag reported that Ryder and Jessie had four kayaks, two canoes, three ATVs and an assortment of fishing gear, all of which would be available for use. The trailer hooked behind the pickup held coolers full of food and drinks, three more kayaks and a variety of floatation devices.

"Bering is bringing a raft, life jackets and extra fishing gear." As the owner of a guide service, Bering always had a supply of quality equipment as well as the latest outdoor gadgets designed to "enhance one's rustic encounter," as his website noted. An oxymoron if Iris had ever heard one.

"Goodie, *extra* gear," Iris muttered, handing off her bag to Hazel, who was chucking backpacks into the pickup bed. "Because a trailer full of stuff isn't nearly enough."

Hazel snickered, took her bag and cast her a sympathetic look. Iris climbed into the back seat. Flynn appeared at the still-open door she'd used as Hazel walked around to the other side. Iris scooted over to the middle. Ally sat next to Tag in the front, Seth got in next to Ally, Tag started the engine and they were off.

For about the first four minutes, Iris tried to relax and enjoy the drive. Then she gave up. Not only was she already battling a crabby mood about spending the day at the lake, but now she also had to deal with this distracting hyperawareness of Flynn's every move. Was it her imagination or did he seem to take up an inordinate amount of space?

The back seat had plenty of room, but his long legs spilled into her zone, making her entire body hum with an electric awareness. Mile after mile, rut after pothole, every bump had his muscled thigh brushing against hers. At one point, he stretched his arm across the back of the seat, his biceps touching her neck. And then there was the fact that he smelled divine. Iris tried to calm the erratic pounding of her pulse while pretending to enjoy the view. Flynn seemed unfazed.

Luckily, there was never a quiet moment with this crew. Stories and laughter abounded, so her lack of enthusiasm went mostly unnoticed. Or at least they spared her from commenting. Flynn, however, kept tossing curious glances in her direction. Eventually, the lake, menacing and dark, came into view. Like the Black Lagoon. Iris couldn't decide which was worse—the Flynn jostling or the day now unfolding before her.

Except, Jasper Lake's water was a lovely shade of green-blue. Flanked by a wide expanse of shoreline, a smattering of houses could be seen peeking out from the brush on one side. At the far end of the lake, lush green hillside slanted up for what looked like miles. Nothing but trees and wilderness as far as the eye could see. Okay, so it might be pretty to the untrained eye, but Iris knew how deceptive the idyllic scene really was.

Ally's teenaged cousin had been attacked by a grizzly bear on a hiking trail there earlier in the spring. Tag had been the pilot who'd flown him to the hospital. For some inexplicable reason, Iris seemed to be the only one who thought it odd that they were planning to hike that very trail today. Well, not *her*, but some of the group.

Tag turned onto a driveway and stopped in front of a sprawling cottage with cedar siding. A chain-link fence enclosed what appeared to be several acres of ground, and inside Ally counted at least eight dogs and puppies in various sizes, shapes and colors. Jessie and Ryder ran a rescue facility, where they rehabilitated abused and neglected dogs. Ryder also trained dogs for police and military use. The vigilant pack, barking madly, tails wagging, shouldered for position along the fence line.

Everyone piled out. Except her. Outside, excited chatter ensued and gnawed at her already frazzled nerves. She was exhausted, and the day hadn't even started.

Nibbling her lip, Iris stalled and briefly considered staying in the vehicle. But only briefly.

"This isn't about you," she muttered. With a weary sigh, she climbed out and hoped she'd packed enough mosquito repellent.

FLYNN DECIDED THE only thing that would have made the trip better would have been if he and Iris were the only ones in the pickup. But as much as he'd enjoyed their close proximity, he knew something was bothering her. She'd been too quiet on the ride. Iris was rarely quiet.

The day stretched out ahead with endless possibilities of getting Iris alone and fixing whatever had gotten her down. Jasper Lake was the perfect place to relax and have fun. A myriad of activities were on offer to distract her. His number one choice was taking her for a ride in a canoe and finding a quiet spot across the lake. A secluded romantic place for their first kiss would be ideal, seeing how he'd missed the opportunity during their shopping trip.

Let the wooing begin! The fact that he was following advice from two geriatric playboys gave him only the slightest pause. Most of their suggestions seemed sound, if a little dated. But he could tweak those for the circumstances.

Ryder and Jessie came out to greet them. Ally introduced everyone who hadn't met. Within minutes, they'd unloaded the supplies and packed them beside the house, where a large expanse of neatly trimmed lawn sloped gently toward the lake. A grill sat on the deck. Two picnic tables were pushed together under one large awning. Farther away, near a line of trees, Hazel and Seth arranged lounge chairs under another smaller canopy.

Bering arrived with his wife, Emily, his sister, Janie, her husband, Aidan, and Laurel Davidson, longtime family friend and owner of the local newspaper, *Rankins Press*. Jonah, Shay, Hannah, her husband, Tate, and their cousin Adele arrived soon after. They were followed closely by Tag's friend and second groomsman, Cricket Blackburn, and Janie and Aidan's teenaged sons, Gareth and Reagan.

A few more vehicles pulled up, guests unloaded, more greetings were exchanged. Soon everyone grew impatient with small talk and three groups began to form—one to kayak to the opposite shore and take a hike to the waterfalls, another to go fly-fishing and still another smaller bunch who'd opted to stay back and swim, float or enjoy the sun. Ryder and Jessie's horseshoe pit looked freshly raked and a badminton net fluttered gently in the breeze.

Flynn watched Iris conversing with Cricket. Flynn knew the guy was like family, but still, he and Iris seemed awfully tight lately. Did he have something to worry about there?

She drifted away from the crowd and settled in a lounge chair under the shaded awning. Digging in her bag, she removed several items—hat, book, sunglasses and a bottle of some sort. After dousing herself with a thick mist from the bottle, she arranged the hat on her head, slipped on her sunglasses and picked up the book.

Flynn waited a few minutes and then approached her. "Hey."

"Hi," she answered, an uncharacteristically tight smile on her face.

He sat on the edge of her chair. "Are you all right?"

"Sure."

"You were awfully quiet on the ride here."

"Was I?" She looked up and then away, and Flynn tried to follow her rapidly bouncing gaze, which didn't seem inclined to meet his. "Is that a mosquito?" She picked up the bottle, aimed and gave the pump a squeeze. "I don't understand why mosquitos even exist."

Flynn leaned sideways, ducking out of the way of the misty cloud. He fanned the air. "You know you were. And no, I think it's a fly. Birds eat mosquitos, so you could argue that they're an important food source."

"You know very well that there are ten quintillion species of bugs on this planet, ninety-one thousand in the United States alone. The birds can eat something else."

"Although, I think Alaska only has, what, like three hundred insect species?"

"Three hundred and four." Iris graced him with a genuine grin.

Flynn gave himself silent props because he knew she was thinking about the biology project they'd done together her sophomore year. Like he wanted her to. They'd turned it into the winning entry in the science fair that year.

"See? Exactly. Poor birds. Very limited options up here. They need the mosquitos."

"Then they should relocate. I don't know why anyone, human or avian, would want to live here, anyway. And then choose a lake in the middle of nowhere to nest."

Flynn tried not to laugh. "Because it's beautiful, peaceful, uncrowded and not corrupted with urban sprawl like the places you claim you want to live." He added a wink to soften the statement.

"Oh, you mean civilization?" she joked.

"I mean smog and pollution and viruses and a mob of people."

"Ahh…" she drawled with a knowing nod. "That would be Heaven you're referring to."

He gave up and chuckled. "I do love arguing with you. Except when I know you're doing it to avoid the real issue. Tell me why you were so quiet."

"Motion sickness."

"Really?"

"No." Tipping her head thoughtfully, she added, "That's actually a problem I don't have."

He shook his head. "What is it then?"

"Nothing."

"Iris—"

She slapped her leg and then pointed triumphantly at the spot. "*That* was a mosquito."

"I think it was a fruit fly."

"Or a tiny mosquito."

"You know very well there are no *tiny* mosquitos in Alaska."

She snuffled out a laugh. "True. I heard they were training some for use as military drones."

He laughed, and then went for it. "How about a canoe ride, just me and you?"

It was hard to see her exact reaction behind the sunglasses, but it looked like she winced a little. "Oh, um, no thank you. Canoes are real tippy, have you noticed that? One wrong move and you're fish food."

"How about a hike? The falls are amazing. We can ride over there in the boat."

Scrunching her nose, she pitched her tone to schoolmarm disapproval. "Flynn, please don't use the *H* word with me. It's right up there with the *C* word. Both of where it is not uncommon to encounter the dreaded *B* word."

"And that would be what? Canoeing and… bugs?"

After an exaggerated huff, she corrected, "Camping and bears."

Barely swallowing his laughter, he gestured toward the fishing crowd now climbing into Bering's raft. "So I'm guessing the *F* word is out, too?" he joked.

She laughed, hard, and Flynn used the time to fantasize about leaning forward and kissing her.

"So, so far out. Like I'd-rather-gargle-burning-hot-lava out."

"Wow. That is far. Swimming?"

"Cold," she countered smoothly. "I don't do cold. Bad circulation."

"Huh." He eyed her doubtfully. "I feel like you might have made that up."

"That's possible," she admitted with a shrug, while her lips fought a losing battle with a smile. "I sometimes forget that you're a doctor and can probably tell these things."

Affection and desire twisted impatiently inside of him as he and Iris exchanged grins. He resisted the urge to kiss away her arguments, opting instead to focus on a modified version of Doc and Caleb's courting advice and let her suggest how they'd spend the day. "What do you want to do?"

"Me?" She seemed surprised by the question. "Nothing."

"Nothing?" Doing nothing in this virtual paradise of a setting was not part of his plan. "Come on, Iris, there has to be something that you like to—"

"Sorry, Flynn," she interrupted. "I'm not interested in hiking or fishing or kayaking or water...frolicking of any kind. Honestly, thank you for asking, but Mother Nature and I share a mutual and abiding dislike of one another."

"Seriously, Iris, how could you grow up here in Alaska, and with the family you did, and not want to do *any* of this stuff?"

AND, THERE IT WAS. Forcing a smile through gritted teeth, Iris said, "Well, Flynn, I..." What would he do if she told him the truth? Pity her, probably. And then try to convert her. Neither of which she wanted.

"I guess you could say I'm like the duckling in a family of swans. Just not a sporty, outdoorsy person. I know it's a difficult concept for people like you."

The stare he leveled at her made her heart hurt a little even though she couldn't quite decipher its meaning. Disappointment? Frustration? Confusion? All three of those and then some.

"People like me?" he repeated.

"Yeah, you know, good at everything."

"Iris, I am not good at everything."

"Really?" She adjusted the back of her seat. "That's not how it looks from where I'm sitting."

"Maybe that's because you always insist on sitting on the sidelines."

Iris glanced away and squirted the bottle at nothing because that did hurt. That always hurt. "Which is where I want to be," she said quietly, hating how petulant she sounded. Even though that was not exactly how she felt. She felt sad and pathetic and left out. Like she often had as a kid.

Seth's voice rang out from the shoreline. "Hey, Ramsey, are you coming?"

Keeping his focus on her, he held up a finger in a wait-a-sec gesture. "How about this—I promised your cousin Reagan I would show him some fly-fishing stuff, so he can catch more fish than Seth. Do you want to ride along at least? I won't make you fish."

"That is sweet," she said. "I'd love to see

someone catch more fish than my braggy brother for a change. But you know what I'd love even more? To hear about it after the fact."

"You're very stubborn, do you know that?"

She shrugged. "I guess. If not liking the outdoors makes me stubborn."

"Fine." Standing, he raked a hand through his hair. "I hate leaving you here all alone. But I'll see you later." When he smiled it held too much of what looked like that pity she wanted to avoid. She pretended to swat at another mosquito.

"'Bye, Flynn."

Iris watched him go as an inexplicable, smothering feeling came over her and left her chest aching. She knew she'd packed her inhaler because it was in her pocket. Like the mosquito spray, it was a constant reminder of her shortcomings. But she knew this feeling didn't have anything to do with her mild asthma, a long-term condition due to the underdeveloped lungs of her premature birth.

"Trust me," she whispered to no one. "I'm good at being alone."

It was true. It had been true her entire life. She was good at being alone. In a room, a crowd, a family full of people—it didn't matter where, she always felt at least slightly removed. So why did it bother her now? It didn't, she assured herself. It was just that when she'd left Alaska, she'd thought she was done with these kinds of situations that left her the odd one out. Soon, she assured herself, she would be gone, and this day would be just another crappy memory.

Flopping her head back, she closed her eyes and tried to enjoy the sounds of nature everyone was always raving about.

Two minutes later, she was ready to give up when a voice penetrated her musing. "Hey, Trippa, are you sleeping?"

Opening one eye, she watched Hazel pull a lounge chair closer.

"Who can sleep with all this noise?"

Frowning, Hazel looked around. "What noise?"

Iris opened her other eye, let out a dramatic sigh and then gestured around helplessly. "The wind, the leaves rustling rudely in the trees, birds screeching in distress, bugs buzzing around and pointing out patches of my bare skin to one other, and I'm pretty sure I've heard growling at least six times. I don't know if it's wolves stalking me, or grizzly bears discussing my choicest cuts."

Hazel burst out laughing. "I have missed you. So. Much."

Iris felt both her heart and her irritability soften. "I've missed you, too. But am I the only one who thinks it's odd that Tag and Ally are having a party at the place where her cousin got attacked by a bear?"

"Louis survived, and this is where they met. I think it's romantic."

"Huh." She hadn't thought of it quite that way. "I guess I can see that. Sort of."

"There are no grizzly bears in Peru."

"But there is some kind of speckled bear."

"Spectacled," Hazel corrected.

"Oh, that's great that they wear glasses," she quipped. "All the better to see their prey. Also, jaguars, poisonous snakes *and* frogs, which is fundamentally wrong because frogs are cute and should not be feared. Then there's that weird river dolphin that lives in the Amazon and makes the hair stand up on the back of my neck. It's like Flipper's demented cousin."

Hazel laughed again, then said, "My goodness, I had no idea you were an expert on Peruvian wildlife."

"We can also talk about crime and disease if you want. Dengue, zika, malaria, yellow fever—"

Hazel held out a hand. "You know what? I'm good."

"Well." Iris shrugged. "You know me, my sister is going there so I have to learn what evil dwells. Then I can worry about you appropriately."

"That is actually really sweet in your special, twisted way." A restless finger tapped against her armrest. "But just so we're clear, I'm not giving up. Someday you're going *somewhere* with me. You can't use school as an excuse anymore."

"I'll go to Paris with you. You could hike up to the top of the Eiffel Tower while I wait at the bottom with *un café et un croissant chocolat*. I'll totally cheer you on, though."

"Deal!" she fired back.

"What?" Iris tipped down her sunglasses to get a better look at her sister's face. "Really?"

Hazel slid a smile her way. "Don't look so surprised. I'd love to see Paris, especially if it means taking a trip with you. How would you feel about a stop in Prague?"

"Um, sure. All that prewar architecture is supposed to be phenomenal." A wave of affection swept through her. Her thrill-seeking, globetrotting sister wanted to take a trip with her?

Hazel's grin reminded her of a satisfied cat.

"Perfect. I cannot wait. Now, what about you and Doc Ramsey the younger? How's that going?"

"What do you mean?" Iris fired off the question and added, "It's fine. We're friends." She cringed inside at hearing the defensive edge to her tone. No way would her sister miss it.

Hazel drew up one shoulder into a casual shrug as she fought a smile. "Nothing. I just meant that you two seem to be spending a fair amount of time together. Back in high school I got it, because you were both geek-leaning *brainiacs*, but since he's a doctor now, too, I'm guessing he doesn't need your help with calculus anymore. So, what's the deal?"

"No deal. And Flynn never leaned geek."

"Um, yes, he did. Granted, he did a good job covering it, but it was there. And, Iris, sharing the back seat with you two was electric, like riding with two coiled masses of balled-up lightning or—" forming her hands like she held a circular object, she kept them there for a few seconds before tossing them helplessly into the air "—something. I just can't figure out exactly what it means."

"It means we're in the wedding together. Ally isn't exactly your typical bride, so we've been helping with the planning—picking out flowers, sampling cake, arguing about the menu, dress shopping, et cetera."

"Dress shopping?" Hazel repeated sharply. "He went dress shopping with you?"

"Um, yes. Last week, the four of us went to Anchorage… And he and I… Flynn picked out my dress. He has really good taste."

"Good taste," she repeated skeptically. "Okay, Flynn Ramsey, busy doctor and devoted outdoorsman, does not go dress shopping with a woman unless there are feelings. This means—"

Iris made a chopping motion with one hand. "No, no, stop, stop. He does. Ally doesn't shop. He was just helping her out by helping me. He picked out Ally's dress, too."

"Shopping together is near the top of the list."

"You are so off base, you know that, right? With this intimacy-infringement list of yours."

Her sister had a laundry list of acts and deeds that she used to gauge a man's degree of interest: giving flowers or thoughtful gifts—generally the *less* expensive and more thoughtful the gift, the more interested they were—calling or texting more than once a day, meeting and/or befriending family and friends, sharing drinks, sharing silverware, sharing dessert… The list went on, and apparently included shopping, and any one of them would earn a guy his walking papers in Hazel's world.

Iris understood. Her sister had been badly hurt. But her rules didn't apply here, not when she and Flynn were already friends.

"How many times a day does he text you?"

"I don't know."

"Answer the question, please."

"What are you, channeling Jonah now? A few. But I told you we're doing this wedding stuff together."

"A few," Hazel repeated. "They can't all be wedding-related?"

"No, but—"

"Has he been over for dinner?"

"Of course. Mom loves him."

"Flowers?"

"Absolutely not. See? Friends." She hoped her sister didn't ask about other gifts. She wasn't going to volunteer the information that Flynn was already a champ in the thoughtful-gift category. The first week she'd been back in Rankins her family had thrown a party to celebrate her birthday and her doctorate. Flynn had brought her a framed photo of her with her cat, Jericho, who had passed away the month before.

"Has he brought you lunch at work yet?"

"We're not talking about this anymore."

"So that's a yes."

"What are you doing here, anyway? Why aren't you fishing or kayaking or out provoking the bears like everyone else?"

"I'm taking a rest day after hiking almost nonstop for the last three months. And changing the subject only makes me more curious, you know that, right?"

Iris blew out a breath. "Yes. But in this case your curiosity is misguided. There's nothing between Flynn and me except friendship. Aside from Ally, he's the only friend I have in town. You and Seth haven't been here, and the rest of our siblings are all attached now in case you haven't noticed. Tag has Ally, Hannah has Tate and Lucas, Shay has Jonah. And now Hannah is running for the state senate and Shay is pregnant. That leaves me all alone. I can only spend so much time with Mom and Dad."

Hazel's speculative gaze homed in on Iris like a laser beam. "If you say so."

"I do. I absolutely say so. Flynn and I are just friends."

CHAPTER FIVE

Two long hospital shifts and one shopping trip later, Flynn parked his SUV behind Bering's pickup in the driveway at the home of Iris's parents, Ben and Margaret James. In keeping with Tag and Ally's inclination for doing this wedding thing their own way, they were opting for a rehearsal brunch rather than a dinner.

Exhaustion nipped at him, but he rallied. The Jasper Lake excursion might not have worked out like he'd hoped, but he was armed and ready to up his game. Reaching into the back seat, he retrieved two boxes from the Donut Den and a shopping bag of provisions.

"Never underestimate the power of the flower," Caleb had advised.

Doc had chimed in, "Thoughtful gestures, trinkets, baubles—the more *thought-filled*, the better."

Iris and Hazel were outside on the covered porch that fronted the large, green-with-white-trim arts-and-crafts-style two-story home. Per-

fect. Flynn climbed the stairs, simultaneously
savoring the sight of Iris and trying not to stare.

"Good morning, ladies."

"Good morning." Iris smiled at him from
where she sat in one of the comfy chairs that
Margaret had arranged on the porch. Flynn felt
that increasingly familiar lightness seep into
him. The first thing he always wanted to do
after coming off a long or difficult stint at the
hospital was to see Iris. If that wasn't possible,
he made do with a text or phone call. She always made whatever good thing had happened
seem better and whatever bad thing seem not
so bad. It was a little addictive.

Hazel said, "Hey, Flynn, how are you?"

There was a resemblance between all the
James sisters, but interestingly Iris and Hazel
didn't look as much alike as their older sisters,
Shay and Hannah. Iris had the lightest shade of
brown hair in the family—almost-blonde, she
called it. She was tall, but with narrow shoulders and a petite build—willowy, where her
sisters had curvier, more athletic frames.

Their hazel-green eye color was the only
noticeable similarity, but the shape was different. If someone didn't already know, they'd
never guess Iris and Hazel were part of triplets, which, he supposed, was a small part of

the reason he didn't think of Iris as "one of the James triplets," like people often did. Mostly, though, it was because Iris was unique in so many other ways.

"Good. Hazel, you look great, by the way. I didn't get a chance to tell you the other day, but clearly, the Himalayas agreed with you."

"Why, thank you, Flynn. I think I could spend the rest of my life there."

"Because, let me get this right, 'it only seems fitting to lay bare your soul among the clouds atop the highest peaks on earth?'"

Hazel's jaw dropped for a split second before she snapped it shut. A sputter of laughter followed. "Yes, that's it exactly. I'm not sure I've ever heard myself quoted back to me. Well done."

Flynn gave her a nod. "I enjoy following your adventures." He handed over one of the bright pink boxes. "I brought pastries for brunch. I seem to recall you sharing Iris's fondness for huckleberry scones back in the day."

"Flynn, you're officially my new favorite person. Wait… Did Iris tell you that I've been fantasizing about these for weeks?"

"Uh, no. Iris and I used to study at the Donut Den occasionally back in high school and she would buy them and always get an extra one for you. And a maple-chocolate bar for Seth. There's a few of those in there, too."

"I can't believe you remember that."

"I have a good memory." For anything Iris-related, he'd discovered.

"Maybe. Or…" Casting a suspicious glance at Iris, she asked, "Iris, did you tell him about the scones? You know I can tell when you're lying."

Iris shrugged and shook her head. "I don't recall mentioning it. Besides, why would I tell him that?"

"Exactly! Ha!" she cried triumphantly, before turning a sweet smile on him. "Not that it would lessen the positive impact of your gesture in the least if she had, Flynn, it's just that Iris and I were discussing something a few days ago, and, believe it or not, these scones prove my point." She opened the box. "So, double thanks from me."

"You're welcome." At Iris's eye roll he added, "I think?"

"Oh, definitely," Hazel said around a mouthful of scone. "Don't mind her. You know how she gets when she's not right."

"I do." He flashed Hazel a knowing grin. "Surly. Is Seth around?"

"No, I don't," Iris countered irritably.

Flynn and Hazel shared a laugh.

Hazel answered his question. "Seth is inside."

"Good. He mentioned that he and Bering were taking Gareth and Reagan up the Opal River for some fly-fishing. I tied a few flies for them to try."

Hazel swiveled toward Iris again, her expression poised with unspoken approval.

Iris gave her a quick glare, then said to him, "They will love that."

Pulling a bouquet of flowers from the bag, he said, "These are for your mom." Then he produced the other bunch and handed them to Iris. "And these are for you." The lilies were nestled in a duck-shaped vase. He hoped she caught the reference.

"You brought me flowers?" Her cheeks tinged pink as she inspected the blossoms.

"Lilies," Hazel said accusingly, "are your favorite."

"Lilies," Iris echoed gently, "*are* my favorite. Flynn…" Soft eyes went velvety green as they latched onto his.

Flynn felt a surge of triumph. He made a silent promise to buy Doc and Caleb dinner ASAP.

"Yeah, I, uh, thought about irises but that

seemed so obvious. And when we were picking out Ally's wedding flowers you mentioned
lilies were your favorite. And ducks are my favorite bird, so…"

Hazel made a noise that sounded like a
chuckle but immediately covered it with a
cough. Then she gave Iris another look Flynn
couldn't decipher but suspected had to do with
him.

Iris ignored her. "They're—" She stopped
in midthought as Flynn slipped the coffee mug
from her other hand. He took a sip and leaned
against the railing.

"Oh, boy," Hazel said and blew out a breath.
"Wow."

"Shut it, Hazel."

"What?" Flynn asked.

Hazel smiled serenely. "I think she means
gorgeous. Is that what you were going to say,
Iris?"

"Did I miss something?" Flynn asked, re-
calling how the triplets often seemed to speak
their own special language.

"No, you didn't," Iris said. "Please ignore
my sister, who has been alone and out of touch
with polite society for several months." Bury-
ing her face in the petals, she added, "I was
going to say beautiful. They're beautiful. And

the vase is…perfect." Then she brought up her gaze, where it latched onto his, and the raw sentiment there had him thinking that Doc and Caleb might deserve more than dinner. Possibly a new fishing boat was in order.

Iris added, "Thank you, Flynn. You've already made my day and it hasn't even started yet."

"You're very welcome." Affection and satisfaction combined nicely inside of him and left him grinning stupidly. But he didn't care. Finally, progress. Opening the other box, he removed a pastry, broke it in half and then offered a portion to Iris. "Split this with me? I want to make sure I have enough room for your mom's egg casserole."

Hazel choked on her scone.

INTERESTING FEELING, IRIS THOUGHT, as she perused the inquiries she'd already received for the position of Copper Crossing's office manager. The juxtaposition between looking for a job and trying to hire someone for a job was a little weird. She had a lesson with Cricket later, so she'd come in early to meet with one of the applicants.

"You really don't need to be here today," Tag

told her a few minutes later, when he surprised her with his arrival.

Iris lounged at her desk, stockinged feet propped up as she reviewed the paltry application from poor Ashley Frye.

"Yeah, look who's talking. You're the one getting married tomorrow. Surely, you have better things to do." Like leaving her and Cricket time for these clandestine flying lessons. "I'm meeting with a potential employee. Get out of here and go chill with Ally before all the chaos begins."

"I wish. Just here to pick up a few things. Today is Ally's last shift at the hospital before the wedding." Tag looked at his watch. "I'm picking her up after I leave here and heading over to the inn. Shay and Emily want us to look at the decorations. You sure you don't want me to stick around?"

"Positive. Honestly, I have very little hope for this applicant. She has a meager work history, next to no experience, no post-high-school education, no bookkeeping or accounting skills. No personality, if her response to 'Tell me why you'd like to work here' is any indication. I'll let you judge. It says, 'Airplanes are amazing and useful.'"

"Well, they are," Tag said with a trace of a smile. "Why are you interviewing her then?"

"I'm not. She's dropping off a résumé and I agreed to test her. If she passes—" Iris gave her brow a dubious scrunch "—then I'll interview her. I agreed to test her because she's enthusiastic and local, and I'd like to give her a chance." Iris glanced back down at the paper. "She moved away and now she's back. I suspect a recent divorce because there's this big chunk of time where there's no work history at all. I'm guessing she hasn't applied for very many jobs in her life and only has a rough idea of how to go about it."

"Hmm. That's really nice of you."

"We'll see. If she can pass the test, I'll have a good idea whether she can do this job. I'm not as concerned about education and experience as I am…mettle. You know what I mean? You have to be good under pressure. You have to understand how difficult a pilot's job is, especially here in Alaska and—"

The door swung open and a woman walked in. Plump, overdressed and clutching her designer handbag like a life preserver, she reeked of trying-too-hard. Iris felt vindicated. She really was good at reading between the lines, so to speak. That is, until Iris recognized the woman, and the blood in her veins turned to ice water.

Thankfully, the woman zeroed in on Tag because Iris was pretty sure the look on her own face would be a dead giveaway to the shock and loathing invading Iris's nervous system. The barely qualified Ashley Frye was Ashley Eller?

"Hi, Tag," Ashley said.

A smiling Tag said, "Hey, Ashley, I heard you were back in town."

Iris had not heard that. But then again, she wasn't exactly tuned in to the local grapevine. Did Flynn know? She doubted he'd care, since they'd broken up in the middle of his senior year. They weren't exactly star-crossed lovers. That gave Iris little comfort, though. Her issues with Ashley had way more to do with Ashley herself than they did with Flynn.

"Yeah, just moved back about a week ago. Congratulations on your wedding."

"Thank you," Tag said.

"My parents have nothing but the most wonderful things to say about your fiancée, Ally. She helped my nana so much when she was in the hospital."

"That's nice, I'll pass that on. She'll be thrilled to hear it."

"Tomorrow, right? Todd Jessup invited me as his plus-one. I'm looking forward to seeing everyone."

More small talk ensued regarding Ashley's family and Ally's job as hospital liaison, but Iris could barely hear past the buzzing in her head. Great. Todd and Ashley would both be at the wedding. She already knew that Faith Monroe and Lorna Howell, Ashley's best friends from school, were going to be there. This just kept getting better and better. She couldn't even escape her past at her own brother's wedding.

Iris willed herself to get it together, and she was ready when Ashley turned her sugary beam of a smile toward her.

Then it was Ashley's turn to react. Like syrup in hot water, her expression melted from eager friendliness to astonishment to what looked like concern.

Ashley stammered, "I-Iris?"

Resisting the urge to glare, she coolly replied, "Yep. It's me, Iris."

Ashley had been the one to give Iris the nickname "Stick" back in middle school. On the surface, the moniker didn't sound all that bad, except Iris knew Ashley and her friends shortened it from "Ugly Stick." They used to shove sticks through the vent into her locker, along with insulting notes. The taunts and mind games continued in high school, where Ashley turned passive-aggressive bullying into an art form.

"It's Dr. James now. Can you believe that? My little sister is a doctor." As if Iris didn't already think Tag was the coolest brother in the world, he added, "But then, I'm sure you're not surprised since you two went to school together."

Ashley's smile wavered but she held on to it like the cheerleader captain she'd been. "Wow. Congratulations. No, I don't think anyone would be surprised by that. You, um, you look different. Really, really different."

"So do you," Iris gushed a little too sweetly, and immediately felt a twinge of guilt. Her nemesis, Flynn's ex-girlfriend, the once curvaceous beauty queen, and Rankins High all-around "it girl" had changed quite a bit, too. Heavy makeup couldn't cover the dark circles under her eyes or the fact that her once porcelain-perfect complexion had turned ruddy.

Ashley's gaze bounced around, but never quite met Iris's. If Iris didn't know better, she'd think the woman was on the verge of tears. She couldn't help but wonder what had stolen Rankins High's most-likely-to-make-it-in-Hollywood's confidence?

"What can I help you with, Ashley? Are you going to be shipping something? Do you need to arrange a transport?"

Uncertainty flickered across her expression before she finally managed a few seconds of solid eye contact. "No. Um…I'm here about the job." She blinked away again.

Iris glanced down at the application on her desk. Yep, Ashley Frye was Ashley Eller, and she was here to apply for the job. Iris couldn't help it, she wanted to laugh. And possibly even dance around and clap. Somehow, she managed to remain composed even as she made a vow—never again would she discount the unabashed power of karma.

"I see. How…interesting."

"Um, Faith told me Tag was hiring a new office person. She filled out the application for me. I—I didn't realize you were working here."

"It's a little more complicated than office person."

"Oh, yeah, of course, I'm sure it is. You're doing the hiring?"

"Yes, I am doing the hiring and the training. What a small world this is, huh?"

"Um, yeah, that's for sure. Here's my résumé."

Iris took it and set it on her desk. "Follow me and I'll show you where you can take the test." Was it wrong to test her when there was no way Iris would ever consider her for the job? Maybe. And she'd certainly gain some satisfaction from "filing" her application exactly where it belonged.

CHAPTER SIX

SHAY HAD DESIGNATED three hotel rooms for the wedding party and family members—one for the ladies, another for the guys and the bride had her own. Iris was the last one out of the ladies' room, and, after a check on a remarkably unruffled Ally, whom she left visiting with her grandfather, Abe, she headed out into the hall. A window overlooked the courtyard and provided a bird's-eye view of the ultraefficient Faraway Inn staff bustling about with last-minute tasks.

Towering, tree-covered mountains glowed against a mind-bogglingly blue sky in the distance. Overhead, the sun was a perfect pale yellow fuzzy-edged ball. Not too bright and not too dim, the soft light would be perfect for the photos that photographer Ginger Weil was already busy snapping away. Iris couldn't imagine a more perfect day for a wedding.

She spotted her sister Shay, owner and manager of the Faraway Inn, unmistakably in charge and rocking her baby bump in a pastel-colored flower-print dress. Hannah joined her, they laughed together, then parted ways to finalize the already-perfect details. Ivory linens decorated the round tables situated around the courtyard. Bouquets of wildflowers and herbs tucked into pale green vintage bottles adorned the center of each table. The DJ was setting up at the far end beside a portable dance floor. Lilah from the Donut Den held a frosting tube, and was fussing around the dessert bar.

Bering, Cricket and Seth, looking tall and handsome in their tuxes, were already greeting guests. Tag knew everyone in town and pretty much everyone had been invited. Summer schedules filled up months in advance in Alaska, which meant the Faraway Inn had been booked every weekend in the summer. Undaunted, Tag and Ally had planned the ceremony for the hotel's least busy day of the week, a Wednesday evening.

Despite the short notice and the midweek designation, the RSVP list was remarkable. Townsfolk were coming out in droves to see Rankins's most eligible bachelor finally part with his title. The devotion and loyalty her big brother enjoyed in this town was well-deserved. He'd spent his life doing things for others. Fam-

ily, friends, neighbors, their pets, wildlife—
anyone or anything who needed help, Tag was
there. And even though Ally hadn't been in
Rankins long, she had her share of fans, too.
They deserved this day.

Meaning Iris could get through the requi-
site hours of socializing, smiling and making
small talk with many of the people who'd spent
her formative years mocking and bullying her.
She would do that for her brother and for Ally.

Smoothing the skirt of her freshly pressed
bridesmaid dress, she squeezed her eyes shut,
inhaled a deep breath and reminded herself of
all the ways she was different than she'd been
back in high school—educated, successful and,
if not exactly glamorous, then at least put together. And confident, something she had no
trouble being when she wasn't about to stare
down the worst of her past.

Determination fueling her, she opened her
eyes and let out a gasp. "Flynn! Yeesh."

"Sorry, I didn't mean to scare you."

"Umm, wow!" she said before she could
stop herself. Flynn in a tux. At least she had
this stunning spectacle to distract her from her
troubles. Clean-shaven, hair freshly trimmed,
he looked like one of those too-handsome-to-
be-real perfume models. It didn't matter what

he was wearing—jeans or tux, suit or scrubs—he was always that guy.

"I—I," she stammered. "You look…amazing."

One side of his mouth curled up, making the dimple appear even deeper on that side. "Thank you." He tugged on a lapel. "I'm feeling pretty dapper. But you…" he drawled. "You are—"

"Please don't say 'gorgeous,'" she interrupted, hating the peevish edge to her tone.

Eyes twinkling, he quirked an eyebrow and teased, "I wasn't going to. What I was going to do is suggest you go get dressed and do something with your hair because we're going to be in a wedding in a very short time and you look like chaos personified. I'm embarrassed to stand up there with you."

One hand went up to touch the elaborate updo her cousin Adele had given her. She couldn't help but laugh. Why did he have to be so…irresistible? Trying to lighten the mood, she gestured at herself. "Sorry. What were you thinking, what were you going to say?"

Voice lowering to a raspy timbre that caused a shiver to skitter across her skin, he said, "Which do you want?"

"What do you mean?" she asked, even as

she knew instinctively that she was wading in over her head.

He took a tiny step toward her and he was already close. "Do you want to know what I was going to say or what I was thinking?"

"Hmm." Infused with an unexpected surge of bravery, she reached up and adjusted his tie. "Which one is better?"

Iris watched his breath catch, as his eyes followed her hands.

"That depends…" His gaze ensnared hers and the intensity she saw there made her breath stall, too. "I'm pretty sure the second one will make you blush."

"Oh." A blowtorch blast of heat filled her cheeks and neck. Served her right for attempting to flirt with the champ. And yet she couldn't seem to stop herself. "Try me," she said.

Surprise flickered across his features before his mouth slowly curved up into a smile. He shifted even closer and Iris held her ground. Was it possible Hazel was right? It didn't matter, she immediately reminded herself. Nothing could happen between them. She hated Alaska. Flynn loved Alaska. She was leaving. Flynn was staying. Those were the facts. And the real truth was that her heart couldn't withstand the damage he could do.

Gaze searching her face, he whispered, "I'd absolutely love to. I—"

"Hey!" a voice called from down the hallway. "Here you guys are."

Flynn winked at her before turning his charm on Iris's cousin-in-law, Bering's wife, Emily. Emily was head of the Rankins Tourism Bureau and an organizational marvel. She and Shay were coordinating the bulk of the reception. "Hi, Emily. You look lovely."

"Thanks, Flynn. You clean up pretty well yourself. Not that you don't rock the whole white-coat-and-stethoscope thing."

If Emily noticed they were standing too close, or that Iris was flustered, she didn't mention it.

"Iris, you look stunning. That dress is... spectacular."

"Isn't it?" She held up her arms. "Flynn picked it out."

Emily quirked an eyebrow in Flynn's direction. "I hear you picked out the bride's exquisite gown, too?"

"That is the truth. I am a fashion maven," he joked.

"Can I just say how impressive that is? Bering would be hard-pressed to tell the difference between a dress and a tablecloth."

"Hey," Flynn answered with an easy shrug. "It's not every day a guy gets asked to take on a traditionally female lead in the wedding performance of the year. I studied up. The eyes of Rankins, Alaska, are on me."

Emily laughed. "Well done, Dr. Ramsey. On behalf of maids and men of honor everywhere, I applaud you."

Flynn executed a little bow.

"Flowers," she said, handing Iris her bouquet. She held up a boutonniere and nodded toward Flynn. "Can you pin this on him?"

"Sure."

"Great. We need you guys in place in ten, okay? I need to find Abe."

"Got it," Flynn said.

"Abe is with Ally," Iris informed her.

"Perfect. Thank you." Emily hurried off down the hall.

Flynn smiled at Iris and she tried to return it. But the ten-minute warning had deflated the moment. Ten minutes until she ran the metaphorical gauntlet of her past. Iris set her flowers on the windowsill and went to work pinning Flynn's corsage into place.

"Hey," he said.

"Mmm-hmm?" she murmured, avoiding his curious gaze.

"What just happened here? What's wrong?"

"What do you mean?"

"More motion sickness?"

She almost smiled. "Flynn, I'm fine."

"Now I know you're lying. In my experience, when a woman says she's fine it means that she either isn't, or that she doesn't want to talk about it. Which is it, in this case?"

"Both."

"How can I help if you don't tell me what it is?"

"You can't help. There," she said, adjusting the flower and patting his lapel.

"How do you know?" Before she could step back, he took her hand and lightly entwined his fingers with hers. When she didn't pull away, he caressed the back of her hand with his thumb. He pressed gently against her wrist and she knew his doctor fingers were tuning into the wild thumping of her pulse.

"'Cuz I know." Forcing a smile, she heaved up her eyes to meet his. "Thank you for the offer, though. We better go."

Instead, he stood his ground, keeping her in place with just the touch of his hand, watching her carefully like they had all the time in the world and he had all the answers.

Finally, he nodded slowly. "Okay…" His voice was so fraught with tension it had Iris holding her breath. "But we're going to talk about something else later."

"What?"

"About…" Pausing, he tilted his head to slay her with one of his roguish grins. "About why you don't want me to call you gorgeous."

They absolutely were not going to talk about that. Instead she blurted, "I'm nervous. There, are you happy?"

"*You're* nervous?" he asked doubtfully. "About what?"

"About what?" she repeated with a chuckle. "How about standing up there in front of three hundred and fifty-two people, some of whom I was hoping never to see again in my life, and then having to make small talk with these same people for I don't know how many hours."

"Seriously?"

"This surprises you?"

He paused and studied her carefully. "It does. You're great at this kind of stuff. You've never had a problem being in front of people. We won the science fair due in large part to your eloquence. You taught classes in graduate school with practically that many students in them, right?"

"Yes, but, science, math, economics… academics in general—that is my safe zone. People inside my zone are fine." She waved a hand toward the window, where guests were already taking their seats in the long rows of white chairs that had been set up on the grassy lawn. "Those people are not. Rankins is not my zone."

"Those people? Iris, a lot of *those people* are your family. Rankins is your hometown. People here love you."

"No, Flynn, they don't. I mean, yes, to the family part, that's true." She was realizing that was truer than she'd believed. The one good thing she could take away from this visit was connecting with her family in a way she never had before. Two good things if she counted Flynn. But she wasn't sure she could. Not exactly. "But the Rankins part, no. Come on, Flynn, you remember what I was like in high school."

"Yes, brilliant, funny, kind, beautiful—"

"Stop," Iris interrupted him. "Dorky, nerdy, clumsy, not athletic, not popular, too skinny, not beautiful—not on the outside, anyway."

"Just because people couldn't see how beautiful you are doesn't mean you weren't."

"Flynn! You didn't think I was beautiful in that way, either. I was teased and ridiculed and bullied—" She cut the sentence short, immediately wishing she could take it back. She didn't want to talk about this and make the day about her. Even though she was terrified.

"Bullied?" he repeated a bit too skeptically for her taste. "Really?"

"Yes, Flynn. Looking back on it now, yes." She sighed. "Look, this isn't one of those conversations you're probably used to having where beautiful, insecure women complain about how fat their ankles are so you'll tell them they're not. I'm not fishing for compliments. I'm not interested in being beautiful." That wasn't entirely true, but she wanted it to be. It mostly was. "My point here is that I'm not looking forward to being on display in front of Ashley and Faith and all the other people who made me feel *less than*, when I knew I wasn't. I'm not."

"Of course you're not." Frustration tinged his tone before his face scrunched with a question. "Ashley Eller?"

"Yes, Ashley Eller. She's divorced and back in town and she'll be here." Iris watched him for a reaction, but she didn't pick up on anything other than surprise.

"Yeah, well, she wasn't a very nice person in general. Which is why we broke up, and also why she and Faith were besties, birds of a feather. But, Iris, we all have bad memories from our childhoods. They don't define us. We overcome them, and we move on."

"Bad memories?" she repeated with a bitter chuckle. "Flynn, you don't…" Understand. She wanted to explain. But what good would it do now? It would sound like whining. She'd worked hard to get past these feelings. She could do this.

Flynn gave her hand a gentle squeeze. "I'll tell you what—I am going to help."

"How are you going to do that?" she asked skeptically.

"I'll stay close. The second anyone makes you feel uncomfortable, I'll swoop in and rescue you."

Despite herself, she smiled. He was so… sweet. If only it was that simple. But she couldn't ignore how the touch of his hand calmed her nerves. "And how will you know that I'm uncomfortable?"

"Trust me," he said. "I'll know."

WITH THE CEREMONY a complete success, guests mingled in the courtyard. Dinner had been enthusiastically devoured, but the subtle scents of lemon, pepper and grilled salmon still wafted through the air. The cake was cut, and spirits were high as guests enjoyed dessert and drinks. Lamps were lit around the perimeter. Music was in full swing and couples migrated to the dance floor.

Flynn didn't have to locate Iris in the crowd—he knew where she was and planned to keep it that way. Not that it was a hardship to look at her in that dress, a phenomenon he'd noticed that other men shared, and one that filled him with both pride and annoyance at the same time.

A voice sounded off to his left. "Flynn, can I talk to you for a minute?"

He turned to find Iris's mom standing before him. "Hello, Mrs. James. Of course. You look incredibly lovely."

Tall and uniquely beautiful, Flynn had always thought that of all the James children, Iris looked the most like their mother. Radiant in her navy-and-gold mother-of-the-groom dress, she could easily pass for a decade younger than her sixty-odd years.

"Thank you. But I wish you'd stop calling me 'Mrs. James.'"

Flynn chuckled and scratched his chin. "That's a tough one for me. You know how old-school Doc is. But I'll start right now." Flynn winked at her. "So, Margaret, how does it feel to have another of your brood happily married off?"

Eyes twinkling, an easy smile lit her face. "Wonderful. It's no secret that I despaired of Tag ever settling down. But for him to find someone as incredible as Ally? I am beyond thrilled. Three down and three to go, another grandchild on the way—I'm a very happy woman."

"I'm so glad."

"I wanted to thank you for helping with the wedding. Tag and Ally and Iris have all been singing your praises. Between you and Iris taking care of wedding details, and Emily and Shay doing the reception, I've barely had to do anything."

"It's been fun. Ally is like a little sister to me."

Flynn glanced up again to see Iris with Cricket. Cricket wrapped an arm around her shoulder, pulling her close to speak into her ear. Iris laughed. Satisfied that she was out of harm's way, so to speak, he focused on Margaret but kept Iris on the edge of his vision. A subtle inquiry about her relationship with Cricket might be in order, however.

"Iris looks exceptionally beautiful, doesn't she?"

He'd only looked away for a second. How had she known? "She does. But then again, she always does as far as I'm concerned."

Expression thoughtful, Margaret tilted her head. "You were always so good to Iris. If it weren't for Jericho in middle school and then you in high school, I don't know what she would have done. I'm not sure what her father and I would have done."

"Jericho, her cat?" Flynn smiled, thinking she might be giving him a little too much credit.

"Yes, she adopted him from Agnes Garner in middle school. Remember Agnes and her cat-rescue program?" At his nod, she went on, "Iris didn't have any friends, except for Hazel and Seth. But they were busy with sports and activities."

Iris didn't have any friends? Their earlier conversation fresh in his mind, a pinch of discomfort nipped at him. Now that he thought about it, she never mentioned anyone from her class. She never mentioned anyone from school, except her siblings.

"Did you know we almost sent her away to boarding school?"

"What? No... When?"

"I'm not surprised. She doesn't talk about her past much, does she? About how difficult her childhood was? She acts like she's overcome it, but I don't know if a person can ever truly get over what she went through."

Flynn paused as a chill went through him. Her childhood? Had she really been that miserable?

As if Margaret could hear his thoughts, she explained, "Iris came to Ben and me when she was thirteen and asked if we would enroll her in boarding school in the lower forty-eight." Margaret grimaced a little at the memory. "She had her argument all laid out, about how she was different, didn't fit in here, had no friends. People always think because she's a triplet that she'd naturally be attached to Hazel and Seth. And she was—is—of course, to a degree. But Hazel and Seth were more like twins than the three of them were like triplets. It's not their fault. It started when they were babies. That seems to be getting better now, but...

"Anyway, Iris almost didn't make it and then

it was one issue after another—lungs, eyes, heart and on it went. Did you know she had nine surgeries before the age of ten?"

"No, I didn't know that." He knew she had a mild asthma condition. Why had it never occurred to him that it had been caused by her premature birth? Probably because she didn't talk about it. But still, as a doctor he should have—he was very aware of the fact that lung problems were one of the most common conditions associated with premature births. Flynn felt his heart clench as he imagined Iris as a lonely little girl, essentially quarantined inside the house.

Margaret went on to confirm his thoughts. "That meant long periods of recovery. Months when she couldn't go outside. All the other kids were running, climbing trees, fishing, skiing and riding bikes. I tried to be with her as often as I could, but it was difficult as we had other children. She spent a lot of time alone, while Hazel and Seth bonded because they developed quicker. They kind of kept pace with one another, spurred each other on even. Unfortunately, Iris got left behind. She missed a fair amount of school and when she did go, she endured teasing. In middle school, there was a group of girls who bullied her. They were so cruel."

Bullied. Ashley and her cronies. Iris had tried to tell him and he'd all but blown her off. Sympathy twisted inside of him thinking about the too-skinny, slightly gawky girl he'd gotten to know in tenth grade. She'd been a year behind him, so he hadn't known her before then. Brilliant, observant and quietly witty, he'd liked her from the first day of advanced algebra, when she'd argued with the teacher over a mistake he'd written on the board.

Seated beside her, he'd watched, intrigued, as she'd taken a sheet of paper and penciled out the problem for the teacher. If only he would have recognized his fascination for what it was. He wished he could go back and shake his sixteen-year-old self. And how could he have been so clueless about Ashley's part in it all?

"Luckily, she was blessed with that brain. And kindness and compassion. And so many other good traits. Although, struggling with the physical stuff always seemed to stick with her."

"It must have been difficult to say no to her about boarding school. Knowing Iris, I'm guessing she didn't take it well."

"Oh, we didn't say no. We knew she was right. It broke my heart, the fact that our baby girl was so miserable. And when she came to us, she was armed with all her research, including a list of schools and the cost of tuition for each one. There were statistics and scholarship applications. We told her we'd think about it. I couldn't bear the idea of her going away, but she was bitterly unhappy. We were just about to allow her to go when she met Agnes and adopted Jericho. She agreed to try one year of high school."

Flynn smiled, feeling more relieved than he should have about an event that happened more than a decade ago. He couldn't imagine his life if he'd never met Iris.

Margaret captured his gaze with a deliberate "Where she met you."

CHAPTER SEVEN

"ME?" FLYNN REPEATED.

Margaret wore a satisfied expression, like she'd been waiting for him to catch up. "Yes, you. And those advanced courses. At first, I was worried about her being in classes where she wouldn't have Hazel or Seth with her anymore. But you gave her a reason to go to school. I thought about seeking you out back then to thank you for being so kind to her, but I didn't want to sound condescending, or put unfair pressure on you. Plus, I knew it would give away her feelings for you."

Flynn swallowed around a massive lump of regret and guilt, and focused on the nugget of hope she'd just given him. "Her feelings?"

"When it comes to her heart, Iris is good at hiding. She had to be in order to get through what she endured. But I knew how she felt about you back then. A mother senses these things."

"You didn't need to thank me—then or now.

Iris was just as amazing in school as she is today. We were…friends." Sort of. Not like they were now. Not like they should have been. "Looking back, I wish…" Flynn paused as the notion sank in that their relationship could have evolved so much differently. How would his life had gone if he'd asked her out back then?

"I was an idiot." The words hammered at his heart like a million regretful spikes.

"You were a teenager," Margaret countered kindly.

"I was a teenaged idiot." This was true. And he hated it. Margaret was right, a lot of teenaged boys were. And probably he wouldn't have been as equipped back then to treat Iris the way he would now, the way he wanted to. He'd dated a bunch of girls, but he'd never been a great boyfriend, or husband, for that matter.

Self-involved, inconsiderate at times, he'd had plenty of his own issues from growing up in the war zone that was his home. Being athletic and dating the prettiest and most popular girls had been his way of getting attention, of boosting his confidence. Neither of which his constantly bickering and self-centered parents had the time or energy to do for him. He'd learned so much in the ensuing years, about himself, about women and especially about relationships. Still, he couldn't help but wish he would have acknowledged Iris's amazingness back then.

Margaret smiled and then echoed his thoughts, suggesting to Flynn that she'd intended this conversation to be about more than the wedding. "Most teenagers are, Iris being a rare exception. Not even Ashley and her friends could break her. They were so…horrible. I wanted to press charges at one point, or at least scare them, but Iris begged me not to. She said she could handle it. I think she was embarrassed, and afraid of what you'd think. Later she told me that because she's a James, she didn't think people would have much sympathy."

Flynn felt nauseated. She'd deserved his help if nothing else, then and now. His own childhood, as rough and lonely as it was, hadn't been nearly as terrible as what she'd gone through. He'd always had school. Where he'd thrived. Sports, friends, girlfriends—he'd had it all. Yes, Iris had her family, but what else? A cat? And, later, if Margaret was to be believed, him?

"She always seemed so confident, mature and above the fray. Looking back, she was a little intimidating."

"That's her skill. She learned the hard way how to play up her strengths. She also knows how to avoid situations that might show her weaknesses."

Flynn thought about that for a few seconds. How had he not seen this sooner? This explained so much. She always declined his and Ally's offers of hiking or fishing or biking... Jasper Lake came to mind, her reticence to partake in any of the activities. He'd thought she just didn't like the outdoors. That was part of it, but Iris's dislike of Rankins was based on way more than he'd presumed. He was worse than an idiot.

"I probably would have screwed it up, anyway."

"Maybe," Margaret acknowledged with a teasing smile.

Flynn chuckled and glanced at Iris.

"What's your excuse now?"

Despite the ache in his heart, Flynn pulled out his best charmer grin. "Margaret, that is an excellent question."

He looked at Iris again, wondering how best to approach this. Cricket was gone, but Todd Jessup was now chatting with her. Seth had told Flynn that he'd heard Todd asking around about her at the Cozy Caribou. That wasn't going to happen.

Two more figures he recognized appeared

in his line of sight—Ashley and Faith seemed to be headed Iris's way.

"If you'll excuse me? I think it's time I tweaked my strategy where your daughter is concerned."

"Nice wedding, huh?"

Iris smiled at Todd Jessup. "Yes, it was perfect."

And it was. Iris was beyond relieved that the difficult part was over. Standing up in front of everyone hadn't been as grueling as she'd expected. Not with Flynn beside her. The dress helped; she knew she looked good.

The real challenge had been holding back the tears as she watched her oldest brother marry the love of his life. Tag and Ally, however, radiated nothing but joy. Apparently it was contagious because despite herself, Iris had to admit she was feeling rather joy-filled herself.

"Your brother is a lucky guy."

"He certainly is."

"But then he's always been lucky where women are concerned. Good-looking girlfriends, good-looking cousin, good-looking sister…"

Iris paused. Was Todd Jessup hitting on her? Todd had been a football player in school. A friend of Seth and Flynn's, and a solid member of the in crowd, he'd dated and married a fellow A-lister and member of Ashley's pack, Treena Scheck, a year out of high school. Two kids and five years later, they'd divorced. He'd never shown the slightest interest in Iris in high school. Then again, no guy had.

"So, I, uh, I was asking around about you, and your brother Seth said he didn't think you were seeing anyone."

A voice off to her left cried, "Iris, hi!" Iris turned to see Faith Monroe descending upon them, a much more somber Ashley by her side.

The black pit in her stomach grew exponentially. That's all she needed, to throw up in front of these women who had made her feel like this nearly every day of her high-school career. Tacking on her best fake smile, Iris braced herself.

Faith went on as if they were old friends. "Oh, my gosh, I haven't seen you since high school. Ashley said you were back."

"Hello, Faith. Ashley. I'm just here for a visit."

"That's right, Hazel told me you were getting some kind of big-shot job. Are we supposed to call you Dr. James now?" While Hazel had disliked Ashley, she and Faith were friendly.

Hazel always said it wasn't in Faith's nature to be truly mean. Where alpha Ashley led, Faith and a whole gang had followed.

"If that makes you more comfortable, then by all means."

"Remember how we used to call you Stick back in school?" She tittered like it was a funny anecdote and not a cruel taunt. Did Faith somehow think the passing of years would make Iris nostalgic?

"How could I forget?" Iris said, infusing her tone with plenty of sarcasm. "You guys were always so *clever*. So imaginative. And what you lacked in originality you made up for with persistence."

"Thank you!" Faith exclaimed. Iris had forgotten how sarcasm was wasted on Faith. "You certainly don't look like a stick anymore, though, do you? Talk about a late bloomer! You're so beautiful now—and stylish. Not like high school at all. I love your dress!"

"Thank you, I think. But look at you! You're the same, huh? It's nice that some things don't change."

"Isn't that the truth?" Faith agreed.

"No small feat, either, considering how many opportunities you've had to grow and…evolve.

It must have taken a lot of self-restraint on your part to resist. Very impressive."

Todd chuckled.

Faith's smile faltered as she seemed to struggle with discerning Iris's meaning. Ashley looked away.

Todd's expression was filled with fresh admiration as it landed on Iris again. "So, after the reception tonight a bunch of us are heading to the Cozy Caribou to sing karaoke."

"That sounds fun." *For you*, she added silently. She'd had enough class reunion-ing to last a lifetime. She was trying to figure out how to move on when Flynn's voice sounded over her shoulder. "That *does* sound fun, doesn't it?"

Iris frowned at him. "Umm…" What was he doing? Trying to encourage her to go out with Todd Jessup? How was that "helping"?

Flynn slipped an arm around her, his fingertips shooting tiny sparks across her bare back. "Too bad we have plans."

That was better. Relief and gratitude fueled her grin. "Yep. Too bad."

Todd looked at Flynn. "Hey, Ram, how you doing, man? I have to say that even though I wouldn't want to do it, you make this man-of-honor thing look pretty fine."

"Thanks, Jess," Flynn responded using Todd's

high-school-football nickname, the same as Todd had done. "That's probably wise on your part. Doubt you could pull it off," he teased good-naturedly.

"That is totally true, dude."

Faith eyed Iris and Flynn curiously. "I see that you two are still…friends?" She gave Ashley an elbow nudge. "We always thought that was the cutest thing, didn't we, Ashley?"

Ashley, to her credit, looked uncomfortable. Brittle smile, shifty eyes, she looked like she'd rather be somewhere else.

Iris looked at Faith. "Yes, Flynn and I are—"

"Friends?" Flynn repeated, and added a little chuckle along with a possessive embrace. "We are definitely that, aren't we?" Dipping his head, he brushed his lips across her cheek and nuzzled her neck. Iris's pulse shifted into overdrive even as anxiety churned inside of her. What was he doing?

Tucked close to his side, Flynn zeroed his gaze in on her. "Can I steal you away for a minute?"

"Sure." Iris settled her face into a smile, not an easy task with Flynn draped all over her and enemies at her flank. Having her back was one thing; her being his fake girlfriend was something else altogether. Still, the gesture was sweet. If only it didn't make her feel like fainting.

Flynn gave the others a sheepish grin. "Honestly, I just want to dance with the most beautiful woman here. Excuse us. Have fun, you guys. Try the salmon. Talk to you later, Jess."

With his hand branding her bare back, he led her to the dance floor. Gentle notes of a popular love song filled the air, so Flynn gathered her in his embrace and made dancing seem as easy as everything else he did. The satisfied smile playing on his lips caused Iris's heart to execute a slow cartwheel inside her chest. She should be used to this, to him, by now.

Lowering her voice to a whisper, she said, "Thank you for that. I owe you one. It was probably a little over-the-top, but I appreciate your dramatic flair. I'm sure they're still talking about it."

He dipped his head, and whispered near her ear, "I could not possibly care any less than I do about Faith or Ashley. And I only care about Todd in that I don't want you singing any duets with him."

"I hadn't planned to but…" Her throat went dry because his hand had returned to her back, where his thumb caressed the skin along the edge of her dress. "What are you doing?"

"Dancing. Is there something going on between you and Cricket?"

"What?" she answered, alarmed by the subject change. Did he know about the flying lessons? She wasn't ready for anyone to know about that yet. "Like what? What do you mean by 'something'?"

Eyes narrowed and assessing, he clarified, "Are you two romantically involved?"

"Oh." She laughed, and then paused to process the question. She didn't want to tell him the truth, but she also didn't want him thinking *that*. "That's not what's going on," she said, and then realized that she'd inferred that something was.

"What is going on, then?"

"Nothing. I mean, he is helping me with something. But we're just friends. He's practically like a brother to me, you know that."

"I do, I was just confirming it before I did something."

"What?"

Then Flynn twirled her around and she could see that Ashley and Faith had been joined by a couple of other women, Lorna included. She also recognized Nicki and Pam, two nurses from the hospital.

"Oh, I get it. They're still watching, right?"

Flynn chuckled softly, shifting his focus to meet her gaze again. His brown eyes seemed to burn into hers. "No, I don't think you do get it," he murmured. "But then again, I didn't really get it, either."

"Get what? Flynn, what are you...?" Her question trailed off because he was staring at her mouth. The heat from her cheeks was apparently burning through to her brain because she could not think straight. Much less talk.

"Maybe this will help."

Then his mouth brushed against hers in the sweetest, most perfect caress. Flynn was kissing her? Yes, he sure was, and his lips were velvety soft and completely perfect, and she couldn't—she wouldn't—think past that. Instead, she kissed him back, pressing her mouth more firmly to his. One hand came up to grip his shoulder. Before she could do more than that, his soft lips were gone.

"Iris," he whispered, "I'm..." He closed his eyes and rested his forehead against hers for a second before slipping a hand around the back of her neck. He pressed a gentle kiss against her forehead and tucked her in close again. "Give me a second."

Iris focused on trying to move air in and out of her lungs, but with her cheek pressed against his chest, every breath was Flynn-scented with hints of spicy soap and cedar boughs. Flynn had just kissed her. What did that mean? What did she do now? Panic welled inside of her because it couldn't *mean* anything.

A chuckle vibrated through him. "That should give everyone something to talk about, huh?"

Of course, she realized, he'd kissed her *for* her, to help her. Thank goodness, he'd broken it off before she'd said something truly embarrassing. Her cheeks ignited with heat as she imagined herself clinging to him like a spider monkey on the dance floor.

She felt a hand on her shoulder and she knew it was Hazel before her sister's smiling face confirmed it. "Hey, Iris," she said. "Ally is going to toss her bouquet in a few minutes."

Somehow, she managed to squeak out an answer. "'Kay, I'll be right there."

Hazel departed. It took effort to drag her gaze up to meet Flynn's. But he was grinning at her like he had the best secret ever and Iris felt her anxiety melt away like wax on a flame. Okay, this was a good thing. It didn't mean anything. He'd been helping just as he'd promised he would. That's why he'd asked about her and Cricket; he didn't want to get in the way of anything. So why did her heart feel like it had just been stolen from her chest and attached to her sleeve? Because Flynn "helping" was a little too much of a good thing.

THAT KISS MEANT EVERYTHING. Flynn watched Iris take her spot with the other single ladies. Sure, it had been quick, but it was enough. Because it had definitely answered the question that had been burning between them for the last two-plus months. He'd seen the hammering of her pulse at the base of her neck, felt her tremble in his arms, the melding of her lips to his. It was the reaction he'd been hoping for, the one that so perfectly matched his own.

And, oh, man… She'd kissed him back and he…he felt like doing a victory punch right there in the middle of the crowd. It had taken every last scrap of his willpower not to take her hand and whisk her away to somewhere private, where he could do it again. But better. And more thoroughly.

But the point here was that Iris could no longer avoid what was so clearly unfolding between them.

IRIS TOOK HER position in the back of the crowd as the DJ cranked up the single-lady song. She spotted Faith and Ashley in the middle row, behind Nicki and Pam. She figured all four of them for solid contenders in the bouquet bout. Iris was perfectly content to let them duke it out while she phoned it in from the last row. She needed a few more minutes to get her bearings, anyway.

Hazel joined her, her knowing grin telling Iris she'd seen what had unfolded on the dance floor.

Immediately confirming it, she leaned in close to her ear and said, "You and Flynn? I knew it! Congratulations!"

"No, no, no." Iris shook her head. "That was…" She waved her off. "I'll explain later," she yelled.

Hazel frowned.

The music quieted. Iris took the opportunity to check her phone. Even though she'd had all calls forwarded to another transport company, it wasn't outside the realm of possibility to have an emergency large enough that Copper Crossing's services would still be needed. Cricket was on call. She didn't want Tag to have to deal with any distractions today.

A loud drumroll ensued, along with clapping and laughter. Iris glanced up to see Ally turn around so her back was facing them. Ally was tiny, but she was strong and athletic, and Iris should have known she'd put some muscle behind it. Those were her thoughts as the bouquet launched high into the air. But then it was sailing straight toward her! Panic shot through her and she reacted. Grabbing Hazel by the shoulders, she ducked behind her sister.

The crowd erupted in cheers as Hazel caught the flowers. The music switched to "Chapel of Love." Iris blew out a relieved breath. Hazel held her prize aloft before executing an elegant bow.

The crowd dispersed. Hazel turned on her with a questioning look. "What was that? It's not a game of hot potato. You could have had it. It was headed right for you."

"I know." Iris gave her a proud grin. "Who knew I could move so quickly and gracefully?"

"Me," Hazel said, placing a bouquet-filled hand on her hip. "I did. I knew. I know," she added, linking her other arm through one of Iris's, "because you are the unqualified queen of the dodge and weave."

CHAPTER EIGHT

IRIS AWOKE THE next morning and tried to sort her jumbled feelings. Stinging nettles had taken up residence inside her foot because her mom's tortoiseshell cat, Micah, was sprawled across it.

Hazel snored softly in the double bed across from hers in the bedroom they'd shared for eighteen years, before they'd headed off to college. Their mom had updated the space a few years ago. Most of their knickknacks, including the shelf filled with Hazel's track trophies and Iris's math and science awards, were boxed away in the attic. Also gone were Hazel's travel posters and Iris's giant periodic table. The once bright purple walls were now a light dove gray. Watercolor prints were artfully arranged on the walls and down comforters with matching duvets covered the beds. But sharing a room felt the same and they still gravitated there when they came home to visit.

Iris flexed her foot. Micah let out a sharp snippet of a meow, conveying his irritation at being so rudely inconvenienced. Contorting her body while simultaneously pulling and shifting the covers and trying to disturb him as little as possible, she slid to the edge of the bed. Golden eyes narrowed disapprovingly before the cat stood, stretched and sauntered to the head of the bed, where he resettled on her pillow. Chuckling softly, Iris rose, donned a pair of sweats and secured her hair in a messy bun.

After the bouquet toss, the rest of the evening had been a blur, a surprisingly fun blur. Wedding-wise, she didn't see how it could have gone better. Tag and Ally were elated. With Flynn glued to her side, Ashley and company had faded nicely into the background. He'd even pulled her up next to him while he delivered what was surely the finest man-of-honor speech in the history of speeches. He'd flirted, held her hand and made her feel more beautiful than she ever had in her life.

In short, he'd put on quite a show. And all for her benefit. But at the same time, she sort of wished he hadn't done it. She'd been so careful about keeping her feelings stuffed down inside where they belonged. Now they were oozing out all over the place.

That kiss.

As fleeting and well-intentioned as it had

been, it was still Flynn's lips on hers. In that short moment, she'd lost her mind. Now that the evening was over, she felt uncomfortable and silly. And smitten. Always that where Flynn was concerned.

Gripping her T-shirt over her achy heart, she let out a groan of frustration. "What am I going to do?"

She hadn't realized she'd been so loud until Hazel rolled over. "About what?" her sister mumbled. "What time is it?"

"Sorry. It's only six. You can go back to sleep."

"Um, yeah, I think I will. Why are you up already?"

"Just a lot on my mind. I'll have coffee ready for you."

"Ohhh… I love you…" Hazel drawled sleepily. "Let's make omelets later and talk about you and Flynn."

"I love you, too. That's a plan, except for the Flynn part."

On the nightstand, her phone began to buzz.

Hazel groaned and buried her head in her pillow. "What is that? Is that a helicopter?"

"Yes," Iris said wryly. "Yes, Hazel, there is a tiny helicopter circling in our bedroom."

Hazel chucked a pillow at her.

Iris ducked and picked up the phone as her stomach did the Flynn flip. He was the only person she knew who would call her this early. Despite her misgivings, he was still her friend—and she didn't want to lose that. Plucking the phone from the charger, she hurried out into the hall.

Except, when she went to swipe her finger across the screen, Dr. Hottie McBrilliant did not light up the display. A Washington, DC, number stared back at her, one she recognized immediately because that's what she did—she memorized things. With a trembling hand, she brought the phone up to her ear. "Hello?"

"Hi…" a tentative voice said. "Is this Iris James?"

"Yes, it is."

"Hey, Iris, this is Sebastien Frieze from The Frieze Group."

"Hello." Okay, already said that.

A brief hesitation followed and then he let out a little groan. "Ugh. You know what? I just realized how early it is up there. I apologize. My assistant left me a note, but I'm only reading that part right now. Should I call back later?"

"No, Dr. Frieze, that's not necessary. I'm up. Early riser."

"Really? Oh, cool. Me, too. I love to watch the sunrise."

"My favorite time of day," she said, surprised at how normal she sounded. Because this could not be a normal phone call. This had to be good news. Sebastien Frieze would not say "Oh, cool" and chat about sunrises if it wasn't.

"So, great, Iris, I'm glad I caught you then. I apologize for the delay in reviewing your résumé. I had a bit of a…family emergency."

"No problem," she said smoothly. "I understand family obligations. I hope everything is okay?"

"Thank you. It is, or it will be… Hopefully, someday." He paused like he wanted to say more, but got to the point instead. "Your résumé is quite impressive and I'm hoping you haven't accepted a position elsewhere by now?"

"No, I haven't."

"Fantastic, that's a relief. Is there any way you can come in for an interview?"

An interview. Two words. Two glorious, life-affirming words it felt as if she'd been waiting her whole life to hear.

"Yes, of course I can. I'd love to."

"Great! I can't wait to show you around." He went on to reveal that the interview was just a formality, as much an opportunity for her to get to know him as it was for him to get to know her. If all went well, the job was hers.

Iris assured him she'd be there as soon as was convenient. She knew for a fact Cricket was flying to Anchorage that afternoon. From there she could catch a flight to Washington, DC, the next morning, which would put her there Friday evening. They settled on a Saturday lunch date.

They chatted for another ten minutes about interest rates, asset turnover ratio, sushi and cats. He had three cats. Of course Sebastien Frieze liked cats. All smart men liked cats. Flynn adored cats. Michah, Sandy and Quartz, her mom's cats, loved him.

Flynn.

A boulder formed right in the center of her chest, threatening to smother the bubble of happiness forming there. She absolutely could not let anything spoil this moment for her. This was the best thing to happen to her since… Uninvited, last night's kiss flashed through her brain. *Ridiculous, Iris. That was fake. This is real. This is the best thing to happen to you, ever.*

Sharing the news would help. Turning around, Iris headed back to the bedroom.

"Hazel." Iris sat on the edge of Hazel's bed.

Pulling the pillow from her sister's face, she added, "Change of plans. Can you wake up now?"

"Maybe." Hazel opened one eye and trained it suspiciously on her. "What would be my motivation? Did you somehow conjure up an omelet already?"

"No, but I have good news."

Her other eye popped open.

"That phone call was from Washington, DC."

That did it—she bolted upright. "Oh, my gosh, Iris! You got a job? *The* job, right?" She threw her arms around Iris and squealed.

Iris laughed. It felt good to share this news with her sister. "Almost." She explained, and then said, "Let's go tell Mom and Dad. Then we'll make omelets for everyone."

IRIS TOOK A MOMENT, as she chopped the ham, to enjoy the excitement her parents had shown at her news. Despite her entire family's emphasis on physical prowess and athletics, her parents had always been proud of Iris's academic success. They were upstairs getting dressed.

Hazel stood beside her at the sink rinsing grapes in a colander. "So, with all the congratulations nicely settled, let's talk about the other major news story in your life—you and Flynn kissing on the dance floor."

"That absolutely was not what it looked like."

"What does that mean?"

"He was sort of pretending to be my boyfriend."

"Why would he do that?"

"To be nice. Ashley and Faith and their cronies were there. He knew I was nervous and he promised to stay close and…help me through it. He just got a little carried away."

"Wow. 'Fake boyfriend to the rescue' isn't even on my list."

"It's Flynn. You know how over-the-top he can be."

"Only where you're concerned."

"That's not true. Look at what he did for Ally and the wedding."

"Ally doesn't count. She's like his family."

That was true. Flynn and Ally were special.

"So that public display of affection was part of some weird playacting thing?" Hazel asked skeptically.

"It was barely a kiss."

"I saw it, Iris. It might have been G-rated but I came up to you guys right after, remember? And I thought the tension was thick on the ride to Jasper Lake. That was child's play compared to that chemical reaction I interrupted on the dance floor."

"It didn't mean anything."

"All I know is that a couple of mornings ago, he violated like ten rules in one fell swoop, and last night he kissed you in front of practically the entire town. And then you two spent the rest of the evening cozied up and acting a whole lot like a couple."

"Ten is an exaggeration."

Hazel popped a grape into her mouth and then tilted her head like she was calculating. Which, Iris soon learned, she was.

"Possibly," she said. "But only slightly." She began ticking off "infringements" on her fingertips. "Bringing you flowers, and not just any old bouquet but your favorite flowers, which means he's paying attention. And there is something between the two of you about ducks."

Iris felt her lips twitch. That had been thoughtful. She shrugged because it was pointless to deny.

Hazel was only getting started. "Bringing Mom flowers, bringing me a gift, bringing Seth and our teenaged cousins gifts—all of them extraordinarily thoughtful. Taking a drink from your mug, sharing a donut. And the fact that he tied those flies for Reagan and

Seth? A thoughtful, *handcrafted* gift gets bonus points and tips him over the edge."

"Bonus points for a handcrafted gift? I've never heard that one."

Hazel gave her a palms-up shrug. "Well, Iris, the list is fluid. Men are crafty in their pursuits. They're always inventing new ways to hypnotize you."

"Hypnotize me?" she said wryly. Unfortunately, her sister's logic didn't seem as ridiculous as it should have. But that didn't mean it applied to Flynn. "You realize how paradoxical a distinction this is, right? The winner of the most intimacy violations perpetrated at one time. According to your rules, I should never speak to Flynn again."

"No, according to *my* rules *I* wouldn't, but you…"

"Me what?"

Hazel moved on to the already-rinsed strawberries, which she began piling in the middle of the fruit tray. "You could acknowledge that what's happening between you is a little more than friendship."

Iris frowned, hating the way those words made her wish and ache at the same time. And she was pretty sure the memory of that kiss would torture her forever.

"He's just being Flynn."

Hazel scoffed. "Right. He probably buys flowers every day and then drops them off to random women all over town. And then kisses them, too, because oh, I don't know—he's Flynn."

Panic gnawed at her logic. These were good points. But she couldn't allow them inside. It would hurt too much if she was wrong. "Hazel, we're talking about Flynn Ramsey. He's a doctor now and even nicer than he was in high school."

"So?" Hazel scowled at her. "I'm standing here looking at Iris James, who is also a doctor. What is your point?"

"Of economics."

Hazel threw a grape and hit her right between the eyes.

"Hey!" Iris cried.

"Listen to me, weaving and dodging is one thing. But do not diminish your accomplishments. Not to me. Not when I know how hard you've worked. And we both know you could have gotten that doctorate in any discipline of your choosing."

"He's... I'm—" She stopped as a surprising flood of tears burned her eyes. She couldn't quite get them blinked away. Swiping at them with a paper towel, she said, "That is so sweet."

Hazel dropped the fruit and grabbed Iris's hands. Voice pitched low and edged with determination, she said, "He's just a guy, Iris. Despite how we build things up in our...young minds. Remember that. He would be lottery-lucky to have you. Even luckier now than he would have been in high school because, even though you can't see it, you're better now, too. In fact, I'm not sure that he deserves you. Although, he is trying very, very hard and gets my respect for sheer effort alone."

"Wait..." Iris clutched her hands, shock and gratitude giving her pause. "You knew?" Iris had never revealed her high-school feelings for Flynn to anyone. Ever.

"Seriously, Iris? I knew. Just like Seth said—we are each other's thirds. Even though he and I had more in common as kids, it didn't, and doesn't, mean we love you or care about you any less. We're like a hand with three fingers... wait, that's kind of weird. We're like a tree with three branches or a three-piece puzzle or...something. You know what I mean."

A surge of love constricted Iris's lungs so fiercely she could barely ask the question. "Why didn't you say anything back then?"

"You would have been mortified if you knew that we knew."

"Wait, Seth knows, too?"

Hazel rolled her eyes. "Of course. Wasn't I just saying that? He knew, like we knew that Seth had a thing for that vicious monster Ashley Eller. And it wouldn't have mattered back then. Flynn *was* different. He was…"

"More like Derrick?" Iris said the words she knew Hazel was thinking. But at the look of pain on her sister's face, she instantly regretted bringing him up. Derrick was Ashley's cousin and the ex-boyfriend who had shattered Hazel's heart. "I'm sorry. I shouldn't have—"

"No, it's fine. The point is that I'm *not* comparing Flynn *now* to Derrick then."

"I get it. But since we're on this subject, imagine if your feelings for Derrick had been unrequited back then? Would you believe that you are so much different *now* that his feelings would instantly change?"

Hazel pondered that for a second. "But I think Flynn sees you now, Iris."

"That's it exactly, Hazel! That's the problem. What does he see? Because I'm not different! Not inside, anyway. If he didn't really see me then, how can I be sure he sees me now?"

"I see what you mean. All I can say is that

time has a unique way of changing things, opinions and perspectives. It can smooth a lot of the rough edges of our emotions."

Iris thought about that, how much easier it had been to face Ashley and Faith with the passage of years. Not easy, by any means, but *easier*, for sure. But that was due more to her than them. They hadn't changed, and neither had her feelings toward them. Except they had a little.

"Iris, if you think there's even a chance that Flynn can make you happy, don't let this opportunity slip away. You should give it a try."

"I appreciate your advice, I honestly do. But I'm going to take this job in Washington, DC, be wildly successful and live happily-ever-after. That's all I want."

"Really?" Hazel eyed her skeptically.

"Yes, really."

"I know you say you don't want to be in a relationship, but do you truly believe this job, any job, is going to make you happy?"

Iris poured the eggs into the pan. "Yes, Hazel, I do. I'm counting on it, in fact. Finally, I will be…someone."

"You already are someone!"

"You know what I mean."

"I do, and I don't." Hazel sighed. "What I do know is that you've always placed so much importance on things that you think will make other people see you in a certain way. Why do you do that?"

Iris tilted the pan to spread the eggs, thought about evading, and then, because something seemed to have shifted, strengthened, in their relationship, she changed her mind. "Because I have to, Hazel. I'm not like you or Hannah, or the rest of our siblings, or Bering or Cricket—or Flynn, for that matter. I can't just *do* anything I want like you guys can. What I can do is think and reason and intuit. And I have to do that, and be good at it, because I won't ever have anything else."

Hazel cocked her head, clearly trying to process it all. "What do you mean you won't have anything else?"

"I mean, I don't want a *f-f-f*—"

"You don't want what?" she asked impatiently. "Flynn?"

A family, she finished silently. She didn't want kids and that was something else she didn't think her own family would understand. Yet another thing to set her apart. But she couldn't bring herself to say that, not even to Hazel.

ROUNDS COMPLETED, FLYNN walked down the hospital corridor and tried to decide how best to proceed with Iris. He didn't want to rush things, but at the same time he knew what he wanted. Should he ask her out on a date and focus on "wooing," like Doc and Caleb recommended? That had worked to a degree and, combined with last night's kiss, the groundwork seemed firmly laid.

So maybe he should just plunge ahead and tell her how he felt? He knew she felt something, too. The problem was that their relationship wasn't typical. He'd been so sure that if he got confirmation that she had feelings for him, then convincing her to stay in Rankins would be a breeze. After his conversation with Margaret, he wasn't nearly as confident. A few well-placed questions to Hazel had confirmed everything their mother had told him and more.

The fact that Iris had sailed through the wedding had to have alleviated some of that old angst. Still, he needed to apologize for the assumptions he'd made. That ignorant comment he'd made before the wedding about "overcoming" bad memories and "moving on" made him cringe. The good news was they were finally on the right track.

Sure, it might take a little more time to win her over than he'd originally believed, but he could do it. They were perfect for each other, and he was going to do his level best to show her that.

Removing his phone from his pocket, he tapped out a text: Good morning, my favorite duck. We need to chat. Can you meet me for a late lunch?

Before he could press Send, a voice off to his left stopped him in his tracks. "Do you know how annoying it is to come all this way and find you on the phone that I can't even get you to answer?"

Deliberately keeping his focus on the screen, Flynn reread the message and made a show of hitting Send before responding, "I'm a very busy man, Sonya, and I only have time to answer the messages that are important to me."

He scrolled through a few already-answered texts before looking up into the face of his ex-wife. Slowly, he registered the rest of her, taking meticulous care not to let his surprise show because it was obvious that she'd intended to blindside him. *Melodrama* should have been her middle name. Flynn's lack of response in these situations had often exasperated her.

He was a master at ignoring and defusing drama. His entire childhood had consisted of it, and he wasn't about to start reacting now, not even when his ex-wife showed up at his place of work unannounced and obviously pregnant.

CHAPTER NINE

"WHAT ARE YOU doing here?"

"Nice to see you, too, Flynn." Sonya pushed away from the wall and stepped closer. The doctor in him calculated that she had to be at least seven months along, while the ex-husband calculated the relief and gratitude he felt that there was no way the child could be his. The idea of being a dad was scary enough—the thought of parenting with Sonya was stone-cold terrifying.

"I never said that—that it was nice to see you."

"Flynn, I'm not here to trade barbs. I need to talk to you."

"So you've said. But what I don't understand is why you couldn't relay the information through my attorney like I requested."

"Because..." She huffed out a sigh. "This is personal. Please, Flynn, can we go sit down somewhere? My back is killing me."

Flynn raked a hand across his jaw. "Sure,"

he said, even though this was not the woman he wanted to sit down and have a conversation with right now. "I'm on my way to the cafeteria to grab a coffee, anyway. I had a late night." He gestured down the hall and she fell into step beside him.

"Thank you," she said. "I was always amazed at the amount of caffeine you could consume and still sleep like the dead."

Flynn gave her a sidelong glance. Surely, she wasn't here to reminisce about their unhappy marriage? He changed the subject to what must certainly be her favorite topic. "It appears that congratulations are in order. You're finally getting that baby you always wanted." Obsessed over, he silently corrected. "How far along?"

"Thirty weeks."

"Boy or girl?" he asked, following up to be polite.

She waited a beat before answering. "Girl."

"That's great, Sonya."

Following her inside the cafeteria, Flynn was glad to see only a couple of tables were occupied. Less chance their conversation would be overheard. Despite her penchant for histrionics, he knew whatever she had to say must be a doozy for her to come all this way.

On her way home from Copper Crossing, where she'd done some paperwork and had a lesson with Cricket, Iris read Flynn's text when she stopped at the grocery store in town. She decided sharing her good news might be an effective way to head off any awkwardness between them, so she took a detour to the hospital. A quick check with Nicki at the nurses' station and Iris learned that he was on break. This usually meant that he could be found in one of four places—the roof, the staff lounge on the third floor, Ally's office or the cafeteria. With Ally away on her honeymoon, and the cafeteria closest, she headed that way.

She spotted him immediately at a small table in the corner talking to a very beautiful pregnant woman. Not wanting to interrupt, she pulled out her phone, intending to text him and see how long he'd be. Too late, she knew he'd seen her when her phone chimed in her hand. Reading the words had her insides tangling with dread.

Help! This is my ex-wife. Remember how you said you owed me? Please come over here, so I can tell her you're my girlfriend.

His ex-wife! No, no, no. A kiss, a probable job and meeting Flynn's ex-wife within a twenty-four-hour span was more than she could take. Maybe she could sneak out… But when she looked up, he was waving her over. She did owe him. Summoning her game face, she approached the table.

"Iris, hi, honey. This is Dr. Sonya Traver, my ex-wife. Sonya, Dr. Iris James, my girlfriend."

Of course Flynn would only have a stunning doctor of an ex-wife. Shiny black hair cut in a chin-length bob emphasized her high cheekbones and sharply angled jawline. Her crystal-blue gaze was openly curious as she assessed Iris.

Iris couldn't help but notice she was thin but puffy at the same time, in that way some pregnant women get. Upon closer inspection, she could see her eyes were red-rimmed and purplish half circles beneath them hinted at exhaustion. All of this suggested to Iris that Flynn's ex-wife was miserable.

Sympathy welled in her and she reached out a hand. "Lovely to meet you, Sonya."

"You, too. Are you a doctor here at the hospital, too?"

"No, I'm not a medical doctor. I have a PhD in economics. For some reason, Flynn thinks it's fun to call me a doctor."

Her smile appeared gracious and genuine.

"Well, you are a doctor. And economics is so interesting, but difficult and confusing, if you ask me. I dropped my Econ 101 class in undergrad."

Iris couldn't help but chuckle. This woman wasn't anything like she'd been expecting. From Flynn's few comments she'd assumed Sonya was disagreeable and wholly unlikable.

"Plus, if it makes you feel better, I don't treat patients, either. I work in research."

Flynn interrupted the small talk. "Sonya decided to surprise me with a visit today."

Iris got the message. He wanted her to know that he hadn't known she was coming. Hmm. "How nice. Flynn, you and I can talk later. I'll be leaving for Anchorage around four, so before that, if your schedule allows it."

Flynn frowned, and Iris knew he wanted to ask about her trip.

"You know what?" Sonya said, sliding her chair away from the table. "Flynn and I are finished for now." She stood and took a few steps away. "Why don't you sit here and join him?"

"What?" Flynn looked back at his ex-wife, confusion stamped all over his face. "You just got here, and you didn't even tell me the reason that you're visiting."

"I know and I'm sorry."

"Not that I mind if you want to go, I just find it odd."

"I know." Sonya's smile was stiff.

Iris was struck with the sense that she'd interrupted something very important. She wasn't sure if it was the hurdle she'd seemed to scale last night, or her new almost-job, but she wasn't intimidated by this woman in the least.

"Sonya, are you sure? Flynn and I can get together later. I don't mind waiting."

Sonya's vibrant blue gaze bored into her, seemingly trying to estimate her sincerity, and adding fuel to her assumption. Desperation and sadness seemed to ooze from her. She pressed two fingers to her temple. "I'm positive. I was going to ask Flynn for a favor, but I've changed my mind. I'm going to go in a different direction." She dug a tissue out of her pocket and used it to dab at tears now sparkling in her eyes. "Do you have children, Iris?"

Iris offered a gentle smile. "No, I don't."

She wiped her nose. "I'm sorry for losing it like this. It's true what they say about pregnancy wreaking havoc with your hormones and emotions."

"Please." Iris reached out and laid a hand on the woman's forearm. "There's no need to apologize. My oldest sister is pregnant right now and she happily proves that point on a daily basis. And Shay is already an extremely, um, passionate person. Yesterday, I asked her if she wanted me to get her a cupcake and she teared up."

Sonya brightened a little and patted her belly. "Same age as mine then. Maybe, someday, you two will see how a child can change your life."

That statement seemed difficult to weave around. Thankfully, Iris didn't have to answer because Flynn chimed in, "Maybe."

"Despite Flynn's fears, he'll be a wonderful dad."

"I'm sure he will be," Iris said. His fears? What fears did Flynn have about fatherhood?

"It was wonderful to meet the woman who finally managed to open Flynn's heart."

"Oh, um, thank you…" Iris stammered. "But I didn't know it was closed."

Flynn reached out and snagged Iris's hand, reminiscent of last evening's performance. "That's because it's not closed for you."

"That's sweet. You two are adorable and that makes me really happy." Sonya managed a small smile. "Goodbye, Flynn."

"Goodbye, Sonya."

They watched her walk away and Iris asked, "Should you walk her out or something?"

"No." Flynn gestured for Iris to sit. "Trust me, she enjoys a grand exit."

"Flynn!" She took a seat.

Flynn raked a hand through his hair. "I know. I'm sorry. I'm extremely snarky where she's concerned. But that woman you just met is not the woman I was married to, I can assure you. She showed more genuine emotion with you in five minutes than she did with me in the entire year we were married."

"You were only married a year?"

"And we only cohabitated for eight months and got along for maybe half that."

"Huh. I… You never talk about her."

"It wasn't a happy time. You've never asked about her."

"I know. I was…" Afraid to hear about how amazing she was, afraid to compare herself to the woman who managed to capture Flynn Ramsey's heart. Now she found herself wildly curious.

"You can ask me anything."

"All right, well, I'm wondering what could possibly go wrong in a year? You were practically on your honeymoon."

"A doctor at the research clinic where she worked."

"What?"

"You asked what could go wrong. He was the main reason it went wrong. She fell in love with someone else."

"Wow."

"We'd only been dating a few months when we got married. I was in med school, stressed and tired. Both of us were looking for a connection. We could never seem to find the time to be together. Neither of us felt comfortable about living together. One day, she jokingly suggested we get married. It didn't seem that unusual. I mean, medical school is so consuming. There's no life outside of it and you feel like it will never end. The next thing I knew we were at the courthouse going through with it. It was a huge mistake and I knew it right away, even before she cheated. We fought all the time. I mean, I think she cheated because she found out…"

"What? Did you cheat, too?"

"Iris, no." He sat back, looking slightly offended.

"Sorry, you've just always…"

"I know, but I'm not a cheater. Sonya wanted to have a baby. Right away. And I…didn't. Having a family is not something I've ever been one hundred percent positive about. The more she pushed for it, the less inclined I felt. And

I certainly didn't want to start having babies while I was in medical school. So she found someone else who would give her that."

Flynn didn't want kids? That wall she'd constructed between them, the one that had already started cracking when he'd kissed her last night, weakened a bit more. "That must have been difficult."

"The cheating hurt, and the disappointment of a failed marriage was tough on me. Especially after my parents' nightmarish relationship. But I'm over it."

"Then why do you still seem angry?"

"It's more that I don't trust her. She got nasty at the end. Once she found out I was leaving, she wanted to go to counseling and try to work it out. After I refused, she got me disqualified from a residency program that I really wanted."

Iris had assumed Rankins was his first choice for his residency. "How did she do that?"

"Her dad, also a doctor, was the head of it. But it all worked out in the end. I was able to come here, which is where I wanted to end up ultimately, anyway."

"I'm glad you see it that way now."

He shrugged a shoulder. "It's been more than two years."

"And you haven't seen her in all that time?"

"Nope."

"Is she remarried?"

"Not that I know of. Trent, the guy she cheated with, was a friend of mine. We have mutual friends. I think I would have heard." He shrugged. "But then again, I hadn't heard she was pregnant, so…?"

"I wonder why she came here? What kind of favor she wanted?"

"Whatever it is, I'm glad she didn't ask because I'm pretty sure I wouldn't want to do it. Trust me, Iris, she's not what she just appeared to be."

"Maybe she is, though. Maybe she's changed. You heard her, motherhood changes people." Iris thought about her conversation with Hazel, about how time can change people, too.

"That would be a really, really big change. I'm sorry if that sounds bad but it's true. Though I honestly hope so—for her sake, and her baby's."

"Speaking of babies, you don't want to have kids?"

FLYNN FELT A fresh surge of irritation at Sonya for forcing this subject. Although he knew it was something they'd need to discuss eventually. If this relationship was going to evolve like he hoped, Iris needed to know where he stood. Still, it was a difficult topic to broach.

"Um, it's… I'm not saying I don't want kids unequivocally. I love kids. You know, I almost specialized in pediatrics. It's just that my childhood was so awful. My parents fought all the time. And they didn't bother to shield me or even keep me out of it. They each used me as a pawn and tried to turn me against the other. If I ever do have kids I want to be positive that I'm not going to repeat that cycle. I want to be like my grandparents. I want to be so in love that I don't have any doubts. And the next person I marry, I'll make sure we're friends first."

Iris was staring at him with an expression so somber it made his pulse stutter.

"What are you thinking? That I'm a terrible, selfish person? I'm not saying I wouldn't do it, period. It would be tough with me as the dad, however, doctor's hours and all. I just think there are a lot of ways to give to the world without pouring all your efforts into parenthood."

"No, I'm thinking how odd it is that this topic came up this morning with Hazel and I couldn't bring myself to tell her."

"Tell her what—that I might not want kids? I know you're intuitive, Iris, but that might fall within the realm of psychic," he joked. "Because I know we've never had this conversation."

"Flynn…" She inhaled, blew out a breath and said, "I don't want kids. Unequivocally."

"Oh." Flynn exhaled a breath of his own and felt a smile slowly fall into place. How incredibly fortuitous because, if he was honest, he leaned this way himself. "I didn't know that."

"No one knows, not even my family."

"Is that why you don't want to get married?"

"Yes. I'd consider marriage with someone who… With a like-minded person, but it's easier just to avoid the topic."

"Clearly you are confiding in the right person. I don't think it's anything to be ashamed of, by the way. I feel it should be a choice more people make, rather than something they just do. But can I ask why?"

"My childhood was…rough, too. And I'm not talking about the bullying that came later. That, I could handle."

"You're talking about your nine surgeries in ten years. And the pain, the medication, side effects, physical therapy and all the ensuing struggles that come along with them."

Surprise flickered across her face.

"Your mom mentioned it last night. Not all

those details, but I can surmise. I have a patient right now struggling in exactly those ways."

Her eyes sparkled with unshed tears and Flynn wanted to hold her and comfort her and help heal all the residual damage that he knew remained.

"I don't want to bring a child into this world and watch them struggle the way I did. Because I would know what they were feeling, and it would kill me. I admit that just because I had problems it doesn't mean my child would. But, honestly, I don't want to take that risk, and if I don't want motherhood unconditionally, I don't think I should want it at all."

"I understand." And he did. It seemed overwhelming, the idea of being solely responsible for a tiny human life.

"I got better, obviously, but I've always had issues. It didn't help growing up in a family like mine that's full of people successful at everything they tried. I was clumsy and uncoordinated. I'm sure you can imagine that when I did try, I only ended up embarrassing myself. In fact, I'm still awkward."

"No, you're not." The idea that she believed that seemed absurd.

She let out a laugh. "Yes, I am. I'm good at

hiding it. But it's fine. I don't care. Nobody has ever asked me to play basketball in DC."

Flynn chuckled. James family basketball tournaments were renowned. He loved her for trying to make light of it. She did that all the time, he could see it so easily now, how she avoided her pain with humor.

"And I know it probably sounds strange because most people want to have kids so they can give them a better life than they had. But what happens when circumstances are beyond your control? What if your child has health problems or other issues and you can't help them? I'm not sure I could manage it."

Flynn reached across the table and enfolded her hand in his. "Iris, I—"

"Hey, guys! It's been a while!" Faith called to them from across the cafeteria. She marched to their table, her stylish heels clicking smartly on the tile floor. "Look at you two all snuggled up. What a party last night! You almost caught that bouquet, Iris. Are we going to be hearing wedding bells from you guys next?"

Iris's smile looked frozen in place. His guess was that she hadn't thought about the repercussions of their show last night. Flynn had. That's what had given him the idea to tell Sonya they were involved. He was hoping to transition their performance into reality.

"But she didn't catch it, Faith. So that probably gives us a little time." Flynn added a wink.

"Ha. True! Is Hazel seeing anyone?"

"Not that I know of," Iris said, seeming to shake out of it. "Her job keeps her on the go most of the time."

"She's so adventurous! I follow her blog. It's so fun to live through her journeys with her. Although, I can't imagine living in a tent like she does for weeks at a time…"

Small talk ensued for a few minutes until Faith finally checked her watch. "Yikes, I gotta run. My sister is having some tests and she should be done soon. I'm driving her home. Good seeing you guys." She waved goodbye and sauntered off.

Iris turned an approving smile on him. "You're good at this."

"What's that?"

"Pretending."

"Thank you, but it's not that difficult." He watched her expression cloud over, but this time he wasn't going to let her get away with it. They were going to talk about that kiss and what it could mean for them.

He decided to wade into it. "What'd you think about last night?"

"Last night was a blast. I had a great time, thanks to you. Thank you again for sticking close and being my boyfriend. It gave me the confidence to get through the night and I'll never forget it. I wish I could repay you somehow."

"You just did."

"Oh, that's not nearly the same and you know it. Although—" waving a hand in the direction Faith had gone, she added "—I just realized that the whole town is probably gossiping about us right now. Why didn't I think about this sooner?"

"Does it bother you?"

"No."

"Me, either."

"Especially since you're the one who's going to have to deal with all the questions when I'm gone. Which is what I want to talk to you about. I have good news."

Flynn felt the flame of confidence that had fired to life last night and burned steady all day begin to flicker.

"Remember the think tank I told you about right after I got here? The one that I've dreamed of working for and applied to but never heard back—"

"The Frieze Group," he interrupted.

"Yes." She grinned. "I'm surprised you remember."

"Iris," Flynn said a little too sharply, "how many times do I have to tell you that I remember everything where you're concerned?" If she noticed the edge to his tone, she didn't react. In fact, her smile was brighter than he'd ever seen it. He felt his flame dim a little more.

"They called this morning and I'm flying to Washington, DC."

That's why she was leaving for Anchorage this afternoon. "For an interview?"

"Yeah. But it's more like an introduction. Sebastien pretty much offered me the job."

"Sebastien?"

"Dr. Frieze, the head of the company."

"I see." The extent of his denial shook him hard. Disappointment followed, working into him and trying to smother his optimism. Was it possible that their kiss hadn't meant as much to her?

Get it together, Flynn. She's sitting right here in front of you, beaming with happiness. Right now, you need to be happy for her. Dig up some joy.

So he did. Pushing to his feet, Flynn took her other hand and urged her to stand. He enfolded her in his arms and held her close. This wasn't over, he told himself, it couldn't be. He wouldn't give up until he knew for sure.

"Congratulations," he whispered against her silky soft, lilac-scented hair.

"Thank you. I'm nervous, but in a good way."

"Iris, you have nothing to worry about. They're going to love you." And that was precisely the problem.

CHAPTER TEN

How INCONVENIENT THAT Iris would think about Jasper Lake's cool breezes at this moment. Because thoughts of Jasper Lake led to thoughts of Alaska, which inevitably led to Flynn. And she couldn't think about Flynn right now.

Still, she couldn't remember the nation's capital being quite so hot last July. Or the streets being quite so crowded. Then again, she reminded herself as she detoured around a throng of tourists blocking the entire sidewalk in front of a white marble statue commemorating someone undoubtedly superimportant, she'd barely stepped outside the previous summer. Between teaching a summer undergrad course, working on a research project and her part-time job at a busy CPA firm, she hadn't had time to notice the weather, much less ponder it.

Opening the door of Bennett's Fine Seafood & Spirits, she was blasted with cool air, which immediately racked her with a shiver. Shivering was her normal state in an Alaskan winter.

Flynn claimed he didn't mind winter. Okay, she really, really needed to stop this.

It was that kiss. Her lips tingled even now just thinking about it. And, yes, she'd sensed a bit of disappointment when she'd told him about the job, but they were friends. They'd spent a lot of time together lately. Surely, he would miss her, too.

"Iris?" A tall man in a perfectly cut suit strode toward her. She recognized Dr. Sebastien Frieze from the photos she'd seen online, but he was even more attractive in person. Lean and fit with a keen, very dark brown-eyed gaze and a crooked smile that made him appear both friendly and enigmatic.

"Yes, hi, Dr. Frieze. It's so nice to meet you."

"Sebastien, please." He held out a hand. It was cute the way a lock of his silky black, stylishly too-long hair slid across his brow. Iris knew the genius economist was only twenty-nine, but he appeared even younger.

"I'm sorry, old-school manners."

He chuckled. "Totally understand. My third-grade teacher, Mrs. Vanderfleet, is a friend of my grandmother's. They've been close since before I was born, but still, she's Mrs. Vanderfleet."

"Mrs. Patterson, my third-grade teacher, is

a friend of my mom's and my brother's neighbor."

They laughed together.

"So, we already have a table. This way." He stepped back to allow her to go first and directed her. "Straight back, take a left through the archway."

The table overlooked the Potomac River. They ordered drinks and chatted. He asked about her trip. Iris asked about his cats. Somehow that transitioned into her education and work history, and Iris had to admire his strategy. He had a nice way of conducting an interview without making her feel interrogated. She felt confident and comfortable and couldn't imagine it going any better.

Sebastien picked up his menu. "I hope you like seafood. But their pasta dishes are amazing, too. What am I saying? Of course you like seafood. You grew up in Alaska, right?"

"Yes, I did, surrounded by seafood my entire life," she joked, expertly evading his mistaken assumption that because she was from Alaska she must love seafood. It was fine if it was well-prepared, but she didn't get the obsession. "My dad and my brother Seth are both professional fishermen."

"Seriously? Fishing in Alaska is at the top of my bucket list."

Iris resisted rolling her eyes. The "Alaska bug," as she secretly referred to the popular obsession with the wilds of her home state, knew no bounds. She didn't get it, but that didn't mean she was above using her Alaska connections to impress her new boss.

"You're in luck, then. My cousin owns a wildlife guide and outfitter service. He offers some of the best sport fishing in the entire state. I could hook you up. Oops, sorry, bad pun."

Sebastien grinned. "Really? What's his name? And I can't wait to tell my assistant, Kai, that we have another employee who likes bad puns. I think it's a sign of intelligence myself." He added a wink.

"Yep. His name is Bering James and he's one of the best at what he does. He's very well-known and respected in the field. Tons of corporate clients. I'll send you a link to his website." Iris pulled it up on her phone and sent the information to him. "Reservations will probably show that he's full for the summer, but don't let that discourage you. He always keeps a few spots open for family and friends."

The waiter appeared. Iris ordered the pasta special, Sebastien the seafood platter.

"So, as I alluded to on the phone, I'd like to formally offer you a position at The Frieze Group."

A mix of satisfaction and joy rolled through her in a gratifying wave. Years of studying and hard work were finally paying off. She did her best to stay in the moment as Sebastien quoted a salary that made her want to weep. Calculating the cost of living in DC paired with her frugality, she could have her school loans paid off in three years. This was it. Dreams coming true at table nine! She wanted to stand up and shout.

The waiter arrived with their meals. Hers was delicious. Sebastien explained that if she chose to accept the position, he'd like her to start in October if possible, the exact date to be decided upon later.

"I'm sure you'll need to give notice where you're working now. We're moving into a new suite of offices next week. Then we have our annual staff getaway in August. I'm taking the week after that off as well, possibly two, depending on how things work out.

"Any chance you'd like to join us for our retreat and get to know me and some of your coworkers? We usually rent a vacation home in the Hamptons or Nantucket or somewhere equally as fabulous. This year it's the Outer Banks."

"That sounds lovely." And it did. She loved the beach. It was one of the few outdoor environments where she didn't have to stress about so many mosquitoes. Iris could almost feel the sand between her toes. "Mark me in the yes column."

"Cool. Are you up for dessert or coffee, or both?"

Incredible how comfortable she felt with this guy already. Iris eyed him carefully. "Honestly? I'd like to order the crème brûlée. But not if this is going to be one of those uncomfortable moments where I say yes to dessert, but you decline, and then we sit here awkwardly while you watch me eat dessert."

The waiter appeared. "Crème brûlée for you today, Dr. Frieze?"

Iris went wide-eyed. Sebastien tipped his head, and then they both burst out laughing. He said, "Yes, thank you, David. Looks like we'll both have my usual. And coffee for me. Iris?"

"Yes, to coffee also." Iris excused herself to use the restroom, but really she wanted to text Hazel.

Sebastien was holding his phone when she returned to the table. "Wow, Iris, I'm blown away here. I'm looking at your cousin's website right now."

"Yeah? He's kind of a big deal. My brother Tag owns Copper Crossing Air Transport, which is mentioned on the site. He handles most of Bering's flights. My whole family is very adventurous and loves the outdoors."

"I have the best idea." Sebastien sat back in his chair, enthusiastic expression confirming the notion. "We could take our retreat in Alaska this year. Do you think… Is there any way that would even be remotely possible?"

Oh. No. No, no, no… A cramp began to form somewhere in her midsection. "Sure, probably. I can call Bering."

"That would be amazing," Sebastien said and then quoted from the site, "'Backpacking, hiking, fishing, wildlife viewing, photography excursions…remote cabins…' Wow, look at the size of that moose rack!

"The fishing…" He looked up and Iris could see the longing in his expression. "I've dreamed of fly-fishing for grayling practically my entire life. But it looks like there's just killer fly-fishing all the way around. Everyone will be so stoked. We've talked about doing something like this for the last few years. Almost everyone, that is. All the, uh, not-as-adventurous folk among us can still go lie around the Outer Banks, but the rest of us—we know where the good stuff is, right?" He winked. "Alaska."

"You got that right!" she said with way too much fake enthusiasm. It was like they were suddenly filming a promo spot for the tourism bureau that Emily headed up. Cue the wildlife footage!

"And this is extra fabulous, because you can be our tour guide."

Tour guide? Perfect, she'd just bragged herself right out of a vacation to the Outer Banks and into more time in Alaska. A pasta-encrusted ball of regret cemented inside her gut.

"Oh, well, Bering has professionals for that. I would just be…" How to describe herself here? A fish out of water seemed apt.

"Our boots on the ground," Sebastien said, finishing for her. "How fun to have insider information, to see the place you know and love so well from your eyes. Isn't this the coolest thing?"

"*So* cool," Iris responded. *Heaven help me*, she thought, *what have I done?*

SETH'S WILD BOUT of laughter propelled him backward against the sofa. "You, Iris James, my Alaska-eschewing sister, are going to show your new boss and your coworkers the outdoor wonders of southeast Alaska?"

"Seth!" Hazel barked. "Not helpful."

Iris had very efficiently used her time on the long trip back to Rankins to work herself into a state of panic. After a day and a half of travel, she was an anxiety-ridden mess. That might explain why she'd walked into her parents' house, where Hazel was helping Seth tie some fishing flies, taken one look at her siblings' pride-filled smiles and blurted out her predicament.

Iris's eyes filled with tears that she was too exhausted to fight. "No, he's right. This is my new boss, at the job I've dreamed about for basically my entire life. I have to work with these people. I'm supposed to be smart and they're going to think I'm an idiot." She swiped at her cheek.

Seth pushed to his feet and hurried to her. Massive arms smothered her with a brotherly hug before he took her by the shoulders, leaned back and said, "Shoot, Trippa, I'm sorry. I shouldn't have said that. But surely you can see the irony here?"

"I can, of course. It's like Mother Nature

is getting back at me for dissing her all these years."

"Um," Hazel said, "I've spent quite a bit of time in nature and am quite sure that's not how it works."

Voice edged with panic, Iris released her brother and let her hands fall to her sides. "Sebastien can't wait to go fishing with me. Me, fishing? I haven't held a fishing pole in my hands since we were fourteen. You guys remember what happened, right?"

Seth snorted with the unsuccessful attempt to hold in another laugh. He looped an arm over her shoulders and drew her close again. "It would have been a beautiful cast if you'd managed to hang on to the pole."

Even Hazel snickered a little at the memory.

"Dad tried so hard not to be disappointed, but I knew. Or how about when the entire family took that Mother's Day canoe trip on the Opal River and I tipped over my canoe? I'm sorry again, Hazel, that I got you wet."

"She was fine," Seth replied, lips trembling. "She's an excellent swimmer. But did it have to be the canoe with our lunches in it? Remember the time we went clam digging and I was determined that you were going to get your limit and—"

"And I lost my rubber boot in the surf? How could I forget?" Iris let out a groan. "See? This is hopeless. I am hopeless when it comes to this stuff and you guys know it. And Sebastien will see me for the fraud that I am. I'll be humiliated and then how can I work there?"

Seth was frowning. "Iris, don't get upset with me. But I don't understand why this matters so much. Why didn't you just tell him that you don't do this stuff?"

Why, indeed. "It's hard to explain. It just sort of happened. It was an interview and I was trying to impress him. Sebastien was talking about how fishing in Alaska is on his bucket list and I bragged about you and dad and your fishing. And Bering—"

One side of Seth's mouth pulled up into a grin. "You bragged about me?"

"You're the best fisherman in the state, possibly the world, aren't you? You've told me that like a billion times, anyway. Sebastien was all, 'Oh, tell me about your brother... What does he like to fish for? Where does he fish? Does he tie his own flies?'"

"What did you say?"

"Um, I said you've been the best fisherman in our family since you were a kid, that you had spent every free minute fishing for something or practicing your casting. I told him you like to fish everywhere and for everything, but that steelhead are your favorite and you love to fly-fish, too. I also told him you're an expert at tying flies."

"Huh. Wow." Surprise flickered across his features. "That is all one hundred percent accurate."

"I know. Just because I don't like to do what you do doesn't mean I'm not interested or proud of you."

He grinned. "Well, I could take your fancy new boss fishing and show him a thing or two—or seventeen."

"I wish," Iris said, and plopped down on the sofa next to Hazel. "I wish we could do some kind of triplet power transfer. Remember how we used to wish were identical so we could trade places and—"

"That's it!" Hazel cried, springing to her feet.

"What's it? Please tell me you've been waiting for this moment all our lives to tell us that we do indeed have special powers?"

"Bear with me for a second. I might have an idea. What is this retreat going to consist of exactly?"

"Let's see… I called Bering while I was in DC and he was so nice and enthusiastic. He asked Emily to get involved and she suggested working something out with Shay at the Faraway Inn. We'll do some day trips and offer choices of activities dependent on their skills and fitness level and what they want to do.

"So, for example, deep-sea fishing, fly-fishing or a wildlife-and-photography tour one day, glacier excursion and whale watching or kayaking the next, then maybe mountain biking or a jet boat ride—that kind of thing. Then the entire group will backpack up to Perry's Meadow and camp for two nights. That'll be fun," she drawled sarcastically. "More fishing and hiking but with extra mosquitoes. Then, the final night will be spent at the Faraway Inn before they head back to Anchorage the next day."

Hazel had been staring at her intently. "Listen to me, you can do this. We can help."

If only. "How?"

"Seth guides for Bering sometimes, so it wouldn't be unusual for him to offer in this case, seeing as how this guy is your new boss and all. We've got a couple of weeks before they get here. Seth can give you a crash fishing course and then he'll cover for you on the trip."

"Done," Seth declared. "What kind of fishing does he want to do?"

"Halibut and grayling fishing are his top two."

"The halibut fishing will be a breeze," Seth declared. "I'm not sure I can make you an expert with a fly rod that quickly."

Hazel waved off his comment like a pesky fly. "We'll figure that out. He won't expect you to be by his side on every excursion. The hiking and sightseeing will be easy. All you have to do is read up on the wildlife, history and fun facts about Alaska. All the bad stuff you already know, but let's try to keep that to a minimum. You know, your bear-attack statistics and all of that. Spin things positively."

"Trust me, I already do plenty of that working for Tag."

"See, you're already ahead of the game! I'll teach you about backpacking and I can even hike in with you to Perry's Meadow. Again, no one will think a thing of me going along—I do it whenever I'm home. And your colleagues will love having another local along, especially your triplet sister."

Iris knew this was true. Bering's family members or friends often tagged along on excursions when there were open spots. Hazel had done it since high school. Charming, knowledgeable and at home in the woods, she'd only be an asset in a group of newbies.

Iris felt a tiny spark of hope, and a blazing fire of appreciation for her siblings. "You guys would really do this for me?"

"Absolutely," Hazel said.

"Heck, yes," Seth said at the same time.

"Do you have any idea what other activity Sebastien might choose?" her sister asked.

Iris grimaced. "Yep. Kayaking."

Hazel nibbled thoughtfully on her lip. "How do you feel about letting Flynn in on this, too? He could have you kayaking in a week."

How mortifying to confess to Flynn what she'd gotten herself into.

FLYNN DIDN'T SEE any reason to beat around the bush. "Iris, we have a problem." They'd met after Flynn's shift at the hospital and were on their way to the Cozy Caribou to grab a bite.

"You already know about my problem? Did Seth tell you?"

"I haven't talked to Seth about this."

Iris shifted on her feet and Flynn could see that she was nervous. Raising her hands up, palms down, she said, "Let's start over. I think we may have separate problems. You go first."

"Sonya is still here."

"Here, where?"

"In Rankins."

"Oh. And?"

"You're not surprised."

"No, not really. She came here for a reason and in spite of what she said I don't think she's ready to let it go."

"That's what I'm afraid of, too. I ran into her at the grocery store while you were gone. She told me she wants to relax for a few days before she goes back to Anchorage. She's says it's peaceful here. I don't know what she's up to. The problem is, she still thinks you and I are a couple."

"Yeah, her and the rest of the town. Even Hazel thinks something is going on."

"It's my fault. I'm the one who kiss—"

"It doesn't matter, Flynn. I'll be gone soon, anyway."

She glanced away and frustration built inside of him. It was so obvious she didn't want to discuss their kiss, which just reiterated to him that it had affected her as much as it had him. Why wouldn't she just admit it?

"It doesn't matter to *you, but* I'm afraid that if Sonya finds out that we're not really together, she'll…"

"What? Do you think she wants you back? She's like seven months pregnant."

"Maybe." Flynn didn't believe for one second that pregnancy would stop her from trying, if that was what she wanted. Flynn wasn't taking any chances. "I'm more concerned about whatever that favor is that she wanted to ask of me. That's why I have a favor to ask of you."

"Sure."

"I haven't even asked it yet."

"It doesn't matter what it is, I'll do it. I want to ask you for a favor, too. Maybe we can trade."

"Great," he agreed. "I was wondering if you'd keep pretending that we're together? Sonya seems to like you and I'm hoping one of two things will happen. She'll either a) give up on me or whatever it is she's doing here and leave, or b) she'll confide in you about what she really wants."

"Done. I only foresee one tiny problem. What will we tell my family? And your grandfather?"

"I think the fewer people who know the truth, the better. Our story is that we were dating and tap-dancing around a relationship before the wedding. I kissed you and it was all over." Truer words had never been spoken as far as he was concerned.

Iris tapped a thoughtful finger to her lips. "I don't see why that won't work. People are already speculating, anyway. We were apparently very convincing at the wedding. But that means we'll have to fake it in front of my new boss and coworkers, too."

"Well, sure, but by the time your company Christmas party rolls around we'll have ended our fake relationship. But I'd be happy to fly to DC and be your date if that's your favor."

She tipped back her head and laughed. "Thank you, Flynn. I wouldn't have guessed making me feel better would be possible right now considering the state I'm in. But now that I think about it, this could work to my advantage."

"Fill me in."

"Right. So, my boss and a bunch of my soon-to-be coworkers are coming to Rankins in a couple of weeks…"

Flynn listened as Iris related her tale and he tried not to be irritated. She suddenly wanted to do all things Alaskan, but not for him or with him. And, she essentially wanted Flynn to help her impress the guy who was, however inadvertently, taking her away from him. Flynn knew it was selfish and petty, but he hoped her boss was a total jerk. He immediately felt guilty about that because Iris had to work for the guy. He decided he'd settle for sort of a jerk, a quasijerk. Ugly, obnoxious, mean—any of those would be a helpful addition, as well.

"So, you actually told your boss that you enjoy all these outdoor activities?"

"Not on purpose and not in so many words. He assumed."

"This is quite a scheme you've cooked up here."

"It was Hazel's idea. Seth agreed to help. So we'll probably have to clue those two in on our fake relationship."

Flynn nodded. "It would be a good idea to have them on our side, anyway. We could use people to cover for us. Sonya is going to be watching."

"Now that you've said that, we'll have to tell Tag and Ally, too, when they get back from their honeymoon."

CHAPTER ELEVEN

"CONCENTRATE," FLYNN INSTRUCTED from where he floated in the comfort of his bright orange kayak, which Iris was convinced worked better than hers. How else could he be so good at this?

"I am concentrating!" Iris cried, and then paddled her kayak in large wobbly circles. She was never going to be able to do this. "I told you this was hopeless."

At least the backpacking and fishing lessons were going better. Hazel was teaching her about "gear." Ironically, there was a mind-boggling amount of gadgetry involved in "roughing it." Hazel had made flash cards of all the terminology and quizzed Iris every evening while they laid in bed. She could "hike-speak" with the best of them. Too bad she couldn't "hike-do." Setting up the tent had been a lesson in chaos. Hazel had laughed until she cried when Iris had tripped, entangled herself in the tent and taken Seth down with her. But Hazel was persistent, and with her insistence and careful instruction, Iris felt like she was finally getting the hang of it, or at least the important parts.

Seth had her "fishing" every day off the "stern" of her parents' deck. Baiting hooks, casting off the "taffrail"—better known as the deck's railing—and practicing reeling in a bag full of laundry. They discussed bait and lures in all their forms, the habits of halibut and other species they may catch on the trip. Tomorrow they were doing a "dress rehearsal" with a half day of fishing in the bay. Seth was absolutely convinced she could pull off a decent imitation of a person who had gone halibut fishing more than once in her life.

Kayaking, on the other hand, was not going as well. After five lessons, she was definitely better, but there was no way she could pass for a mediocre paddler, much less a skilled one like Flynn.

Flynn, she suddenly realized, was quiet. Too quiet. When she managed to circle her kayak around so that she faced him, she stopped paddling. He had his face pressed into the crook of his arm against the inside of his elbow—his favorite way to squelch laughter, she'd discovered over the preceding days.

"I'm so glad you're enjoying this."

Still grinning, he raised his head to look at

her. "I am." He added an apologetic shrug. "I'm sorry, but I've never seen a person who has one arm that is so much more dominant than the other."

"At least I haven't tipped it over today." Come to think of it, she hadn't tipped over since lesson three.

"True."

Iris sighed. "What am I going to do?"

"Maybe you could be sick on kayaking day."

"Acting sick always comes back to bite me somehow. Maybe you could find me some bad chicken and I could literally get sick. You're a doctor," she joked, "so you could cure me."

He laughed. "I'm just happy to get you out here on the water. I don't care how good you are at it."

Iris couldn't even make a smart comment. Because, honestly, she was happy, too. Spending time with Flynn like this was...dangerous. The thought popped into her head without prompting, or maybe it was the movement off to her left—something rising up out of the water that she instantly knew was too large to be a seal or an otter. They'd seen plenty of those in the last few days.

More of the creature surfaced—it was impossibly huge and menacing and so close she could see the rubbery texture of its skin. Adrenaline coursed through her, prickling her skin and making her pulse pound like a frenzied drumbeat. She thought about paddling, but her arms had gone numb.

"Flynn!" She tried to shout but it came out like a wispy croak. "What is that? Oh, crikey… It has a fin!" Terror lodged in her throat and she wanted to scream. Why couldn't she scream? Seriously? A whale was going to swamp her kayak and drown her and she couldn't even scream. Iris twisted around helplessly, which made her kayak bob and dip erratically. She squeaked out another feeble "Help."

But Flynn was too busy watching the show, paddle lying across the bow of his kayak.

Whipping her head back around, she saw that it was gone. But for how long?

"Awesome," Flynn said, his voice filled with wonder. "That is without a doubt the closest I've ever been."

Was he crazy? This was not at all awesome. But she couldn't say that because she was still speechless. Before she could even gulp in another breath, a series of black-and-white humps surfaced—thankfully, this time a little farther away. But not far enough.

Sensation seemed to be returning to her

arms, but when she stuck her paddle in the water it seemed to flip a switch because another whale went airborne, its black-and-white form glistening in the sunlight. And it was angled right toward her.

A new burst of panic exploded inside of her. "Oh, no!" Her voice, at least, was working. "Why do they keep jumping like that? They're heading this way. Flynn, please, help me!"

Maybe it was the increase in volume, or even the hysteria. It didn't matter because suddenly Flynn was there, right by her side, and he pulled her kayak close to his.

"Iris, hey! Look at me."

She did.

"We are fine. They have no interest in us. Nothing is going to happen."

"Are you kidding me?" she whisper-yelled and pointed. "They are right there, I could literally hit one with my shoe. I hope they didn't hear that and if they do I hope they understand hyperbole." She cringed and squeezed her eyes shut.

"Whales are known for both their keen sense of hyperbole and sarcasm," he returned calmly.

"Flynn, this isn't funny!"

"I'm sorry. I know you're scared, but you

don't need to be. Now, open your eyes and just watch them for a minute, okay?"

"I doubt that's going to dissuade them from swamping us with their giant breaches."

He chuckled.

She growled in frustration.

"Seriously, you didn't mean that to be funny—swamping us with their giant breaches? And please note that I didn't say anything about you hitting a whale with your shoe."

"I don't even want to paddle because then they'll know I'm the weaker one."

"They're not here to hurt us."

"Flynn, they're called killer whales for a reason. They are the wolves of the sea. They'll cut the weak one from the herd and eat it. So of course you're not scared because you know that's me."

He snickered some more and then said, "Iris, please. Will you do this? I won't let anything happen to you. I promise. If you want to leave after this, we will. I will hook your kayak to mine and get us back to shore so quickly you won't even remember the trip."

"Fine." She opened her eyes in time to see another whale launch out of the water and land with a huge splash. She would have screamed, but then a baby immediately followed. More jumping and splashing and showing off. Flynn reached for Iris's hand and she tried to pretend like she wasn't in a kayak right next to the big guys, but watching from the comfort of her living room.

It didn't really work, but the animals were fascinating. And when they finally calmed down, she was calm, too, and that's when it hit her that they were chilling with a pod of killer whales. Which was beyond cool, now that she didn't think they were trying to murder her. For the first time since she could remember, outside of the view from an airplane, she was awed by her home.

"Flynn?" She looked at him, only to find him staring so intently at her that it caused a new rush to her bloodstream. But this time there was no fear involved. She smiled and hoped he could see the sincerity and the affection she felt for him. "Thank you," she whispered, "for making me stay."

"IRIS, CHECK OUT this app that Candace found." Flynn watched Sebastien Frieze sidle up next to Iris.

Twelve employees from The Frieze Group had arrived along with Sebastien that morning. The troupe was now gathered in the dining room of the Faraway Inn, where Adele, Iris's cousin and the restaurant's manager, had arranged a private buffet lunch. After a hearty meal and a social hour of meeting their hosts and guides, the group would be taking off on a half-day tour of Rankins, which included a short hike, followed by a boat ride around the bay.

In addition to Bering, Hannah, Seth and Hazel, who would all be leading excursions over the next few days, three of Bering's regular guides, Freddie, Ian and Tony, mingled with the crowd. Emily, Shay and Adele were on hand to answer questions and make everyone feel welcome. Tag and Ally, newly returned from their honeymoon, were also there.

Tag and Ally had taken both the fake relationship and fake Iris-the-adventurer news like the good brother and sister-in-law that they were. Tag had even volunteered to give airplane tours to anyone interested.

"That is so clever." Iris studied the display on Sebastien's phone. He stepped close and whispered something Flynn couldn't hear. Iris laughed. Sebastien touched her arm.

They acted like friends who'd known each other for years. Flynn squelched the tinge of jealousy and reminded himself that Sebastien was just her boss, while he, Flynn, was her fake boyfriend. Which, now that he thought about it, allowed him certain fake liberties.

Stepping up next to her, he slipped a casual arm around her shoulder and forced himself to objectively analyze Dr. Frieze. Much to Flynn's disappointment, he was the opposite of ugly, and he had to admit that under normal circumstances it would be difficult not to like the guy. Witty, charming, respectful and polite, his intelligence managed to shine through without coming off as condescending. But these were not normal circumstances. Besides, something felt…off. Maybe Flynn's judgment was clouded because of how often Sebastien kept touching his new employee.

"So, Sebastien," Flynn said in an effort to get to know the guy, but mostly to draw the man's attention away from Iris. "Did you grow up in the DC area?"

Sebastien met Flynn's gaze head-on. Was it his imagination or was there a challenging glint in his eye? "No. I'm from Maine. I may not be quite as ruggedly cool as you supreme northern folk, but I'm no stranger to the great outdoors."

"I've always wanted to visit Maine," Iris gushed.

"It's a pretty small state, though, isn't it?" Flynn said. "And there's not much for mountains, right?"

Sebastien's brow knitted. "I suppose so, if you compare it to Alaska." He turned and picked up his glass from where it was sitting on the table behind him.

"I compare every place to Alaska. That's what you do when you're from here." He shrugged. "It's true what they say, everything's not only bigger, it's better."

Iris gave Flynn an odd look, which he probably deserved. He pretended not to notice. Timing it perfectly so that Sebastien would see, he kissed Iris on the temple.

Sebastien grinned and held up his glass in a toast. "A true patriot of the last frontier. I like that." He took a sip and used it to gesture between them. "How long have you two been dating?"

"Three months and nine days," Flynn answered immediately. They hadn't discussed that detail, but that's how long Iris had been back in town and exactly how long Flynn wished they'd been dating. That wasn't quite true. He wished they'd been dating for ten years, but that obviously wouldn't be believable. "But we knew each other in high school."

"Oh, so is this like a reconnection thing? High-school sweethearts reunited?"

"No, we were just friends back then," Iris answered.

"Really, really good friends, though," Flynn clarified.

"Well…" Iris drawled. "We were—"

Flynn interrupted, "We never wanted to ruin that friendship. I regretted it after I went away to college and realized how truly amazing Iris is. All these years, I couldn't stop thinking about her. No other woman could compare. No other woman will ever compare, honestly." This wasn't nearly as difficult for Flynn as it seemed to be for Iris, who was peering up at him with barely concealed curiosity. Flynn gave her shoulder another squeeze to snap her out of it.

"Yep," she chirped brightly, shifting her gaze back toward Sebastien. "Flynn was a year ahead of me, but it was a small school and we had a lot of the same classes. We used to study together. But I always, um, wished it could be more."

Ha, Flynn thought, finally she admits it! Then he remembered that she was putting on a show. He needed to get a grip.

"Ah, study buddies," Sebastien said in a joking tone. "Guess she's my study buddy now, huh?" He added a wink.

Iris laughed.

Flynn fake-laughed. *Game on, Dr. Bossman Economist.*

SALTY SPRAY MISTED Iris's face while she stared out at the horizon as Seth had instructed. At this point, she couldn't tell if her gut was roiling because of nerves or if it was from the motion of the boat. Either way, she needed the bacon-egg-and-cheese biscuit she'd had for breakfast to stay put. Seth had recommended plenty of protein to keep her stomach "solid," right before reminding her that nothing shouted "deep-sea-fishing newbie" like seasickness.

Iris hadn't been this far out on the ocean since that day she'd mentioned. The three of them had just turned fourteen and Hazel had begged her to go fishing with Seth, their dad and a boatload of Seth's buddies, so she wouldn't be the only girl on board. Iris hadn't gotten sick then, but that felt like ages ago. She also didn't have to pretend to enjoy fishing that day. She'd spent the entire trip devouring *The Count of Monte Cristo* on calm seas.

Today, the ocean was not calm, and she wouldn't be reading. It was one of Sebastien's bucket-list days, for halibut fishing, and she needed to be all in. While Seth captained the boat out to his "secret spot," Iris played his instructions over and over again in her mind. They'd practiced for untold hours, and it was safe to say she owed her brother. If she managed to get through this outing without falling overboard or making a complete fool of herself she'd officially be in his debt forever.

The boat slowed to a crawl and soon began bobbing and dipping in the waves.

"All right," Seth announced a few minutes later. "Let's get some lines in the water."

Iris ticked off items on her mental checklist and soon had her pole squared away. She dropped her line into the water and turned to find Flynn, who had been acting weird since the night before at the meet-and-greet, watching her curiously. She felt better about the approving glance Seth tossed her way as he helped get Candace's line in the water. Candace was fiftyish, hailed from Ohio, had a PhD in history and had never been out on the ocean. She seemed sweet, even though she was turning green.

On graceful sea legs, Flynn stepped up beside Iris. "What's wrong?" she whispered as she turned in her spot at the stern and pretended to watch a puffin gliding by. "Did I do something bad? Did you see me almost forget the bait?"

Flynn grinned like he found that particularly amusing. "No, but that's easier to do than you'd think. You nailed it."

"Great. Now, let's just hope I don't catch anything."

He prepared his pole, baiting the hook, dangling it overboard and then letting out line.

Minutes later the first passenger doubled over and let out a groan. It was Timothy, who, Iris had learned, liked to play tennis and seemed smitten with his wife and young girls back home in DC. He leaned over the side of the boat, where he promptly lost his breakfast. Candace immediately followed suit.

Sebastien winced at Iris. Iris returned the sympathetic gesture. Flynn tore open a granola-bar package and offered her a bite.

Like a chain reaction, Sebastien's assistant, Kai, joined Timothy and Candace. Then RJ, a six-foot-five, muscle-bound mathematical genius and extreme-sports adventurer, moaned pitifully and disappeared below deck. A short time later Iris realized the only passengers not getting sick were her, Flynn, Seth and Sebastien.

"Oh, no…" Iris whispered a few minutes later. "I think… Yep, here it comes."

Flynn took her arm. "What's the matter? Are you going to be sick? Don't worry if you are—it's a little rough out here today."

"No," she huffed and pointed. "My line is jiggling. Dang it, I think I have a bite."

"What…?" Flynn followed her gaze.

"Fish on!" she shouted, exactly the way her brother had taught her.

From the bow, Seth beamed and gave her a thumbs-up. It was shaping up to be a good day on the water, for Iris and Sebastien at least.

A FEW HOURS LATER, Flynn watched Iris reel in her seventh fish of the day. Thankfully, the wind had died down and the ocean had settled. Most of the passengers were upright, albeit their complexions still sported various shades of green. A few had even caught fish. Sebastien was thrilled to have reeled in three halibut, including one monster at 200-plus pounds that Flynn was sure would be the largest of the day.

Flynn looked at Seth, who stood beside him beaming at his sister. "How is it possible that she's catching all these fish?"

"Obvious." Seth grinned. "She's one-third me, isn't she? That's how."

"You do know that's not how it works, right? You three are not any genetically closer as siblings than Tag, Shay or Hannah."

Seth answered with a disbelieving shrug. "This is exactly how it works, my friend. You can spout that genetic stuff all you want, but after you try living naked in such close quarters with two other people for eight months, sharing the same blood supply, then we'll talk. Right, Trippa?"

Flynn would have argued the point, but Iris radiated happiness as she brought in yet another catch. "Aye, aye, Captain." She cast Flynn a contented grin, and said, "And, Seth is right, that is exactly how it works."

WHEN THEY RETURNED to the dock, Emily was waiting to collect the tired and hungry fishing guests. The group was now en route to the Faraway Inn for a rest before they enjoyed a grilled halibut feast for dinner.

Iris and Flynn stayed to help Seth clean the boat. They were having dinner later at the Cozy Caribou with Sonya. Iris wasn't sure which was worse—playacting for her boss and coworkers or Flynn's ex-wife. The whole thing would be comical if she wasn't exhausted.

Like a seasoned expert, Flynn started on the

chores. Iris pitched in, sorting and storing the life vests, gathering the trash, scrubbing and cleaning, and it wasn't long before Seth stepped back and nodded with approval.

"Thanks for the help, you guys. I can take it from here." To Iris, he said, "I think your boss was impressed with you, Iris. Heck, everyone was impressed."

Iris smiled. "Thanks to you. It's too bad so many people got sick, but it kept them distracted from my missteps. I could never have pulled this off without you, Seth. Thanks again. And I have to admit it was extraordinarily fun."

That earned her a hug from her smelly brother, although as he embraced her she recognized that she couldn't be entirely sure who smelled worse. As relieved as she was about the day's success, anxiety was already mounting about the next item on the agenda.

"Halibut fishing is much easier to fake than kayaking."

Seth loosened his hold, and said, "But that's just it, Trippa." He kept an arm around her shoulders and gave her an enthusiastic shake. "You weren't faking it. You did it!"

Huh. Iris grinned up at him. "That's true. Turns out, deep-sea fishing doesn't take much athletic ability. Although, I definitely need to start working out before the next time I go. No wonder your arms look like tree limbs. I'm going to be so sore tomorrow, which should make kayaking interesting. My wrist is killing me." She hadn't noticed how much so until that moment.

"Where does it hurt?" Flynn asked. Iris liked how his brow furrowed with concern.

She showed him. "Right here." Gentle fingers probed around the area, which had begun to throb. She hissed in a breath.

"Sorry," he said with a wince. "Let's go."

They said goodbye to Seth and headed for their cars in the marina parking lot.

"Ice that when you get home. I want to look at it again," Flynn said as she climbed into the borrowed car her parents were letting her use for the duration of her stay. "And I'm picking you up early for dinner. I'll text you when I'm on my way."

CHAPTER TWELVE

FLYNN WENT HOME, showered and changed his clothes. He had some extra time, so he swung by the hospital to check on a patient. The elderly gentleman was recovering nicely, and they chatted for a while before his daughter arrived with his grandkids. Flynn said goodbye and went downstairs to Ally's office.

"Hey! How was the fishing trip?" she asked.

"Fantastic." Flynn settled into his customary chair across from her desk and filled her in on the details. "Iris killed it."

"That reminds me, don't you have today off?"

"Yep, the next three days, but I wanted to check on a patient. I'm on my way to pick up Iris in a few minutes. We're meeting Sonya for dinner."

"Dinner with the ex. Iris is the best fake girlfriend ever."

"Believe me, I know. I still can't figure out what Sonya is up to."

"What makes you so sure she's up to something?"

"Now you sound like Iris."

"Thank you. Iris is brilliant. How's the interviewing going, by the way?"

Flynn scrubbed a frustrated hand across his jaw. "Terrible. She got a job, you know?"

Ally chuckled. "Not that interviewing, but I heard, and I'm truly happy for her. I mean the Flynn-and-Iris interview."

At his look of confusion, she explained, "You once told me that any time you spend time with another person in a romantic way it's like an interview for a life partner. Remember that?"

That made him smile. He'd been full of advice when Ally and Tag were dating. So easy to give when he wasn't the one suffering in love. "In case you've forgotten, my romance with Iris is fake."

"Is it?"

"I don't want it to be. But in a normal, healthy relationship, both parties need to agree that it is, indeed, a romance."

Ally laughed. "Well, maybe you need to push it a little."

"What do you mean?"

Ally did her signature Mona Lisa impersonation for a few seconds before explaining. "Iris is more like her oldest brother than she realizes. She has this idea about what will make her happy and she's so firmly on that track that she can't see that there's another, better track out there."

"You know, this whole being-girlfriends thing that we do—" he gestured between them "—is a lot more fun when I'm the one giving advice."

She chuckled. "I bet. And you don't have to take my advice. Although, I am going to point out that one of us is now blissfully wed, while the other is still miserably single."

"Excellent point." Flynn laughed. "I've already taken advice from two extremely enthusiastic senior citizens. Why not go with something from the opposite end of the age spectrum? What do you suggest I do?"

"Make a move. A real one. Not a fake-boyfriend kiss in the middle of the dance floor. Approach her, sincerely, when it's just the two of you and see what happens."

Flynn gave her the truth stare. "Did you really do that with Tag?"

"Yep. Until, finally, he admitted that he had feelings for me."

"Wow."

Pulling one shoulder up into a shrug, she

said, "I knew what I wanted, and I knew what he wanted. He needed help figuring it out. And that's what I do, Flynn—I help people."

He took a second to laugh and then pondered what she'd said. "You might be right."

"I think I am. But be prepared, because if she's as much like Tag as she seems, there might be an initial moment of panic."

"WHERE ARE WE GOING?" Iris asked from the passenger seat of Flynn's SUV. As promised, he'd picked her up early. She'd had just enough time to shower, dress and ice her wrist as she filled in Hazel on the events of the day. Her wrist was even more sore and swollen now and she had no idea how she was going to paddle a kayak.

"You'll see," Flynn said, and turned a corner onto a side street.

"Okay."

He pulled into the parking lot of his grandfather's medical clinic and turned off the engine. "Come on, we're going inside for a few minutes. I have an idea that might make tomorrow easier."

"Excellent. Did you get ahold of a body double or a virus you can inject me with?" she joked.

"I couldn't handle two of you, and it's not quite as showy as a virus but it might help."

Flynn got out and she followed. The clinic was closed for the day, so they headed around back, where Flynn unlocked the employee entrance and held the door open. Once inside, he led her to an exam room, where he turned on the light.

He pointed to the paper-wrapped table. "Have a seat."

"Um, you know I was joking about the virus, right?"

"Sit."

"Yes, Dr. Bossy-pants."

He opened a cupboard and muttered under his breath while he rifled through what appeared to be medical supplies. Pulling out a plastic-wrapped package, he opened it and held it up for her inspection.

"What is that?"

"A brace for your wrist. Hold out your arm."

"Flynn, that's nice, but it's not brace-worthy."

"Yes, it is. And I was thinking if your doctor diagnosed you with a sprained wrist it would be really difficult for you to paddle a kayak."

She let out a gasp and held out her arm. "That is brilliant!"

"We'll take the two-person kayak and you can ride along with me."

She grinned. "This just keeps getting better and better."

Moving a little closer, he captured her gaze with his. "I think so, too." Iris felt her breath catch as something told her that he meant more than kayaking.

"How does that feel?"

She straightened her arm, bending and flexing her fingers. "Much better, actually."

"That's because you really did strain it. I'm going to give you an anti-inflammatory and a pain reliever. As your doctor, I don't want you gripping a paddle or lifting anything heavy for at least a couple of weeks."

"Thank you, again. For doing all of this for me."

"You're doing something for me, too, remember?"

"I got the best part of the deal. I couldn't ask for a better friend. I'm going to miss you when we fake break up," she joked. "Do you think we can we still be real friends?"

His answer was a stare that made her stomach flip. "What if I told you that I don't want to fake break up?"

"Oh, Flynn, everyone knows fake long-distance relationships are tough," she quipped, trying to lighten his mood because did he realize what he was saying here?

"No, Iris, I mean I want to end this stupid charade right now."

"Flynn, we can't break up yet. We're having dinner with your ex-wife and we still have kayaking with my boss tomorrow and…" Her words trailed off as he stepped closer.

Iris froze, her heart pounding, sending her pulse rocketing into overdrive. Flynn's face was only inches from hers and there was no mistaking the emotion in his eyes.

"What—what are you doing?" she stammered, voice a little hoarse from his extra-close proximity.

"What am I doing?" He repeated the question with a chuckle. But nothing about it, or the expression that followed, suggested he thought this situation was funny.

"We should probably get going…"

One hand cupped her cheek and Iris wanted to press her face into his palm. The scent of him surrounded her. Freshly showered with that hint of spicy soap and fresh-cut cedar, it was a delicious, heavy, distracting dose of Flynn.

Locking his eyes onto hers, he said, "Iris,

please don't run from me right now. I have some things I need to say, okay?"

She nodded because her throat seemed to be sealed shut. And because she wanted to listen. She did, even though she was terrified of what he might say.

"What I am doing is something I should have done a few months ago when you first got back to town. I thought about it the day of your birthday party at Bering and Emily's, when you were wearing that green dress and I couldn't take my eyes off you." He angled his head.

He was going to kiss her, and Iris knew that if he did, there was no going back for her this time. She'd explained away the first kiss by insisting it was simply him getting carried away trying to help her, but this...this was different. The end of this would hurt too much.

"Flynn, I don't know..." she whispered.

His thumb caressed her cheekbone and she closed her eyes because it was painful to look at him. She couldn't bear for him to see what might be showing on her face, how much she wanted this.

Gently, he smoothed her hair behind her ear. "I should have done this back in high school, when you were the smartest, most beautiful, most fascinating girl in school, and I was the stupidest boy, who refused to see it. Which means I didn't deserve you. I still don't. I don't think anyone does, honestly. Not even Sebastien, who, I admit, is a cool guy, to borrow his words. But I want to be the one to try because I promise you, Iris, I will try the hardest."

Her heart clenched tightly inside her chest.

"Iris, open your eyes." His lips grazed her ear, and a shiver went through her.

"I can't."

"Please."

She did, but it took a lot of effort.

He drew back far enough to meet her gaze, to search for an answer to the question before he asked it. "Do you really not know? Because I want to kiss you now, Iris."

And that was it. She knew she was done. Her heart had decided it all for her. She wrapped her arms around him. "No, I mean, yes, I do know. I want you to kiss me, Flynn."

FLYNN DID.

Slipping his other hand around her back, he flattened his palm between her shoulder blades to bring her closer. His mouth found hers, and this kiss wasn't a brush of lips witnessed by a crowd of people.

It was just him and Iris.

And he kissed her in the way he'd been dreaming about for three long months. But it felt like three hundred years of emotion that he'd been holding at bay. The feelings he'd had for other women seemed shallow and silly when compared to Iris. Sonya was right—his heart had been closed for business. This was all for Iris, and she was everything he wanted.

Her kiss told him she felt something, too. The fingers of one of her hands dug into his shoulder while the other hand gripped his bicep.

Trailing his hands down, he settled them on her hips. Lifting his head, he captured her gaze with his. As difficult as it was to stop kissing her, he had to see her, to look at her and assess her reaction.

She didn't give him a chance. Entwining her fingers in his hair, she urged his mouth back to hers. And he happily obliged. Gradually, reluctantly, he recognized that he needed to rein this in. They did have somewhere to be. Moving his lips to the side of her neck, he found that spot just below her ear. Finally. And nibbled.

She let out a little gasp, which only made him want to start all over.

"Iris?" he whispered before he gave in to that temptation.

"Yes, Flynn?"

"Are you going to stop calling me your friend now?"

"Yes, but—"

Silencing her with another soft kiss, he then said, "There are no *buts*, right? There's just me and you and all of this is real?"

"Mmm-hmm..."

"And what we have is more than friendship, and more than a fake relationship?"

Iris nodded. "Definitely more."

WAS THIS TRULY her life? Iris wondered. She'd gone from the most intimate, romantic moment of her life with her high-school-crush-turned-friend, turned-fake-boyfriend, now real boyfriend, to dinner in a crowded restaurant with said boyfriend's pregnant ex-wife in a span of ten minutes.

"So, how are you feeling?" Iris asked a visibly pale Sonya as Iris and Flynn settled in the booth across from his ex in the Cozy Caribou.

Sonya responded with a small smile, and Iris could see it required effort. Beneath the table Flynn held Iris's hand and, despite this odd situation, she felt content right in the deepest part of her soul. It was a part she was convinced had been reserved for Flynn because she'd never felt like this before. She wondered if she was glowing. Should she feel guilty about this new-found happiness when Sonya was clearly still down? Iris resolved to cheer her up.

Sonya blew out a sigh. "Honestly, I've been better. But thank you for asking. It will be a relief when this is all over."

Poor thing was nervous, which was under-standable. Just the thought of going through a pregnancy terrified Iris.

"I bet," Iris said. "How long will you be stay-ing in town?"

"I'm not sure yet. I didn't intend to stay this long, but it's so peaceful here. I've taken a leave of absence from work, so I don't have a sched-ule right now."

The back of Iris's neck prickled. She wrote it off to the concern welling inside of her. "But what about doctor appointments? Shouldn't you be seeing your OB-GYN every couple of weeks right now?" She knew Shay was a spe-cial case with her history of miscarriages, but she thought regular appointments were stan-dard at this point.

"Oh, um…yeah. I had an appointment before I got here, so I'm good for a while."

The waitress materialized before Iris could

ask more questions. They all ordered. Sonya asked about Iris's family.

Iris gave her the basics, and she seemed to hang on to every word. Sonya admitted to her fascination at belonging to such a large family. "And your sister is pregnant. Will that make you an aunt for the first time?"

"No, my sister Hannah, who is currently running for the state senate, has an adopted son, Lucas. And then there are my cousins, Bering and Janie, and their spouses, with seven kids among them. I'm like an aunt to those kids, too. We're no strangers to babies in our family."

"That's so wonderful. I always wished I had a big family. I'm an only child."

"I can't imagine what that's like." Iris wouldn't have traded her siblings for anything in the world. She knew her issues would still be her issues, regardless of her family. And she was especially grateful for her sisters and brothers now, when they had her back like they so clearly did.

"It's not that great, is it, Flynn?" Sonya said. "At least Flynn had his grandparents. And still has Doc."

Flynn's phone went off. He glanced at the screen. "Speaking of, will you ladies excuse me for a second? This is him and he's doing rounds for me tonight."

"Of course," Iris said.

When he was away from the table, Sonya shifted in her seat and asked, "You guys seem so comfortable together. And happy. You're both just...radiant. How long did you say you've been dating?"

"About three months," Iris answered without hesitation, inwardly cringing at the lie but wishing it were true. At least they were dating now, sort of. Although, she had no idea how they were going to manage it. For the time being, she was going to ignore the *what-ifs* and *buts* like Flynn suggested and enjoy the sensation. Not to mention, she had bigger fish to fry right now. "But we were friends in high school, so we already knew each other."

As if the words *high school* had summoning powers, Iris looked up to see Ashley Eller approaching their table. She barely managed to smother a groan.

"Hey, Iris. I saw Flynn by the door and I was hoping that was you."

"Hello, Ashley. Ashley, this is my friend Sonya. Sonya, Ashley. We also went to school together."

"Nice to meet you," Sonya said. "Another

great thing about small towns, huh? The way
you all know each other? What a wonderful
place to raise a family."

"It can be," Iris said. "Depending on your
circumstances."

"Yes, so true," Ashley said, making direct
eye contact with Iris. "I won't keep you guys,
but, Iris, I've been meaning to call you. I was
wondering if we could get together one of these
days soon? Lunch or coffee? My treat."

Iris focused on not looking as stunned as
she felt. Would this evening of surprises never
end? Flynn's ex-girlfriend had just invited her
to lunch with Flynn's ex-wife seated across
the table. She did not have time for this. And
that's when she truly comprehended that Ashley no longer held the same power over her.
Gone were the resentment, the fear and the
jealousy. In fact, maybe she did have time for
this. She had a few things she'd like to say to
Ashley in private.

"Sure, coffee would be great." She couldn't
imagine what Ashley could possibly want to
discuss unless it was the job at Copper Crossing. Did she think she could somehow sweet-
talk Iris into hiring her? It wouldn't take Iris
long to explain how she lacked the necessary

experience and encourage her to put her application in elsewhere.

Ashley's smile looked relieved as she suggested a day and time. Iris agreed.

Then Ashley said, "I'll let you get back to your evening. Nice to meet you, Sonya." With a final wave, she walked away.

Sonya smiled. "She seems nice."

"She does," Iris responded, because Ashley did come across that way.

"I went to boarding school in New York. The only time I've ever run into an old classmate was in Switzerland at a clock shop, of all places."

If only she could be so lucky, Iris thought, but she returned Sonya's smile instead.

Sonya shifted in the booth. "Listen, Iris, I don't want to make you uncomfortable by talking about Flynn and me. But I do want to say… I know Flynn doesn't trust me, and I don't blame him. But I was a different person when we were married. I'm not here to get him back and the last thing I want is to come between you two." Sonya's blue eyes were wide and sincere, and as they locked onto Iris, she felt a stirring of…something. That same disconcerting sensation that told her things were not right in Sonya's world.

"The absolute last thing," Sonya repeated.

"I appreciate you saying so. It's good to hear, but honestly, I'm not worried. Flynn and I have a very strong relationship. We both feel like this was meant to be. It would take a lot to come between us." With every piece of her, she hoped this was true.

"I can see that," she said. "And it's such a relief."

Iris thought that seemed like an odd response, but then again, this was a rather odd situation.

"What's a relief?" Flynn asked as he joined them again.

"You and Iris," she answered brightly. "I'm very happy for you guys. Oh, yum, here's our food. Smells delicious. I can't remember the last time I was this hungry."

CHAPTER THIRTEEN

"FLYNN?" IRIS SAID from her seat at the front of the kayak.

"Yes, my queen," he joked as he led the entourage of Frieze Group kayakers near the shoreline.

She laughed, and the sound worked right into him in an even better way than usual. Less anxiety, more…possibility. Iris asked, "Does that make you my loyal subject?"

"Obviously."

"I do kind of feel like Cleopatra. All I need is a hot guy up here feeding me figs and wine."

"I'm sure we'd have no shortage of recruits. Although, I want you to know I'll only hire guys who have no potential."

"That's funny. I want to see the whales again. Can you manage some whale calls?"

"Do I need to remind you that you almost capsized your kayak when you saw them the first time?"

"I know." She sighed dramatically. "Can you

believe how inexperienced I was back then? Thank goodness for Sebastien, right? In more ways than one."

"For Sebastien?" he asked, a little sharper than he intended.

"Yeah, you know, if it hadn't been for him I never would have learned how to kayak or fish. I'm seeing this place in a whole new light."

"Iris, I've been trying to get you to do some of these things ever since you got back home."

"I know, but…"

"But what?"

"I guess I never had the proper motivation."

Flynn felt a rush of irritation and tried to decide if he was being irrational. He had mixed feelings about helping her succeed as it was. He wanted her to like Alaska for her own sake. And his. *Theirs.* Not Sebastien's. All of these things that she was studying, attempting and "seeing in a new light," he'd repeatedly invited her to do. With him. So that she'd see that it wasn't as bad as she thought. So she might want to stay.

"Spending time with me isn't a good reason to try," he said drily, "but trying to impress some stranger is."

Not surprisingly, she seemed to pick up on

his mood. "Flynn, you know what I mean, he's my boss and—"

"Hey, what's going on up here?" Sebastien asked, gliding up beside them in his kayak.

"We were wishing we could summon the pod of killer whales we saw last week," Flynn said.

"Killer whales! That's awesome!"

"It was pretty awesome," Iris agreed.

"Sorry about your wrist," Sebastien said, and then teased, "But that's what you get for catching the most fish."

"But you won the pool with the biggest," Iris pointed out. "A two-hundred-and-three-pound halibut is nothing to sneeze at."

"True." Sebastien grinned. "It was a trip of a lifetime. I'm still in shock. Are you going to be able to go backpacking with that bum wrist?"

"As long as my doctor clears me."

The temptation to say no danced across Flynn's tongue. And yet, he wanted her to be happy, too. At the end of the day, he wanted that more than anything.

Pushing aside his personal feelings, he said, "She should be fine. No fly-fishing or lifting anything over five pounds."

"Lucky for me, Hazel is going along so she can help. My sister is literally an expert hiker."

Sebastien said, "I know! She's so cool! I follow her blog and I love it. I just didn't make the connection between you guys. I can't wait to talk to her about some of the places she's been. Your family is…outstanding when it comes to this stuff. When you said they were outdoor lovers, I didn't comprehend exactly what you meant."

"It's a difficult thing to describe. People don't tend to believe it when they meet me."

Flynn stifled a laugh. She was so good at this. Hedging really was one of Iris's special gifts.

Sebastien kept an easy pace beside them. "So I know you're not officially working with us yet, but there's this fund-raising gala in DC soon. I would love to have you attend and help me represent The Frieze Group. There will be tons of lawmakers and lobbyists and important people there. It would be nice to introduce you to some of those whose policies we'll be helping to formulate."

"Yes!" Iris answered immediately. "I would love that."

Flynn tried to ignore the twist of jealousy. Flynn wasn't the jealous type. He'd always been too confident for that. But the vision of Iris and Sebastien attending a fancy party materialized before him. Iris, all dressed up in the very place she wanted to be with Sebastien, the guy who was the embodiment of everything she wanted. It wasn't jealousy, he told himself. Not exactly. It was the uncertainty of knowing where he and Iris stood that was the problem. They needed to get some things sorted between them.

Thinking about the long-distance relationship they were now facing filled him with dread. But not as much as imagining no relationship at all. They would find a way to make it work. They had to. He loved her, but he knew it was too soon to spring that one on her.

"Flynn, you should come, too. I know it's probably difficult for you to get time off being a doctor and all, but you're more than welcome."

"I could probably swing that. A trip to DC to see what it is Iris will be doing when she moves roughly four thousand miles away from me sounds like just the thing."

IRIS EXAMINED THE worn and tattered backpack Hazel had placed in front of her. It appeared barely useable.

"What is this—twine?" Iris fingered one

of the pockets where her sister had resewn a frayed pocket.

"Yes, handwoven. A woman in Nepal gave it to me and I borrowed a needle to sew it. The needle was carved from a piece of bone."

"Do you know how charming that sounds? I wish I could tell that story."

Hazel gave her an encouraging shrug. "You can. I don't care. I've never written about it. No one would know."

"No, I mean, I wish it was my story to tell." Iris hugged her. "But thank you. And thank you for letting me use one of your backpacks. This should help avert suspicion." Iris knew from her time at Copper Crossing that nothing said "inexperienced outdoorsperson" like a shiny new backpack.

Hazel grinned. "Lucky for you I keep all my old packs, huh?"

"Beyond lucky. Which is how I'm feeling for the first time in like…ever."

"I'm guessing that's not due entirely to this worn-out pack."

"Is it that obvious?"

"To me, it is. So, are you guys finally…?"

"I think so. He kissed me. For real this time." Saying the words aloud made it feel real, too.

Tangible and a little terrifying at the same time. "And we agreed that we're more than friends."

Hazel chuckled. "Congratulations!"

That's when the reality of the situation sank in. How could this possibly work out? Her legs felt funny. She needed to sit down.

"Oh, no. I can see in your face that you're freaking out."

Iris backed up and sank down onto the edge of the bed. "Flynn said we'd work out the details later, but I don't see how… I haven't had time to think it through yet but now that we're talking about it, I'm…" Anxiety churned inside of her. "Geographically, we couldn't get much farther apart and still be in the same country. He's committed here with his residency and he's made a deal with Doc to take over his practice when he finishes. But I can't stay here, Hazel." Her apprehension rose several notches at the thought.

Sure, things were better. She felt like she'd finally carved out a place within her family. Muddling through this Alaskan adventure was proceeding better than she anticipated, but it wasn't really her. Her dream was in Washington, DC. Not Rankins. She could never be as successful, as important, here as she knew she could be there. Not to mention that she didn't relish the thought of running into Ashley and Faith and company on a regular basis. Then there was Sonya, whom she couldn't begin to figure out.

"I can't."

"All right, Trippa." Hazel stepped closer and lightly gripped her shoulders. "I can see all those gears and wheels that make up your complicated brain spinning at light speed. Stop it! You can't think everything through all of the time. Sometimes you just gotta go with your gut."

"Now you sound like Flynn."

"It's possible that Flynn is brighter than I thought. He fell for you, didn't he? Love has a way of sorting these details."

Love? Did she love Flynn? Yes, of course she did. She always had. And she knew that in a lot of cases what Hazel said about love was true. She'd known it in the depths of her soul when she was offering advice to Tag and Ally. The problem was, she didn't know if it was right for her. She did know the stats on divorce. She'd read the anonymous polls about how much people, especially women, sacrificed for love—and regretted it later. She'd worked so hard to earn this career. And yet, being with Flynn felt so right…

Hazel gave Iris's shoulders a little shake. "I said stop."

"Okay."

"Besides, maybe you'll realize you don't like him as much as you think."

"Really? That would actually be great!"

"No, silly. That was a joke." Hazel shook her head. "You two have been dancing around this thing since high school. I know the timing isn't ideal but name a time in life when it is. You need to relax and see where this goes. And right now, no more talking about it. Just enjoy it. Meanwhile, we've got a big day tomorrow."

Hazel held up an object. "Do you remember what this is called?"

"Personal locator beacon."

"That's right." She added a proud, approving nod and pointed at the backpack. "Now, stuff it."

"So, what do you think? Isn't this magnificent?" Hazel swept an arm toward the landscape behind her as Iris approached. Five hours into the hike, Hazel had stopped to wait for her at the end of a switchback in the trail. There was a stunning forested view, where a creek cut through a lush, green meadow below.

Iris joined her and planted her good hand

on her hip. Her wrist ached, one heel burned where a blister was forming, her lips were dry and her shoulders felt bruised from the straps of her pack. Beads of sweat snaked uncomfortably between her shoulder blades, and her forehead was saturated with more perspiration, which, mixed with sunscreen and mosquito repellent, trickled down and burned her eyes. At least she hadn't had to use her inhaler.

"Do you want me to be honest?"

"Yes."

Iris glanced around to make sure none of their fellow hikers was nearby. The group included Bering, Cricket, Hazel, Iris, Flynn and the Frieze Group employees, including Sebastien. They'd started out together but as the hours wore on, differing speeds, points of interest and varying fitness levels had them splitting up into pairs and threesomes. Bering had reiterated the importance of the buddy system.

Flynn, bless him, had joined Cricket and Sebastien. Iris assumed it was to keep her future boss occupied so he'd be less likely to pick up on her inexperience. She was extra appreciative.

Because this sucked.

She opted for more diplomacy in an effort to not hurt her sister's feelings. "It is very pretty.

And I am eternally grateful that you prepared me. I am trying to enjoy it, I swear. But in addition to being uncomfortable, I feel like a sitting duck. I'm trudging uphill with a heavy pack strapped on my back like I'm not already at a disadvantage where bears are concerned. Not only am I weighted down, I'm also carrying bait and I'm on their turf."

Hazel chuckled and patted the bear spray hanging from the holster around her waist. "That's what this is for."

Iris frowned. "If you say so. I've watched YouTube videos of bears charging. You know they can run like thirty miles an hour? I'd never have time to use that."

"Remember when Gareth used it on a bear?"

"Gareth saw the bear coming and he has reflexes as fast as Hannah's. And not even a fire hose blasting pepper spray would save me from an angry moose if I got between her and her calves."

"Maybe." Hazel laughed. "I am proud of you, though. No one would know that you weren't enjoying this."

Iris grinned. "Thanks to you and Flynn. It's nice how he and Sebastien are hitting it off."

Hazel flashed her a look of surprise and then

burst out laughing. "You think that's what's going on here? That they're *hitting it off*?"

"Um, yeah, don't you?"

"I don't understand how you can be the smartest, most perceptive person I know, and still be rather dense when it comes to the matters of your own heart."

FLYNN'S STRATEGY WAS definitely intended to keep Sebastien away from Iris. Pretending to befriend the guy seemed like the logical way to go about it.

He, Sebastien and Cricket finished the hike and had arrived at the campsite before the rest of the party. Bering and one of his guides, Tony, were already there. The five of them made short work of setting up camp.

When they finished, Flynn suggested, "How about if Sebastien and I head upstream so he can try out his new fly rod? When the rest of the party gets here, Tony can bring whoever else wants to fish."

Bering agreed. "Excellent idea, Flynn."

A satisfied Flynn headed off with Sebastien. Not only would this make Iris happy, but it was also less time the guy would be able to spend with her.

BY THE TIME Iris and Hazel made it to camp, Iris knew she'd made a terrible mistake. She was officially miserable but resolved to keep it from Hazel.

Hazel helped her remove her pack. "You all right?"

"Great," she lied. Hazel had worked hard to get her this far and there was no way she was going to wimp out on her now. She could get through this.

"Let's set up our tent and grab a bite to eat. I smell food and I'm starving," Hazel said.

"Sounds good."

Iris was relieved to learn that half their party had continued on to do some fishing, Flynn and Sebastien included. She needed a few minutes to regroup.

Tent in place, Hazel wandered off to eat dinner. Iris took a hand towel from her pack and headed toward the narrow brush-lined stream that ran along one edge of the campsite. She soaked the cloth in the cool water and rinsed the sweat off her face and neck.

A flat rock a few yards upstream beckoned. She sat and decided to remove her boot to inspect the hot spot on her heel. Wincing, she probed at the puffy blister. She'd ask Flynn what to do when he returned. Leaning back on her hands, she closed her eyes and tipped her face toward the sky. The cool air drifting up from the glacier-fed ripples felt amazing.

Relaxed for the first time all day, she never even heard a buzzing sound, but the telltale sting below her right eye was unmistakable.

WHEN FLYNN AND Sebastien returned from fishing, Flynn left a content Sebastien to tell fish stories around the campfire while he went in search of Iris. He found her inside the bright blue tent she was sharing with Hazel. At least he assumed the rustling sound inside was her.

He kneeled before the zipped enclosure and softly called to her, "Iris?"

The flap moved to reveal Iris's face, green eyes flashing with what looked like panic. "Flynn, where have you been?" she whispered. "Can you please come in here?"

"Fishing with your boss," he answered, crawling inside the tent. "Correction, out-fishing your boss." Flynn could handle a fly rod and he'd enjoyed showing Sebastien a few moves.

The rustling sound he'd heard was obviously her. She was at it again, frantically rummaging through her pack.

"What are you looking for? Why do you only have one boot on?"

"I got bit."

"On your foot?" What could have gotten into her boot? "By what?"

"No, I have a blister on my foot. I got bit on my face by a mosquito. I have to treat it, and I don't—"

He barked out a laugh. "Iris, sweetheart, I know you don't like them, but a mosquito bite is not going to kill you."

"Flynn, you don't understand! There's a reason why I hate them so much—I have Skeeter Syndrome."

"You're allergic to mosquitoes?"

"Yes. I've never had an anaphylactic reaction, but I will swell up like a puffer fish, and sometimes I get a fever. This one bit me right under the eye and I can guarantee you it will be blistered and swollen shut if I can't find..."

"How do I not know this?"

"It's embarrassing! That's why I'm always running around armed with mosquito repellent. I had it on today, but I was sweaty, so I cooled off in the creek. Between that and the sweating, I must have washed it all off. Two minutes without my diethyltoluamide perfume and this is what happens! Just one more reason why I hate this place."

"But there are mosquitoes everywhere, all over the world."

"That is not true, they are not everywhere, and they are not all like these pterodactyl-sized, voracious, Alaskan vampire mosquitoes," she muttered and went back to burrowing. Flynn noted that her belongings were scattered around and figured there couldn't be much left inside her pack by now.

"What are you looking for?"

"Antihistamine. I thought it was in a side pocket, but maybe I forgot to transfer it—"

"Hey." Flynn reached out and placed a hand over hers. "Look at me for a sec."

She did. He liked how his touch seemed to calm her. "I'm a doctor, remember?"

She nodded.

"I have a first-aid kit that will blow your mind."

"Really?" she squeaked. "Please tell me this magic pack includes an antihistamine."

"Oral and topical."

"Oh, my…" She slumped to one side. "Thank you. Can you get it, please? Hurry."

"My pack is right outside." He crawled to the entrance, lifted his pack inside and quickly fished out the kit. He removed two pills and handed her his bottle of water. She swallowed them. He dabbed the topical on her bite.

"How does it look? My eye feels funny."

"As predicted, it's swelling and blistering a bit, but the meds will kick in. And we'll give you another dose later. I have plenty."

"Thank you."

"Now, let me see that blister."

She reclined to rest on her elbows, taking care to lean on the side that didn't have a sprained wrist. She exhaled sharply to blow a lock of wayward hair away from her face. Flynn tried not to laugh as the movement rendered her momentarily cross-eyed.

"Just for the record, I hate backpacking. There is nothing good or fun about this. I don't know how Hazel does it. I will admit that fishing and kayaking both have redeeming qualities, especially kayaking with you. But this, out here in the middle of nowhere with nothing but what you can pack on your back? This is…" She paused to dredge up the right word and finally exclaimed, "Foolishness!"

Flynn knew he needed to reassure her. "Iris—"

But she was just getting started. She sat up. "I love hot running water and refrigerators and cars. Cars are awesome. And…beds! I love my bed. Why would a person purposely hike *away* from their bed to deliberately sleep on the ground with bugs and bears? Why, Flynn, why? Can you answer that? I can't even—"

He cut her off before she could rile herself further. "Lean back and let me look at your blister."

She scowled. "You're bossy when you're doctoring, are you aware of that?" But it seemed to work. She followed his suggestion and produced her foot.

Crossing his legs, he placed her foot on his lap and examined the area. "Ouch, that looks sore."

When she didn't respond he looked at her and felt his heart squeeze hard inside his chest.

Fat tears pooled in her eyes. She blinked and one escaped. Head shaking, her voice came out a raspy whisper. "I don't know what I was thinking when I thought I could do this… Look at me, I'm a mess."

One foot was bare, her opposite hand sported a brace, there was a smudge of dirt on her cheek, tendrils of hair hung loosely around her face and her lips were chapped. Another tear followed.

"Yes, you are. But—"

"Thanks a lot. You—"

"Shh," he said, and lowered her foot. "I was going to say that you are a mess but at least you're a hot mess…"

"That's not—"

"A very, very hot one."

"Oh, well, um," she stammered, almost smiling and looking pleased by the compliment. "That's…"

He furrowed his brow and pretended to study her face. "Is that a blush or a sunburn? I should probably get the aloe vera next."

"What? No!" Touching a hand to her face, she said, "I'm wearing SPF fifty, waterproof. It's—"

"Iris, I'm joking. It's not a sunburn…"

"Oh." The pink intensified as the gist of his comment sank in. She smacked him on the shoulder. "Very funny."

But she laughed, and that had been his goal.

Flynn chuckled and resumed his task. He applied a thin layer of antibiotic ointment to the area and secured a piece of moleskin on top of that.

"There, that should hold."

"Thank you." He tried not to chuckle at her dramatic sigh.

"This is fun." His hand slid up her pant leg

while his eyes roamed over her. "Anyplace else I need to play doctor?"

She barked out a laugh. "Not at the moment, but I am going to need you to be on call…"

"Maybe we should do a more thorough exam," he whispered. "Or possibly I should kiss you and make it all better."

Her eyes closed as her lips welcomed his for a scorching kiss. And then a few more.

"Hey! You two," Hazel called a few minutes later from outside. "We're making s'mores out here."

Flynn watched Iris's eyes flutter open. "Did she say s'mores?"

She shifted like she was going to get up. Flynn shook his head, and said in a teasing tone, "Yes, but you hate all this, remember? There's nothing good about backpacking. So you should probably just stay here and rest."

"Fine." Mouth wrestling a smile, she said, "There might possibly be one good thing about this trip."

"Only one thing?" Flynn glared playfully and kissed her again.

Grin firmly in place, she conceded, "Fine, two things. There are exactly two good things about this trip."

CHAPTER FOURTEEN

"IRIS, THANK YOU so much for everything. Your family rocks." Sebastien and company were gathered in the Faraway Inn for a farewell dinner. They were departing first thing in the morning after having had a fun-filled week that could only be described as an unqualified success. Sebastien was talking about making it an annual event.

Flynn watched Iris smile at her new boss and felt a measure of pride. Despite his frustration and the possible threat level Sebastien presented, Flynn admired the lengths she'd gone to in order to impress the guy. Regardless of her "motivation," she'd knocked it out of the park as far as Flynn was concerned.

"Thank you," she said. "I have to agree. My family is pretty special. I'm so glad everything worked out."

"It was one of the best weeks of my life. My only complaint is that it went by too fast. I'd love to take another run at those grayling. Man, that was fun. I'd stay longer if I could swing it, but I've got a...a really important thing I've got to get back for. You're lucky that you get to call this place home."

"I know, extremely lucky. You're welcome again anytime."

Flynn wanted to roll his eyes. Instead, he slipped an arm around Iris's waist and gave her a little sideways hug.

Sebastien grinned. "Only a few more weeks and we'll get to see each other every day. I love how we've hit it off. I'm so stoked to have you on board."

"I'm excited about it, too."

Sebastien looked at Flynn and said, "It's great that you'll be joining Iris in DC for the gala. I look forward to introducing you guys to some very cool people."

"Thanks for the invitation. Should be fun," Flynn remarked.

"Iris tells me you're still doing your residency—how's that going to work out? The long-distance thing? That can be hard on a relationship."

"We're not worried about that. I only have another year or so." That was fudging slightly, he thought, but whatever. "In the meantime, we're hoping to accumulate enough air miles that we can take the most incredible honeymoon ever."

"Oh." Sebastien's eyebrows went up. "So, you guys are engaged?"

"Um," Iris answered.

Oops. "Yes," Flynn said.

"Congratulations! Where's the honeymoon going to be?" Sebastien asked.

"Iceland," Flynn answered.

"Bora Bora," Iris said at the same time.

Flynn chuckled. "Actually, we haven't completely decided yet if it will be Iceland, Bora Bora, New Caledonia or Seychelles."

"Huh. That's kind of an odd yet very specific assortment."

"Not really. Those are the four places in the world outside of Antarctica where there are no mosquitoes."

Iris was gaping at him, so he took the opportunity to brush a quick kiss across her lips. Then he looked back at Sebastien and said, "You'd never know it, but Iris *hates* mosquitoes."

A SPRAINED WRIST, a blistered heel, chapped lips, two chafed shoulders, an aching back and one scabbed-over mosquito bite later, and a nice combination of accomplishment and relief settled into Iris. She'd done it.

With the help of Flynn and her family, she'd not only survived, but she'd also proven that she could "Alaska" with the best of them. Okay, maybe not the best, but she wasn't the worst, either. She was officially exhausted. Thankfully, fatigue seemed to be afflicting most of the crowd and Iris was glad when the evening wound down early.

"So, how are you feeling?" Flynn asked as he drove her home. "Like you conquered the world?"

"Ask me again after I sleep for twelve hours straight. In my bed."

Flynn laughed, happy that she could joke about the experience. "You should be really proud of yourself."

"I am. I'll admit it. But I know I never could have pulled it off without you and Hazel and Seth. Thank you again, especially for getting me through my meltdown."

"You're welcome. But you deserve the credit. You're the one who persevered. My part wasn't much of a hardship, doing all the things with you that I've wanted to do for a long time, anyway."

"Yeah, I'm sorry about that."

"About what?"

"When we were kayaking the other day and I said I never had the proper motivation. You seemed upset and I thought about that and I get it. It wasn't that I didn't want to do this stuff with you, it was that I was too afraid."

"I know. I just wish that I could have been the one to make you want to conquer that fear."

"Well, you might not have been the one to make me want to, but you were instrumental in helping me do it. And in keeping me from being completely miserable."

"Are you admitting it was fun?"

"Parts of it," she conceded.

Flynn slid her a smile. "Good."

"Why did you tell Sebastien that we're engaged?"

"Honestly? I feel like he's less likely to try asking you out if he thinks we're engaged."

"Wait, you're jealous of Sebastien? He's my boss."

"No… Of course not—I don't do jealousy."

She chuckled. "You don't *do* jealousy? Is it that easy? Must be so nice to have everything work out for you all the time," Iris said wryly.

"Not everything," Flynn countered, thinking about how things were playing out with him and Iris. "But he's into you, Iris."

She sputtered out a laugh. "Flynn, trust me on this one. Sebastien is not into *me*. But, *oh, my gosh…*" Peering at him carefully, she added, "Hazel was right."

"About what?"

"About a whole list of things actually, but what I'm referring to is that she told me you were deliberately trying to keep Sebastien away from me—is that true?"

"No. Maybe," he conceded. "A little."

"I can't help it, I love the idea that you're jealous, as long as it's only a little. I promise, you have nothing to worry about where Sebastien is concerned. You're all I want."

The words made his heart soar even as reality flooded in to deflate the sensation. "I know, I mean I trust you. It's not him, exactly…"

"Then spill it, what's the problem?"

When he'd kissed her, he'd assured her that they could work things out. But the truth was that he hadn't thought it through. Not completely, and Sebastien had put his finger right on the four-thousand-mile-wide wound. Painfully. The long-distance relationship wasn't even the issue so much as their long-term status. They could survive the distance for a while, but then what?

Because, despite Iris conquering the last

week, nothing fundamental had changed regarding her feelings about Alaska; she wasn't going to live in Rankins and he wasn't going to move to Washington, DC.

It was a bitter pill to swallow but Flynn was beginning to see that Ally and Iris were right—he was used to things going his way. Selfishly, he'd wanted her, and he'd wanted her to admit that she returned his feelings. Stupidly, he'd thought that would be enough. They'd declare their love and then live happily-ever-after here in Rankins.

But now that her leaving was bearing down on them, he didn't have any idea how they were going to be able to do this. But he couldn't bring himself to tell her. Not now. Not when they'd finally gotten here, to this point. He had no idea what they were going to do.

As if to underscore his thoughts, she leaned forward and took his hand. "What is it?"

"Okay," he said, and turned on his most rakish grin. He held up his finger and thumb about an inch apart. "I'll admit to maybe this much jealousy."

"You feel like company?"

Flynn hadn't heard his grandfather coming

up the stairs to his deck, but he was glad to see him. "Hey." He waved him over. "Yeah, sure."

Years earlier, when Flynn was in high school, he and Doc had converted the space above the garage into a mother-in-law apartment, which his grandparents then used as guest quarters. Flynn secretly suspected that they'd been anticipating the day that Flynn would move to Rankins permanently and need the affordable apartment.

He'd finished his shift at the hospital but was too keyed up to sleep. It happened sometimes, and when it did he'd come home, sit outside on this deck, gaze out at the view and try not to think about anything much at all. Until Iris had returned to town. Since then, he'd spent most of his free time thinking about her, dreaming about the life they could make here together. How was he going to tell her that he didn't have it all figured out?

His grandfather handed him a frosty cold bottle of beer and lowered himself into the chair next to Flynn's. Flynn opened the bottle and took a long drink. Doc did the same. A cow moose and her calf emerged from the edge of the brush and began munching on a willow tree.

"How was the backpacking trip?"

That brought a trace of a smile. Despite her "motivation," Flynn was proud of Iris for pulling it off. She'd overcome some serious obstacles.

"Successful," he said.

"Good news."

"Thanks again for the advice. You and Caleb should consider writing an advice column or a blog or have a radio show."

Doc grinned. "Glad we could help. We'd be great on a radio show, wouldn't we? But, I gotta say, you look kinda miserable for a man in love."

"I may have jumped the gun a little."

"Let me guess, you're sitting up here and stewing about how you kids are going to manage a long-distance relationship?"

Shrewd, his grandfather was. "Pretty much." He added a slow nod and decided to confess. "When she first moved back, I thought if I could confirm that she had feelings for me then I could convince her to stay. I thought it would be easy if she cared about me even a fraction as much as I do about her. I was confident that she didn't really hate Rankins as much as she thought she did. I thought, you know, that love would prevail." He added a shake of his head.

"And now?"

"I've discovered that there's a lot more to her dislike of this place than I realized." He paused to watch the moose for a moment. "It's difficult because the same way this place embodies my best memories, it exemplifies her worst. And I get it, it's easier to avoid the past than face it." Basically, what he was doing with Sonya. "I can't ask her to stay here."

"I see."

"And I can't leave."

Doc peered at him like he was thinking this over. "Can't or won't?"

"As you well know, I still have over a year of my residency to complete and then I'm buying your medical practice."

Expression set to pondering, Doc leaned back in his seat. "You know, your dad and me, we've never had a strong father-son relationship. He always wanted… Heck, I still don't know what he wants. I have no idea how your grandmother and I could have raised such a selfish individual."

Flynn laughed. He didn't know, either. His parents had been perfect for each other in that sense.

"But you're a good man, Flynn. Better than your grandmother and I ever hoped you'd be.

I'd like to think I had something to do with that."

Flynn reached over and gripped his grandfather's hand. "You had everything to do with that—you and Gram, both. I don't know where I'd be right now if I hadn't had you guys to turn to."

"My point is, I'm so grateful for the time we've had together."

"Me, too."

"All I've ever wanted is for you to be happy. Iris makes you happy, Flynn. Just the idea that you've found a love that's anything like what I had with your gram makes me even happier than watching you follow in my footsteps."

"She does, and I want to make her happy, too."

"But?"

"But I don't know if it's possible to have everything we want in life. I think I was too confident, maybe a little selfish. I didn't stop to consider the logistics before I…told her how I felt."

"That's not an easy thing to admit."

"It's even harder to deal with."

"There's something your grandmother used to say that seems fitting in this situation. She used to tell me, 'Teddy, I would be happy in a garbage dump if that's where I had to live to be with you.' And if you could have seen the apartment we lived in during medical school, you'd know it was true."

Flynn laughed and scratched at the bottle's paper label with his thumbnail.

"You know we settled here because she fell in love with it?"

"I did not know that." Flynn had never thought to ask what had brought his grandparents to Alaska.

"I wanted to live in Colorado, where our folks were. We came up here one summer on vacation with some friends and she didn't want to leave. It was important for your gram that we have our own life."

"Do you regret it? Did you ever wish you would have stayed in Colorado?"

"Not for one minute. I've never been one of those people who believes that where a person lives has all that much bearing on their contentment."

Flynn thought about that. "I see what you mean. I've spent my entire life trying to get home, here to Rankins, but when it comes down to it, that was due largely to the fact that you guys were here. This is where I've always seen myself."

Doc watched the moose. "However, in Iris's case, I can see where that would be different."

"Me, too. That's why I can't ask her to stay."

"So don't."

Flynn was tired, so it took a bit for Doc's words to register. "What are you saying here, Doc?"

"I'm saying there are a lot of opportunities for a young doctor in Washington, DC. You have options, Flynn, you just haven't taken the time to explore them."

"But…" He felt an outpouring of love for his grandfather so strong it made his eyes burn. "What about me buying your practice?"

"The practice is still valuable. You're not the only doctor to want a practice in small-town Alaska."

Flynn nodded. That was true. But there was a deeper issue, the one he'd spent his entire life struggling with after a lonely childhood of feeling like a drifter. It wasn't easy to admit that he liked belonging somewhere, feeling needed, being liked and, yes, being loved. The first three he got from this town and the latter was sitting beside him. Although, Iris loved him, too. Even if they hadn't exchanged the words yet, he knew it to be true.

"You're the only family I have. I don't want

to leave you. I don't want to leave Rankins. And since I'm being honest here, there's a part of me that can't understand Iris not wanting to stay here. She's got this big, amazing family who will do anything for her. How can she want to leave them? Sure, she's different from them in a lot of ways, but they don't care."

"But she does. Just as you want to be a part of the crowd, Iris wants to stand out from the crowd. She needs to believe that all those ways that she's different aren't bad. It's tough to do in a family like hers."

Doc was right. Even though she'd proven to herself, and to her family, that she could do this Alaska thing, the bottom line was that she didn't want to. Somehow, Flynn needed to accept the fact that she wasn't going to change her mind.

"KEEP IT STEADY AND…there we go. Nice. You're a natural with that yoke, Iris."

"Cricket, I would love to smile at you right now, but I can't tear my eyes away. Am I really doing this?" A rush of adrenaline blasted through Iris's bloodstream and left her tingling all over. The thrill of being in complete control of something so powerful was heady.

"You're really doing it. I've seen pilots with

hundreds of hours of experience who don't have your gentle touch."

"Then there's the fact that I have the best instructor." This time she managed to toss him a quick grin. Brotherly-type pride danced in his luminous green eyes.

His compliment meant a lot to her for two reasons. One, Cricket wouldn't give it if he didn't mean it, and two, she was flying a real airplane! Okay, so she was flying it with Cricket, but that didn't matter. Her solo flight would come soon enough.

Iris relaxed into the movements she'd memorized and practiced and memorized some more. Gradually, the beauty of their surroundings sank into her—the cerulean blue of the sky, velvety green mountains rising from the crystalline water of the coast.

"It's wild how different piloting a plane is than being a passenger." Growing up in small-town Alaska and having an older brother for a pilot, she'd been no stranger to flying in small aircraft. But this—this was exhilarating.

"It is," Cricket agreed.

With a slow, steady push of her foot on the rudder, she banked the aircraft gently to the right. The plane swung around, then she adjusted the yoke and brought the nose down gently. The power at her fingertips and the picturesque view combined to steal her breath.

After a moment she glanced at Cricket again, and asked, "Does it ever get old?"

"Not for me."

For the first time in her life Iris thought she might understand her thrill-seeking family a little better. Floating among the scattered clouds, and the majestic mountains that appeared to rise from the sea. Nestled along the shoreline of the bay, the tiny town of Rankins appeared quaint and beautiful. Rooftops glowed in the sunlight, making it easy to spot the Cozy Caribou, with its characteristic red roof. She could imagine people walking along the streets. The riverfront park adjacent to the bay looked inviting with its verdant patches of green grass, picnic tables, paved pathways and state-of-the-art play structures.

Viewing her hometown from the air on a pristine day like today, she could almost forget the hurt she'd endured at its hands.

Almost. After a while, Iris relinquished control and Cricket landed the plane. They sat there for a few seconds in silence and she could feel Cricket's gaze on her. She belted out a joyous laugh and beamed at him. "I love it! Cricket, thank you! I'm… Wow. This flying thing is incredible!" Kayleen was right—she did belong here. They'd been in touch, and Iris couldn't wait to email and tell her.

"It is and I knew you'd be great at it." Peering at something out the window, he said, "Uh-oh."

"Uh-oh? What 'uh-oh'? Is something wrong?"

"Looks like we've got an audience. Your brother is here."

"Oh, boy..." Iris winced. "I guess this is one way to tell him, huh?"

He laughed. "I like how positive you're being."

They exchanged encouraging smiles and climbed out of the plane.

Tag stood by the hangar, hands on hips, gaze narrowed on them. But Iris quickly noted that he wasn't the only one there. Ally and Flynn were next to him. Flynn's expression said that he was both impressed and surprised. Ally looked like her usual calm and cool self, with possibly a hint of pride in her expression.

Iris and Cricket joined them and Iris said, "Hey, guys, what's up?"

"What's up?" Tag repeated flatly. "You have been, apparently. What's going on?"

Iris chuckled. "That's funny. Total unintentional pun. Um, I've been taking flying lessons."

"Cricket has been teaching you to fly?"

"Yes."

Ally smiled and confirmed that pride Iris thought she saw. "It's a very valuable skill, Iris. Good for you."

"Why didn't you ask me to teach you?" Tag asked, and for once, she couldn't tell what he was thinking.

"Well, the answer's obvious," Cricket said. "When you're smart and you want to learn something, you naturally seek the best instructor. Iris is brilliant, so the rest follows. I'm sure she would have asked you if I'd been too busy."

Flynn chuckled.

Tag rolled his eyes.

Iris watched her brother, trying to gauge his reaction. "Tag, I hope you're not upset. I didn't want… It didn't have anything to do with you. I didn't want anyone to know until I knew I could do it."

Ally said, "He's not upset, Iris. He's thrilled. Right, honey?"

Tag shook his head like he couldn't quite believe what had transpired. "Of course you could do it. I am so proud of you. But I am a little upset…"

"Tag, I'm—"

Tag pulled her in for a hug. "About having to give you one of my airplanes."

Iris laughed. "You won't have to do that."

"You heard Kayleen, a deal's a deal."

"Wait, what?" Cricket asked. "What plane? What deal?"

Iris told the story of meeting Anne, Chloe, Summer and Kayleen.

When she finished, she added, "I'll admit Kayleen inspired me."

Cricket chuckled. "Well, now I'm inspired, Iris, for you to get your license even quicker."

They all laughed.

Flynn hugged her next. With his mouth close to her ear, he whispered, "Way to go, Duck. I guess there was something going on with you and Cricket, huh?"

CHAPTER FIFTEEN

"YOU KNOW HOW people always say they want to get a bridesmaid dress that they can wear again, but it never happens?" Iris said as she and Flynn stepped into the elevator of their Washington, DC, hotel. Sebastien's assistant had secured them rooms only a few blocks from the museum where the gala was taking place. "It's fun to actually get to do that."

Flynn pushed the button for the lobby. "It's fun for me, too."

"Why's that?"

The doors closed. "Because it means I get to do this." Flynn placed his hand on her bare back, spreading his fingers to achieve maximum surface area.

"Ohh…" He watched her breath catch and it made him feel like a superhero. A teasing glint sparked in her hazel eyes as she then slew him with a dazzling smile.

They'd flown in the day before and her skin had a sun-kissed glow from the time they'd spent sightseeing. They'd hit some of the key tourist attractions, like the White House, the Washington Monument, the National World War II Memorial, and Vietnam Veterans and Korean War Veterans Memorials, as well as parts of the Smithsonian. Tomorrow's agenda included the Tidal Basin and the Lincoln Memorial because, she'd informed him, she wanted him to see it at sunset.

Some of his favorite moments had happened when she'd showed him the not-so-popular spots she loved, like her favorite town house in all of Georgetown, the best place to buy fresh-cut flowers and the bagel shop where they still made everything from scratch. She'd bought six different flavors and made him try every one.

He drew her close for a kiss and Flynn quit thinking about where they were and where they'd been because he still couldn't believe he could kiss Iris whenever he wanted. The bell dinged, indicating they'd arrived at the lobby. Flynn released her, enjoying the fact that she seemed as breathless and disoriented as he felt.

"Elevator kissing," she teased as she moved toward the door. "So cliché."

Flynn took her hand and pulled her back,

pressed the button to close the doors and kissed her again.

"Flynn," she protested weakly and kissed him back until the doors opened once more.

Laughing, they exited the elevator into the spacious lobby. Once outside, Iris tapped the app on her phone to call for a car. Less than three minutes later, their ride pulled up. They arrived at the venue, where men in tuxes and women in cocktail attire headed inside.

Sebastien and another man met them out front. "Hey, how are my favorite Alaskans?" Iris gave him a hug. Flynn shook his hand.

Sebastien gestured to the man beside him before taking his hand. "I'd like you to meet my partner, Drew Carter. Drew, Iris James and Flynn Ramsey."

Flynn barely had time to process just how unfounded his jealousy of Sebastien had been because the sight before him all but took his breath away.

Inside the grand, marble-floored foyer, a young couple dressed in elegant formal wear checked them in. A chamber orchestra played to an empty room beyond. The woman gestured up the stairs, where the party appeared to be in full swing on the second floor.

They ascended the elegant staircase and

Flynn immediately appreciated the brilliance of the acoustic setup. The music drifting up from the first floor wasn't too loud that conversation couldn't easily flow. Black-and-white-attired waitstaff carried sparkling silver trays with offerings of wine, champagne and ice-cold water. A long seafood bar was laid out with prawns and oysters on the half-shell, and crab sat chilling on a thick layer of ice. Fancy appetizers filled tiered platters at one end. An artistic display of desserts stood on another table.

Before long, Flynn had met so many people his eyes began to glaze over. Iris was deep in discussion with a philosophy professor she knew from graduate school, so he excused himself to get a drink. An hour and countless conversations later, he was getting ready to devour a double-chocolate cupcake when a beaming Iris found him again.

"That looks delicious."

He offered her a bite and enjoyed watching her eyes light with joy as she took a taste. Moments like this stretched out before him.

"Mmm," she said, "I love it when a cupcake tastes as good as it looks."

Flynn took a bite and had to agree.

"Are you having fun?" she asked, and there

was no mistaking the hopefulness in her expression.

"Yes, I am. Sebastien introduced me to…I think it was maybe the surgeon general."

"That's awesome. Did you talk about important stuff like heart disease and diabetes?"

"No, we discussed bow ties versus regular ties for formal wear, the necessary inconvenience of road construction and the Lincoln Memorial, which I'm looking forward to visiting tomorrow, by the way. Then I had a conversation with a guy who thinks these tiny soft-shell crabs are better than ours. Can you believe that?"

"I hope you set him straight regarding the size and superiority of all things Alaskan."

"Absolutely not," he joked. "Our state is getting crowded enough as it is. I generally let people wallow in their misconceptions with the hope they won't discover how great it is and move there."

She laughed and linked her fingers in his. "Well," she said, "I just met a Supreme Court judge. I think I managed to sound not as intimidated as I felt. I also talked to Senator Marsh— you know, Bering's friend?" At his nod, she went on, "He asked my opinion on Alaska's most pertinent economic indicators. He's a smart guy. I can see why Bering and Tag like him. And he told me he honestly believes Hannah is going to win the state senate race. She's a natural, he said, and people gravitate toward her. I already knew that, but isn't that great?"

Lifting a hand, Iris waved at an attractive older woman in a floor-length sequin gown. "That's Dr. Olivia Dormand," she explained. "She's completely brilliant, a specialist in macroeconomics, a consultant on a project I worked on. She's written like six books on the subject."

And at that moment, Flynn truly understood—Iris belonged here. This was her "zone," just like she'd talked about. She would never be as happy in Rankins as she would be here. The realization left him with one last important question—could he be as happy here as he was in Alaska?

Maybe Doc was right; Flynn felt like he belonged in Rankins because his best memories resided there. A lot of them now featured Iris. Sure, it was also about the tiny close-knit community he loved, nestled in the vast wildness of Alaska, and the endless opportunities to do all the activities he enjoyed. But mostly, it was about the people. His life, he realized, was about Iris.

This weekend together in the nation's capital had been amazing. It had shown him that he and Iris could create memories anywhere. It was a beautiful city. So long as he was with her, it didn't really matter what they were doing, whether it was quiet visits to the bagel shop or fancy parties like this one. It felt just like what his grandparents had. Different locale than he'd imagined, same kind of love. The notion was exhilarating.

"Hey," she said, squeezing his arm. "What are you smiling about?"

"I was just thinking about something."

"Do you want to share?"

"I do. I will. As soon as we get out of here."

"We can go now. Sebastien and Drew are leaving."

"Okay, then." He took her hand and they headed for the door.

"It feels so good out here," Iris said when they stepped out into the cool night air. "I'm not sure I'll ever get used to these East Coast summers. It's like I'm either melting in the heat or freezing from the air-conditioning."

"One nice thing about them is that the kayaking season is longer here. The fishing isn't as good, but I hear there are places in Maryland that are decent. We can go on charter boats all along the coast and explore the Atlantic Ocean.

If you thought catching halibut was fun, wait until you land a bluefin tuna."

Iris stopped in her tracks and turned toward him. "Flynn, what are you saying?"

"I'm saying that when I finish my residency I'd like to move here and be with you. And until then we will make this long-distance thing work."

"But…what about Doc? What about your medical-school bills and buying his practice?"

"My wise and extremely generous grandfather pointed out that his practice could be sold to anyone. And my medical-school bills can be paid off the same way other doctors pay them off, but at a much lower interest rate."

"You talked to him about this?"

"He talked to me."

"But what about what you want? I know how much you love Alaska, how much you love Rankins."

"I do, but I also understand now how much you don't. And what it all comes down to is…" He searched for the right words and finally decided to borrow some from his gram. Pulling her into his arms, he said, "Iris, I'd live in a garbage dump if it meant I got to be with you."

"AUNT IRIS! IRIS!" Lucas and Violet ran to her. Iris picked up her nephew and her little cousin, one at a time, gave them hugs and set them down again.

"Jeez, you guys are getting big. Pretty soon, you'll be picking me up."

They giggled. Lucas said, "That's funny."

Ally, along with all three of Iris's sisters, their cousin Janie and Emily were congregated around a picnic table. Nearby, the play structure, monkey bars and brand-new swing set were all getting plenty use from assorted James kids.

Janie's twin boys, Gabe and Finn, swarmed around her next, hugging her legs in turn. "We're playing sorcerer-sorceress," Gabe informed her. "Do you want to play?"

"I absolutely do." She had no idea what it entailed but it didn't matter. "Let me talk to your mom and the other big people for a bit and then I'll be over."

Iris and Flynn had returned home from Washington, DC, the previous day. Iris had a ton of stuff to accomplish in the next few weeks, including hiring and training a new employee at Copper Crossing, but she was determined to soak up as much family time as she could before she left. When Janie had texted that morning to invite her to an impromptu gathering of James women in the park, she couldn't refuse.

"How is my little niece or nephew?" she asked Shay when she descended upon the group.

"Fabulous. He's kicking all the time."

"You keep calling it a 'he.' You know how weird that's going to be if it's a girl, right?" Shay wanted a boy that they could name after their paternal grandfather, Augustus "Gus" James. He'd founded the Faraway Inn and left it to Shay when he passed away.

"I don't know…" Shay pulled one shoulder up into a shrug. "I think Gus is cute for a girl."

"So do I!" Ally said.

"Hmm. That is pretty cute," Iris agreed. "What about Augusta?"

Shay grinned. "We're negotiating."

The women discussed baby names while Iris asked Hannah about her state-senate campaign. Hannah glanced at Emily, who was serving as her campaign manager. They exchanged smiles before Hannah answered, "Really well."

Emily added, "Your sister is being modest. She's a rock star."

Iris told them about her meeting with Senator Marsh and his optimism regarding Hannah's win. Everyone was smiling with satisfaction when she finished.

"Okay, Iris," Janie interrupted impatiently. "Enough of this chitchat, as sweet and important as it is. How was your trip to Washington, DC, the one you took with Flynn?"

"It was great."

"How are things with you and Flynn?" Hannah asked.

"We're…" She shrugged. "It's…good." And it was. Except, she and Flynn hadn't discussed the details of how they were going to manage a new relationship across so many miles. Turning over possible scenarios had kept her up the night before. She really wasn't up for answering questions from her family that she had no answers for.

"How good?" Janie asked.

Violet, bless her, saved Iris from having to answer by bringing her the "wand" and the "robe" and informing her it was her turn to be sorceress.

Iris gave her family the whadda-ya-gonna-do? shrug and jogged to the grassy expanse of lawn, where the kids were waiting. After a quick rundown on the important yet ambiguous rules that only kids could conceive, she was ready to roll.

Blanket draped over her from head to toe, sorceress arms stretched wide, stick-wand firmly in hand, Iris cast her best "spell," and then chased after the kids, which wasn't easy considering the blanket kept flopping in front of her eyes. The excessive giggling and squealing spurred her on and made the element of danger worthwhile.

Gabe tripped and fell, laughing all the way. Iris tagged him with her wand, then scooped him up and gave him a loud smooch on the cheek before lowering him again. She caught Violet next and gave her the same treatment. Holding her beneath her armpits so her little feet dangled just above the ground, she said, "Should I plant you here?" Then she spun her around. "Or here?"

"Iris!" she screeched and then burst out laughing. Iris joined in because the kid had the cutest belly laugh she'd ever heard.

"Well, you're a flower like me so I have to plant you somewhere, right?"

"No! I want to run."

"Can flowers run, though?"

"Yes!" More giggling ensued.

"Well, okay," Iris conceded. "But don't stay in one place too long because you might sprout roots and get stuck."

Violet stilled, and in a too-serious tone, she asked, "Really?"

"No, absolutely not."

She lowered the child down and Iris's "robe" slipped off. Violet could be rather literal, so Iris reiterated, "That was just a joke. You will not actually grow roots."

"Iris?"

She looked up to find Sonya standing nearby. "Sonya, hi! What are you doing?"

"I have an appointment later. It's such a gorgeous day I decided to take a walk." Iris wondered if she meant a doctor's appointment, although she waved an arm in the opposite direction of most of the town's businesses. Concern warred with discretion. She decided it wasn't her place to pry.

"It is. You look great, by the way."

"Thank you. I'm feeling better." A new OB-GYN had recently opened a practice in Rankins. Maybe she'd already seen a doctor.

Violet took a step forward. "Hi, I'm Violet." She loved how Emily's daughter was so friendly, but in such a polite way.

"Nice to meet you, Violet." Sonya held out a hand, which Violet shook. "My goodness, your eyes are almost the same color as the flower, aren't they?"

Violet flashed the smile she'd inherited from her dad and nodded. "Lots of people say that. Tag says it all the time. He calls me wildflower. Because my name's a flower, too, like Iris's."

"It is! That's so neat to have that in common with your…"

"Violet and I are cousins, second cousins technically. Our families are very close, though. She's like a niece."

Violet nodded vigorously. "Nice to meet you," she said. "Goodbye." She scampered off to join her cousins.

Sonya watched Violet go and Iris knew she wasn't imagining the affection she saw in the woman's expression. Then Sonya looked at Iris and said, "She's adorable. You're really great with kids."

"Thank you. I love kids." Iris glanced toward the group of giggling children. "This is going to be you pretty soon. You must be so excited."

Sonya sighed. "And nervous. Now that the time is close I realize how little experience I have. How do you know what to do with them? Like that game you were playing. My parents never played games with me."

"Hmm. When you grow up in a big family like ours you get together a lot and kids are just always around. I used to babysit my little cousins when I was a teenager. They're fun and I guess if you pay attention they'll let you know what they like. My personal strategy is to keep them as engaged as possible—play games, talk to them, make them laugh." Iris could tell from the look on Sonya's face she wasn't convinced. Iris didn't envy the fear and uncertainty Sonya had to be feeling. Reaching out, she laid a hand on Sonya's arm. "Don't worry, you'll know what to do. That maternal instinct will kick in and you'll be a pro in no time."

Sonya tried to smile but it looked more like a grimace. Iris's heart went out to her. Easy for her to say when she wasn't the one facing it. Pointing toward the picnic table, she said, "Hey, do you want to meet some of my family? Lots of moms over there to give you first-hand advice, more than you probably want. Emily, mom of Violet and Brady, baked cookies and my cousin Janie made some delicious brownies. Janie has five kids, aged eighteen to infant, including that set of twins there." Iris pointed in the general direction of Gabe and Finn. "She's an expert in motherhood. Plus, we've got chips and dip... Oh, and a fruit tray."

Sonya's smile went a little wider and almost reached her eyes. She nodded. "I'd like that."

CHAPTER SIXTEEN

"So Sonya thinks we're engaged now, too?" Iris repeated what Flynn had just told her as they strolled hand in hand along the path that fronted the bay. Iris had taken a long lunch. She'd gotten sandwiches to go from the Cozy Caribou and met Flynn at the hospital on his break. Given his shifts at the hospital and Iris trying to find her replacement at Copper Crossing, this was the first opportunity they'd had to be alone since they'd returned from DC two days ago. "We managed to ease our way out of one fake relationship only to get into another, much more serious fake one?"

"I'm sorry." Flynn grimaced. "But I ran into her again at the hospital yesterday morning. I don't know if 'running into' is apt because I had the feeling it was on purpose on her part."

A gentle, balmy breeze blew in from the water as they neared the spot where Iris had seen Sonya. "I ran into her yesterday, too. Like right here, in the afternoon. I introduced her to everyone. She seemed a little better, less despondent."

"I agree. But that's..."

Flynn took the bag from her hand and set it on the table. "That's what?" she asked.

"I don't know... She was asking questions about our relationship and making me nervous. I felt like I needed the added layer of protection of an engagement. I really am sorry, but please don't make me tell her the truth."

Iris laughed and gripped his hand a little tighter. "Flynn, it's fine. After everything you've done for me, I'll do as much pretending for you as you need."

"Thank you. Hopefully, she'll be gone soon, and it won't matter. She can't stay here forever."

Why not? Iris wondered, but didn't ask the obvious question because Flynn was putting his arms around her. Eyes blazing, dimpled smile in place, Iris felt that now-familiar warmth spread through her. Would she always feel this way in his embrace? He dipped his head and kissed her. Question answered, she thought, as joy and affection blasted through her like a million sparks from the most brilliant fireworks show. He broke off the kiss and pressed his forehead to hers for a few long seconds. She liked how he always seemed as affected as she did.

"We need to talk about what we're going to do."

Iris swallowed nervously and nodded. She knew this was coming but it hadn't stopped her from worrying. What if Flynn had been thinking about the difficult logistics, too, and realized it wasn't worth it?

"What about not doing this?"

"What do you mean?"

"I mean how about not pretending anymore? Listen…" He pulled back to look at her and the intensity she saw in his eyes had her already agitated heart jumping. "I know this is going to seem fast, but I feel like I've wasted so much time where we're concerned. I love you. I'm so in love with you, Iris. It's like all the loose ends in my life feel tied when we're together."

Relief washed over her fast and hard and left her a little dizzy. She gripped his shoulders. "It's not too fast," she assured him. She'd been in love with him for more than a decade. "I lo—"

"Hold on." He held out a hand to halt her declaration.

"Let me finish and then you can tell me you love me, too. I think this is worth the wait."

"Fine," she answered with a playful huff and an eye roll.

"Here's the thing… I've been thinking about this a lot. We're facing more than a year of a long-distance relationship. But when you're visiting Rankins and when I come to DC, I want us to be together, you next to me, me beside you. In fact, I want to wake up next to you in the morning and fall asleep beside you at night. I want to make you breakfast and I want you to kiss me when I have to leave at whatever gruesome early hour in the morning it is."

Okay, so he was right, that had been worth waiting for. Joy pulsed through her veins, flowing into every inch of her body. She'd never experienced this kind of happiness in her life. Ever. Contentment was the best she'd hoped for. Academic success, the job of her dreams, those were good, satisfying accomplishments. She'd believed that was enough. Now that she'd tasted this kind of euphoria, she finally understood.

Love. It hugged her heart and made her feel whole and complete at the same time. Like she could float away. She didn't think there was anything she wouldn't do for this man. Tears formed, burning her eyes, and she realized it was the first time in her life she'd ever cried tears of joy. A short burst of laughter followed at the thought.

"I want to do that as your husband."

She nodded. "I want that, too."

"Good. Okay, go ahead." Flynn's smile was brighter than the sun and even more beautiful.

She laughed and shook her head. "I love you, Flynn."

He nodded, and despite his usual confidence, he looked relieved, too. "Good. That's so... perfect, actually. Will you marry me, Iris? You're all I want."

"Yes, I will. Of course I will. I can't wait to marry you."

He pulled her to him and hugged her close. "Shortest fake engagement ever."

"Even shorter than our fake relationship."

IRIS WAITED FOR Ashley in the Donut Den. Nervous energy churned in her stomach, and not in a good way. She couldn't stop the fleeting thought that she was being set up. Like the prom scene in *Carrie*, where Carrie's classmates pretend to be her friend and then humiliate her in front of the entire school. If Faith and Lorna came through the door along with Ashley, Iris didn't know what she'd do. Unfortunately, she lacked Carrie's telepathic powers.

She couldn't help but feel relief when a lone Ashley dashed through the entrance, spotted Iris and hustled over. Exhaling a single sharp breath, she said, "Sorry I'm late. My babysitter flaked on me and I had to run the kids out to Mom and Dad's. I try not to ask them too often, you know what I mean? I don't ever want them to think I'm taking advantage."

"You're fine. It's only a couple of minutes."

Swinging an enormous purple-and-white striped bag from her shoulder, she let out a little yelp and an "Oh, no!" before smacking a hand to her forehead. "I did it again."

"You did what again?"

"I left my bag at Mom's and brought the baby one with me. My brain still isn't fully functioning since Devon was born. And the poor little mite was up for hours last night…" Ashley dropped the carry-on-sized bag onto a chair and began rummaging around inside it. "Which means I don't have my wallet."

"Do you need some money? I can buy your coffee." Iris held her cup aloft.

Ashley looked up and frowned at her. "You already ordered? You were supposed to let me buy you coffee." She shrugged out of her jacket and Iris noticed a brown stain on her wrinkled blouse. No makeup, faded leggings, messy ponytail—Iris couldn't wrap her brain around how different Ashley seemed than the perfect, put-together femme fatale she'd been in high school.

"I got here a little early, so…"

"Motherhood steals your brain cells, but it also…channels them in very helpful ways. It forces you to levels of ingenuity you would not believe." Ashley dove into her bag again. "This is not the first time I've done this, so I've taken to stashing emergency cash in one of the pockets. Plus, it's nice, in case I forget to leave money for the babysitter and she needs to buy something." She waved a handful of dollars in front of Iris. "I'll be right back."

Iris watched her. As she chatted with Hailey, the young woman working behind the counter, Iris couldn't help but notice how engaging she was. When Ashley turned on the charm, she was magnetic. Hailey produced a box and began filling it with pastries. Ashley came back to the table with an extra-large coffee and an assortment of goodies.

Tossing Iris an enticing grin, she said, "You're not going to make me eat alone, are you? I hate that."

"Me, too, actually." Iris smiled, grabbed a napkin and chose a bear claw.

Ashley removed the lid from her cup and picked up the creamer. Iris had never met anyone who put as much cream into their coffee as she herself did. It was disconcerting to have anything in common with Ashley Eller. Iris considered making small talk but decided to let Ashley take the lead.

The fact that Iris was even here facing down her past was a milestone. She credited her courage to braving so many Alaskan elements, physical and mental, over these last weeks. And flying an airplane. Admittedly, there was a little bit of Flynn-related engagement confidence mixed in there, too. They were going to make the announcement to everyone at their regular James family Sunday dinner.

Ashley took a huge bite of her donut, then another, and one more before wiping her mouth with a napkin she plucked from the dispenser. "Sorry, I skipped breakfast." Ashley finished off the donut and took a chug of her coffee. She then chose a glazed huckleberry muffin and began peeling away the paper. "I can't wait to find a job. I adore my children, but we all need to get into a routine. Between the divorce and the move, it's been mayhem." She sighed. "This single-mom thing is challenging, not that Roy was any help when he was around, which is a big part of why we got divorced and why I need a jo—" Eyes wide, one hand went up and made a chopping motion at the air as if to cut off her sentence. "Which is not why I asked you here. To talk about the job. I mean, I want the job, but I'm not begging or pressuring you for it or anything."

Iris gave her a reassuring smile and started to say she understood, but then Ashley's diaper bag fell over. An object toppled out and hit the floor with a thud. The lid flew off the container and a million Cheerios skittered across the floor.

Ashley covered her face with a hand while Iris tried not to laugh. She stood but an efficient Hailey was already hustling around the counter, broom in hand. "I got it. Don't worry."

"I'm so sorry," Ashley said. "I can do that." She reached for the broom.

"Don't be silly." Hailey waved her off with a kind smile. "This is my job."

"Thank you, Hailey."

Iris couldn't help but feel the tiniest twinge of compassion. Ashley was a hot mess. A hot mess of someone trying at least, Iris reminded herself as she tore off a chunk of her own pastry.

Hailey soon departed, not a trace of cereal

remained. Ashley seemed to fortify herself with another long pull from her cup. She set it down. "I'm sure you're curious about why I wanted to see you."

"I am."

Dropping the half-eaten muffin onto a napkin, Ashley wiped her fingertips and then folded her hands on the table in front of her. She fidgeted with her chipped nail polish before meeting Iris's gaze head-on.

"Here goes. Iris, I owe you the hugest apology. I know you can probably never forgive me and I wouldn't blame you if you didn't. I was such a nasty person in high school. And I'm…" She trailed off with a shake of her head. "I'm so, so sorry about the way I treated you. It keeps me up at night."

Iris stared blankly. She opened her mouth to respond, then closed it again to give it some more thought.

"Like days, if not minutes, after Bette was born it hit me. The thought of anyone treating her how I treated you makes me sick to my stomach. For the last six years I've thought about tracking you down and apologizing. It didn't feel like something I could do over the phone and then I thought why would she even talk to me? If I were you, I would hang up on me. I certainly don't think I'd be here listening to me, either. But then again, I'm not kind and classy like you are. Like you've always been."

As shock settled over her, Iris did more staring.

Ashley went on, "I was so jealous of you."

That produced an involuntary snort of disbelief. "You were jealous of me?"

"Yes! Gah! I wanted to be smart like you so much."

"Um…"

"You know my dad's an engineer?"

At Iris's nod, she continued, "He wanted a son so badly, a smart boy like he is. Like my cousin Derrick is. He got three girls instead, two artistic scatterbrains like our mom. But Callie and Stef don't care what he thinks. Why would they? They're both incredibly talented. But me, I didn't get their artistic abilities. And I didn't get my dad's brains, either. I'm… I've always felt like such a nothing."

Iris was taken aback. "But you're so… You were the most popular girl in our class."

Ashley glanced away for a second before meeting Iris's gaze again. "I know, but who cares? I mean, I know I was pretty. I am pretty," she corrected quickly, like she didn't believe it anymore but was trying to convince herself. "It was the only thing I had back then. It was…" She smiled but it looked more like a grimace. "It was the only thing I *thought* I had. I'm realizing, slowly, that I do have other gifts. Despite how I might appear this morning, I'm organized, efficient and I can multitask like no one's business. I'm calm under pressure. All of that helps make me a good mom. And I was a good wife. Roy couldn't have run that car dealership without me—in fact, he's figuring that out. His cheating had nothing to do with me."

Iris didn't know what to say. It was a lot to process.

"There's something out there for me, I just need to find it. I've been seeing a therapist. I feel like I've taken myself apart and now I'm putting the pieces back together, but the way I want them."

"That sounds like a good idea." Iris managed a smile. "I was jealous of you, if it makes you feel better. I wanted to be pretty."

"Well, you got your wish, didn't you? Your beauty spread from the inside out."

"Ashley, that's a really nice thing to say."

"It's true." Ashley smiled again, and it looked so heartfelt, so genuine, that Iris was struck with the thought that Ashley was so much lovelier now, too, than the high-school beauty queen she'd been. Ashley's beauty, it seemed, was spreading inward.

"Once you hit rock bottom, it's easy to be honest. You probably don't remember, but Flynn and I started going out right around the time you two became close. I couldn't handle it. I came unglued. I used to ask him to study with me. Looking back, that would have been pointless because we didn't have the same classes. I used to complain that he spent more time with you than he did me. Which he did, by the way, did you know that? Because being the obsessed teenage girlfriend that I was, I kept track."

Iris shook her head. "I didn't know. But it wasn't like that with Flynn and me. We were just study partners. Friends."

"No, you weren't." Ashley barked out a laugh. "I mean you both thought that's all you were because you... I don't know." She shrugged. "Because Flynn was a teenage boy and neither of you could see how amazing you are. But I knew you'd end up together someday. And if you didn't, it would have been a tragedy."

SUNDAY DINNER WAS a long-standing tradition in the James family. It had been going on for as long as Iris could remember. This week, Aunt Claire, Bering and Janie's mom, was hosting.

Two picnic tables had been placed end-to-end outside in a freshly mowed expanse of the grassy yard that fronted her home. Another table was next to that. Lawn chairs were scattered about where people chatted and finished their melt-in-your-mouth pork roast and potato salad. Laughter and teasing mingled with the joyful squeals of the kids, who were playing a game of whiffle ball a short distance away.

Talk soon turned to the assortment of pies laid out for dessert. Iris fidgeted in her seat beside Hazel. Hazel slid her a knowing smile. There was something about sharing a room with your sister that invited the sharing of confidences. She'd told Hazel about the engagement the night before. Flynn had already informed Doc, who sat beaming beside Ally at the next table.

"Where's Flynn?" Hazel whispered.

"Talking to Mom and Dad."

"Such a gentleman. I found out before Mom and Dad?"

Flynn had insisted on speaking to her dad first even though Iris felt like the tradition was a little antiquated.

"You're the only person I've told."

"You didn't tell Tag?"

"Nope."

Hazel smiled triumphantly, and then scooped up her last bite of potato salad.

Flynn emerged from the house along with her parents. Grin in place, Flynn caught her eye and winked.

He walked straight toward her and then leaned down and whispered in her ear, "Permission granted."

"What a relief," she said sarcastically. "I'm so glad we don't have to secretly run off to Vegas now."

Flynn chuckled. "No, we can make arrangements and fly like normal people. Do you want to do it or should I?"

"You, please."

Iris untangled herself from the picnic table to stand beside him.

"How do we get everyone quiet?" Flynn asked.

Hazel looked up at them over her shoulder. "May I?"

"That would be great," Iris answered and plugged her ears.

Hazel's whistle was loud enough to stop traffic. Every head turned their way.

"That was for us," Flynn said with a wave to the crowd. "Nicely done, thank you, Hazel."

Iris heard Flynn's phone chime inside his

pocket. He ignored it. "So this will surprise some of you more than others, I'm sure." He grinned at Tag and Ally. Tag's gaze narrowed. Ally smiled knowingly. "Iris and I are getting married."

A chorus of congratulations erupted around them followed by roughly three thousand questions.

"When? Do Emily and I get to help plan another wedding?" Shay asked.

"Where?" This from Janie. "Because I think someone needs to get married at Bering and Emily's. We could—"

"Um," Iris interrupted. This was the part that wasn't going to go over well. "It's sort of tentatively planned for two weeks from now. In Vegas and you're all invited. But don't feel obligated. If you can make it, that's great. If not, that's fine, too. We just want to be married, we don't care so much about the *getting-*married part."

"I THINK THAT went well," Flynn said a short while later, scooping up a spoonful of dessert. "Your aunt makes the best huckleberry pie in the world."

"It did. And I know, she does." Iris stole a

bite. "The Vegas thing went over better than I thought it would. You know how my family likes a gathering."

"A gathering in Vegas will be fun, too. Especially for me."

Playful smile dancing on her lips, she leaned toward him. "Me, too," she said just before pressing her mouth to his for what should have been a quick kiss.

Flynn slipped a hand around the back of her neck to hold her in place. Joy pulsed fast and hard through her veins. They were going to do this. Love really did conquer all.

"Remind me why we're waiting two weeks?" he whispered.

"Airfare prices, remember?"

"Oh, yeah…" He sighed dramatically. "I'm not sure it's worth it."

A voice sounded nearby. "Hey, lovebirds."

Flynn gave her another quick kiss and they both looked up to find Ally standing before them.

"I'm sorry to interrupt, but Doc is leaving."

"Emergency?" Flynn asked.

"Yeah, I'm afraid so." Ally looked from Flynn to Iris and back again. "Flynn, he said your ex-wife is in labor."

A bolt of concern shot through Iris. "But she's not due for another three weeks. Flynn, we need to go and be with her. She doesn't have anyone…except us."

CHAPTER SEVENTEEN

"FLYNN, I DON'T UNDERSTAND…" Tears clouded Iris's vision, and why did her fingers ache? Glancing down, she realized how tightly she was gripping Flynn's hand. She loosened her grasp. "How could this have happened?" She inhaled a breath, but the pungent smell of hospital seemed stronger than usual and only heightened her helplessness and despair.

Flynn's head was shaking, signaling he, too, couldn't believe what had just transpired.

They'd arrived at the hospital and found out that Sonya was in the middle of a cesarean-section surgery. The baby survived, but Sonya had suffered a seizure and died.

The nurse appeared at the door of the hospital room where Iris and Flynn were waiting, a tiny bundle held in her arms. "Do you want to hold her?"

Iris nodded. "Yes, Nicki. I do."

Nicki passed the baby to Iris. Concern jolted through her. The infant felt too light.

Iris thought of a flannel-wrapped pack of feathers. She studied the tiny, perfect, adorably scrunched face and could barely breathe. The baby opened and closed her lips and shifted, and something inside of Iris shifted, too. With a staggering force, Sonya's fate and the baby's plight landed hard on Iris's heart. Tiny and completely defenseless with no mom to protect the baby, it felt unfair, and this moment utterly surreal.

"What a pretty girl you are," Iris whispered, swallowing a sob. Remaining calm and positive for the baby's sake, Iris suddenly felt like it was the most important thing in the entire world. She lowered herself into the hospital room's rocking chair. After brushing a kiss to one velvety soft cheek, she looked up at Flynn.

Keeping her tone gentle, she asked, "Sonya never mentioned having preeclampsia?"

Flynn seemed to be in a similar stupor as he kneeled beside the chair. "No. But I've been in touch with her doctor in Anchorage. She was diagnosed and had medication. She's lucky she even carried the baby this long."

Iris felt fresh tears spring to her eyes and quickly blinked them away. "I knew something was wrong. I wrote it off because she freely admitted the pregnancy was stirring up her emotions. Maybe if I hadn't been so pre-occupied with my own life, with my job, with us. I wish—"

"Shh, Iris," Flynn interrupted softly. "I wish, too. But this isn't your fault. Or mine. I don't understand what she was still doing here. She should have been back in Anchorage in the hospital. We… I don't know what she was thinking."

"What's going to happen to this beautiful little girl, Flynn? I know Sonya's relationship with her parents was strained, but should we call them? She doesn't have siblings… Who should we call?"

"I don't know… I'm going to get ahold of Trent and see where he is and why he's not here and find Sonya's parents. When I asked Sonya about them last week she said they were traveling. I think she said they were in Europe."

Iris gave him an encouraging smile. "That sounds like a good place to start."

"I'll go do it now. Will you be okay? Do you want me to get Nicki or one of the nurses?"

"We'll be fine. I just… She needs someone to hold her, I think. I'm going to text Mom, Hazel and Shay. Hannah is in Juneau for that campaign event. You know how my family loves babies and I don't want this one to be alone, not even for a second. Maybe we can take shifts."

FLYNN FELT A combination of sorrow and pride so intense he could only nod. The woman he loved was showering affection on his ex-wife's child. He pressed a kiss to Iris's temple before caressing the baby's soft cheek.

Clearing his throat, he said, "That would be exactly the right thing for her. Doc and Dr. Grant are conferring about whether to send her to Anchorage. She's a little small but her lungs sound good and vital signs are excellent. We just need to figure out where she belongs."

Iris smiled up at him with so much trust and sympathy in her eyes Flynn felt his knees go a little weak. She was the most incredible woman he'd ever known, and he hadn't thought it was possible to love her any more than he did.

Flynn pulled out his phone and stepped into the hallway. Allowing himself one deep, fortifying breath, he then texted a mutual friend of his and Trent's to ask for his number, which he'd deleted after he'd found out about him and Sonya. Minutes later, he had the number and made the call.

Trent picked up on the third ring with a tentative "Hello?" that suggested to Flynn that he hadn't deleted the contact on his end.

"Trent, hi. It's Flynn."

"I know. It's great to hear your voice, buddy. How're you doing?"

"Not great. I, uh, I have bad news."

Trent listened silently while Flynn did his best to gently deliver the shattering news. When he finished, Trent said, "I can't believe it… It's hard to understand. That's so sad."

Seconds ticked by as he waited for Trent to tell him he was on his way. When that didn't happen, he asked, "Trent, is the baby yours?"

Silence echoed from the line before he answered, "Mine? No, Flynn. No, it's not. Sonya and I broke up too long ago for the baby to be mine. We… I don't think she really loved me. Or, maybe she did, I don't know. But she wanted a baby so much it…scared me."

"Yes, she did. I'm just… I don't know. This is a weird situation."

"How is the baby doing?"

"Remarkably well. She's small but otherwise healthy."

"Good. That's good."

"Do you have any idea who the father might be?"

"Maybe." There was a long pause, and then he said, "Not precisely, but…"

"What do you mean?"

"Flynn, this situation might be even weirder than you know. Listen, last fall there was a break-in at the lab. Laptops were stolen, electronics, a few pieces of medical equipment and you're going to think I'm making this up, but... You know Saul and his photographic memory?"

"Sure." He and Trent had been amicably jealous of Saul DeMarco in med school.

"A couple of the coolers were unlocked and he noticed..." Trent trailed off with a pained sigh.

Flynn broke out in a cold sweat. A sound like a freight train roared inside his head because he knew what Trent was going to say.

"Saul noticed that several sperm samples were missing. We couldn't prove it, because the records that go with them were gone, as well as the computer where all the info was stored and the flash drive. The backup drive, too."

"Nothing stored in a cloud somewhere?"

"Nope. That was part of the confidentiality agreement, that there would be no outside storage of donor names or DNA or anything else. None of the samples were ever supposed to be used to fertilize anything. In fact, these samples were all slated to be destroyed in a few weeks."

"Unbelievable." Flynn didn't mention just how much he wished he didn't believe it. A painful stab of fear sliced through him. "Are you saying that you think Sonya used one of these samples to get pregnant?"

"I'm not saying that for certain. But you knew her, Flynn. You were married to her and you know how badly she wanted a baby. All I'm saying is that the timing works. She quit three weeks after the break-in and I haven't seen her since."

After talking it over for a while, they ended the call.

The adrenaline rush had left him shaky. He needed to get his bearings. He walked over to the window that looked down on the bay and tried to calm himself. There was no evidence that Sonya had done what Trent suggested. Except for the fact that she'd quit her job and disappeared after the break-in. As Trent pointed out, Flynn knew her. He absolutely believed her capable of this. If she had gotten pregnant this way, would she have used his sample?

"Flynn?" a voice interrupted his reverie.

Inhaling a breath, he turned and faced his grandfather. "Hey, Doc. Baby okay?"

"Yep, baby is fantastic at this point. Marcie and I agree that we don't need to transport her. Unless, you want her sent to Anchorage for a second opinion." Marcie was Dr. Grant, Rankins's new OB-GYN.

"Me? No, I trust the assessment completely. You've delivered a lot more babies than I have. I'm glad Marcie was here to do the C-section."

Doc nodded. "Me, too. She sure is a welcome addition around here."

"I just got off the phone with Sonya's ex-boyfriend. He claims he's not the father. I'm going to call her parents and see what they know."

Doc was staring at him in a way that had Flynn's anxiety churning all over again. "You don't know, do you?" he asked.

"Know what?"

Doc reached up and absently scratched the back of his neck. "I thought this was all very odd."

"What are you talking about?"

"When Sonya got here to the hospital she knew she was in medical distress. Dr. Grant's exam confirmed it. Sonya asked for a pen and paper, so she could write down the baby's name and the father for the birth certificate in case she didn't make it."

Flynn felt an instant shot of dread solidify in his gut even as he silently praised Sonya for having the presence of mind to do so.

"And?" he prompted his grandfather.

"She named you, Flynn, as Lily's father."

IRIS FELT THE blood rush from her head as Flynn told her that his name was on the birth certificate. She tightened her hold on the baby because she felt a little light-headed.

"She's yours?" Iris forced air into her lungs.

"No. I mean… I don't know."

"Flynn, you told me that you hadn't been together in over two years. You said—"

One hand went up, effectively interrupting her. "That's the truth, Iris, I swear. But you need to listen to me carefully, okay? This is a strange story."

She nodded for him to continue.

Taking a second to gather his thoughts, he scrubbed his hands over his jaw before linking them together around the back of his neck for a few seconds. Releasing his grip, he blew out a breath and said, "When Sonya and I were first married, she was working at a research clinic."

"Yes, she mentioned that." Iris urged him on. The baby squirmed. Iris looked down in time to watch her yawn. Baby yawns equaled unparalleled cuteness.

Flynn moved so that he was facing her and then waited until he'd captured her focus again. "A fertility clinic."

"Oh." Iris's brain quickly shuffled through the possibilities. "Flynn, did you donate your sperm?"

"I did. They needed test subjects. We were told the samples would be destroyed. But Trent said there was a break-in at the lab and some samples appeared to have been stolen." Flynn recited the rest of the details.

"You think she used yours?"

"I don't know."

"What's her name?"

"What? Who, Sonya?"

"You said she wrote down the baby's name, too. What is it?"

"Oh. Of course. Lily, Lily Justine. Justine was Sonya's grandmother's name. I don't know where Lily came from."

The words washed over Iris, bringing a million tiny needles that prickled every inch of her skin.

"I do," she said. "Or at least I think I do." She told him the story of meeting Sonya in the park and introducing her to Violet. "She loved how we were both named for flowers."

"You don't think that's a coincidence?"

"I don't. Oh, Flynn, don't you see? I think she knew she was going to die… Maybe that's too dramatic, but she was afraid of that at the very least. That's what she was doing here in Rankins. You told her we were getting married and this was her way of telling me…" A fresh sob gathered and stole the rest of her words. Swallowing it down, she continued, "I think this was her way of telling me that she wanted me to be Lily's…"

She couldn't bring herself to say the word because Sonya had made a terrible mistake. Iris couldn't be any child's mother, not even for this perfect, precious little one who was likely Flynn's. Tears rolled down her cheeks, but she didn't bother trying to stop them this time.

Flynn deflated right before her eyes as the weight of the truth bore down on him. The blood seemed to have drained from his face and he looked so pale she feared he'd collapse.

"Flynn, you need to…"

Before she could get the "sit" out he slumped in the chair opposite her. His gaze narrowed in on the baby like he was seeing her for the first time.

"What do I do?" he asked.

"I don't know." For Iris, this explained so much of Sonya's behavior. Flynn, she suspected, needed a little more time. And possibly a nudge toward the truth. "Right now, I think you should hold your daughter."

"We don't know yet if she is my daughter. I know you like her, liked her, Iris. I mean Sonya. But the woman I knew could be devious and manipulative. This is—"

Iris scooted forward and passed him the baby. Lily kicked her little legs and then settled in his arms like she belonged there. Iris couldn't stop the stabbing pain in her heart as he gazed down at the little pink bundle. Wonder, curiosity, admiration and affection were written all over his face.

Of course, as a doctor, he had experience with newborns. But this was different. It was like she could see the possibilities flashing through his mind.

But when he looked at her, she could see there was still doubt there, too. "Let's keep this between us for now, okay? I'll get a DNA test and then we'll go from there." His eyes searched her face and Iris knew he was trying to see her feelings, read her thoughts.

"Okay," she agreed. She tried to smile but

her face felt paralyzed, her happiness was paralyzed. Because she didn't have doubts. Inside, it
felt like her soul was being torn apart because
at that moment she knew that she and Flynn
were being torn apart, too.

Iris was bombarded with emotions. Sorrow,
sadness, anger, guilt, happiness, joy. Sonya was
dead, and Lily had no mother.

But Flynn now had a daughter.

She was a horrible person for even thinking what came next because who was she to
wish that Sonya had never come here? That
she'd never sought out the father of her child?
What she'd done to Flynn was so wrong. Yet,
it wasn't Lily's fault. And Iris reminded herself that Sonya had undoubtedly been hoping
for some kind of shared custody or visitation
between Flynn and his child. And then, after
meeting Iris, she'd planned for that, too.

Sonya couldn't have known that Iris didn't
want a family. All she'd known was that Iris
and Flynn were a happy couple and why
wouldn't Flynn want to be a part of his child's
life? She and Flynn had only encouraged this
with their fake engagement. Iris's ramblings
about her large and loving family, and Sonya's
meeting them, had probably added to it. Why

wouldn't she want her daughter to be a part of that?

Why wouldn't Flynn want this for himself? Iris couldn't allow herself to wish away this chance at fatherhood for him, especially when he would never have it with her. And she certainly couldn't let herself wish that Lily would never know the love and comfort and kindness that having a man like Flynn as a dad would bring. Lily was innocent and perfect, and she needed a parent.

All Iris could do was cling to the thought that Flynn loved her. And at least she'd had him for a little while.

"HOW'S THE BABY? How's our granddaughter?" Cynthia Traver looked up from her where she sat, crying, next to her husband, Richard. They were side by side on a navy blue sofa somewhere on the eastern coast of Norway.

Flynn cleared his throat and focused on keeping his gaze on the camera. Informing relatives that a loved one had passed was one of the most difficult aspects of being a physician. Telling your ex-wife's parents via Skype while they were vacationing in Europe was indescribably horrific.

Sonya's relationship with Richard and Cynthia hadn't been great when Flynn knew her. Flynn hadn't spent a lot of time with them, but he liked them both. He believed the feeling was mutual.

Richard was a widely respected immunologist and Cynthia a psychiatrist with a thriving private practice. She'd gotten in touch with Flynn when he and Sonya had filed for divorce, expressing her and Richard's disappointment at the breakup. When Sonya waylaid his residency, Richard called to tell Flynn the decision wasn't personal, on his part, anyway.

"She's doing remarkably well," Flynn said. "Especially considering she was three weeks early." He recited her vital signs and Dr. Grant's assessment, knowing they would want every detail.

"That's wonderful news, at least. Is she with Trent?" Cynthia asked.

"No." Flynn pressed his palms together and inhaled a fortifying breath. Obviously, Sonya had led her parents to believe Trent was the father. "Cynthia, Richard, there's no easy way to say this so I'm just going to tell you that Sonya and Trent broke up more than a year ago. Trent says the baby isn't his."

They both stared blankly as the meaning behind his words sank in. "Well, then…who is?"

"We're not sure yet."

"What do you mean?" Cynthia's face twisted with confusion. Flynn felt for her. "There's more than one candidate—"

"Flynn," Richard interrupted, "what in the world is going on?"

Flynn explained as best he could, leaving out the part about his sample likely being among the ones taken and his name being on the birth certificate. Cricket was flying the DNA samples to Anchorage the next morning. Trent's lab was putting a rush on the test, so Flynn would know for sure in a couple of days. No sense in muddying the water until he had the facts.

Cynthia cried some more and then shook her head. "You know, I blame myself. I tried so hard to keep my work separate from my parenting. Too hard, I see that now. I knew she needed help and I…" She broke down again.

Richard curled an arm around her shoulders. "Cynthia, dear, we've discussed this. It's not your fault. Look at all our friends and their kids, all the methods we've seen employed— too much affection, not enough attention, too much or not enough discipline… Parenting is like a roll of the dice with the best of intentions. Our daughter was a troubled soul, but we loved her and raised her the best we knew how."

Then he looked up, right into the camera's lens, and his electric blue gaze reminded Flynn of Sonya's—so much so, it left him a little disoriented. Would he see his own eyes looking back at him via Lily someday? Or his dimples? What about—

"Flynn, if you could take care of things until we get there, we'd appreciate it."

"Of course, sir. I'm already on it."

Cynthia dabbed at her cheeks, and asked, "Who is caring for the baby?"

"Me, my girlfriend and her family. Your granddaughter's receiving the best possible care, I can promise you that."

CHAPTER EIGHTEEN

"SHE'S SUCH A good little baby, aren't you, Lily of the valley? Oh, you are the sweetest thing," Margaret cooed, rocking Lily in her recliner.

Iris sat beside Hazel, watching from the sofa. The sight of their mom cuddling Lily made Iris feel as warm and cozy as the baby looked all bundled in her flannel blanket. Lily let out a squeak.

Iris's grin collided with Hazel's. Hazel said, "She seriously makes the cutest noises in the world."

Operation Baby Emergency was in its third day and turning out better than Iris had even hoped. Emily and Janie had both brought over spare baby items—onesies, pajamas, bibs, blankets, bottles and assorted gadgets and gizmos. Janie had also supplied a crib. Emily loaned them a car seat. Babyhood fresh in both their lives, they were full of helpful advice. Between Iris, Margaret, Hazel and Hannah, baby Lily always seemed to be in someone's arms.

Flynn was there between shifts and Iris marveled at his lack of fear and wholehearted willingness to get down into the trenches. Feedings, diapers, crying, baths—nothing fazed him. And then there was Doc, who came over daily to dote on her.

"Mom," Iris said, "how did you do it? How did you and Dad handle everything when the three of us were babies? With me being sick and needing so much care."

"We had a lot of help—your aunt Claire was a godsend." Bering and Janie's mom had lost her husband when the kids were babies and the two families had always spent a ton of time together. "Tag and Shay were thirteen and twelve when you triplets were born. They pitched in, so did your cousin Janie. Your Grandma Taggart came and stayed while you were in the hospital. They let Hazel and Seth come home after a few weeks, but you were there for seven weeks. Your dad and I took turns so that one of us was always with you and the other home with your siblings."

"That must have been so hard." Iris smiled as tears burned behind her eyes. She didn't truly realize how emotional this baby thing made a person. Especially when the baby in question likely belonged to your fiancé.

"It was a tough time, but you don't think of it like that when you're going through it. You discover that you just *have* the strength, it's a built-in part of parenthood. All I could focus on was how much I loved you and wanted you to live. I begged you to live. I prayed for you to live. I willed you to live."

Iris thought she understood. She desperately wanted Lily to be healthy, to feel safe and loved. That was her mission until Lily's grandparents arrived. Sonya's parents were on their way and then Lily would have the love of her mother's family, too. Flynn said they were good people. That was enough for Iris.

Affection and protectiveness mingled with the looming disappointment about her and Flynn's uncertain future. She didn't feel selfish about that because her overriding concern was for Lily.

What was important was that she stay in the moment. Where she worried about everything.

Even though Flynn reassured her that thirty-seven weeks was only borderline premature, Iris couldn't shake her fears about Lily's health. Was her breathing too shallow, was her pulse too weak? Too fast? Should she feel so warm? Was she too cold? What was that spot on her cheek? Were her cries normal? Did she eat enough? Anxiety constantly floated on the surface of her consciousness, snatching her peace of mind and sending her imagination reeling.

She kept reminding herself that Flynn was a doctor. Between him and Doc they'd pick up on anything amiss. The bottom line was that even this tiny taste of parenting was exhausting. However, there was an end in sight.

Because the fact remained that as much as Iris adored Lily, caring for her only solidified her intrinsic belief—she wasn't cut out for full-time motherhood.

"HEY, JONAH, WHAT'S UP?" Flynn took a seat across from Iris's brother-in-law at a corner booth in the Cozy Caribou. Jonah had called and requested the meeting, but had revealed nothing other than it was in his professional capacity as an attorney and it was regarding Sonya.

"You want coffee?" Jonah asked.

"That'd be great."

"Good, because I ordered you some."

The waitress brought two cups over. She filled them and said she'd be back to take their orders.

"This is important and urgent, so I'm just going to get to the point."

"That works for me," Flynn said before lifting the cup and taking a sip.

Keeping doctor's hours was good baby training. Lily had been up for the first three out of the six hours he'd had off the night before. After finally rocking her to sleep, he'd caught a few hours of rest in Seth's old room. He smiled, affection bouncing around inside of him, as he thought about how Iris insisted the crib be placed in her and Hazel's room. For someone who didn't want any kids of her own, Iris was a champion foster mom. Of course, she had a team of experts on hand, as well. If he didn't already adore her family, he did now.

Gratitude made his chest a little achy. Flynn didn't know what he'd have done if this duty had fallen to him and Doc alone. Thinking about Lily churned up so many emotions. He was so anxious to know if she was his. What would that mean for his future? What would it mean for him and Iris? They hadn't talked about it. It had to be on her mind as much as it was on his. He loved her even more for keeping her focus on the baby as they existed in this unsettled state.

"Your ex-wife came to see me a few days before she died."

"About what?" Flynn had already checked

online to make sure they were truly divorced. He'd heard stories where the papers never got filed.

"She asked me to draw up a will."

Cup halfway to his mouth, Flynn froze. Not unusual, he reminded himself, for new or expecting parents to draw up a will. Especially a single mom with a medical condition. He set down the cup.

Jonah went on, "It was simple, and she asked for it to be expedited. So I did it. Unfortunately, she didn't have time to sign it, but her wishes were clear. You're her sole heir. She left you everything and gave you custody of Lily."

"Me?"

"Yes. She also asked that I add 'and your future wife.' I assume she meant Iris, even though you guys announced your engagement after she came to see me."

Flynn nodded.

"That part has no legal meaning because you're not married. I explained that to Sonya, but she insisted I put it in there."

Flynn took a moment to think, a difficult task with his brain spinning a million miles an hour. Sonya had been quizzing him about their relationship not because she had designs on him for herself. It was for Lily. Iris was right. Sonya had been afraid she was going to die, or at least the thought had occurred to her.

"Jonah, thank you for telling me. I'm—I'm sure you can imagine how difficult this situation is. I don't know…?"

Jonah held out a reassuring hand. "Flynn, I want you to know that even though Sonya has passed away I'm still bound by attorney-client privilege here. Although, the law states unequivocally that if I believe that the deceased would want the information disclosed then I can act on that. Without a doubt, that is the case here. As her intended heir and personal representative, you can submit the unsigned will to the court. I'm not going to tell anyone about this until you decide how you want to proceed. But I do have to ask if the baby is yours. It makes a difference in what I disclose to the Travers."

"I understand." Flynn heaved out a breath. He'd been trying not to think of Lily as his daughter until he knew for sure. Jonah's information only seemed to strengthen the notion. Sonya's parents were still alive. Why would she grant him custody if he wasn't the father?

Over the last few days, he'd gone from praying the baby wasn't his to wondering how he'd feel if she was. It was impossible not to adore her. He cautioned himself to wait a little longer for the DNA results even as the love, the fatherly feelings, he'd been holding at bay started to spill over. When he'd told Iris that he was ambivalent about having kids, he'd meant it. But he couldn't possibly have known what this would feel like.

A daughter. Would Iris want Lily to be her daughter, too?

Iris adored her. He knew she did. He just wasn't sure what that would mean to her. Did she feel this same overwhelming love and fierce protectiveness, too? Would it change anything for her? It had to, right? It wasn't something he had any control over, and it was changing things for him.

"The answer is that I'm not sure."

"I see." Jonah remained poker-faced. Flynn was impressed.

"But it's not what you think. Can I assume what I'm about to tell you is confidential, too?"

"Absolutely."

Flynn explained about the fertility study.

"Wow," Jonah said when he'd finished. "That's so wild. Like soap-opera wild. And categorically wrong. If she were alive, I'd recommend a lawsuit. That's theft. There have been lawsuits over similar incidents, women using sperm without permission from ex-boyfriends and husbands."

"I know. And the thing is, if I'm not Lily's father I don't think there's any way to find out who is. According to a friend of mine who works at the lab, the samples and the records were all destroyed."

Nodding thoughtfully, Jonah picked up a spoon and lightly tapped it on the table, then said, "I contacted Richard and Cynthia Traver. I informed them about the circumstances surrounding Sonya's will. Not what's in it, just that she'd had one drafted. They said they'd spoken to you and asked you to take care of things until they arrived?"

"Yes, they did."

"Good. I'm glad that it's amicable among you all. When will you get the DNA results?"

"Should be tomorrow morning. A friend of mine is fast-tracking the test."

"Okay, good. Knowing whether or not you're the father will make a big difference here. Like I mentioned, an unsigned will can be submitted to the court for consideration."

"I don't care about anything but custody. I mean, if Lily is mine, then of course I want her."

Jonah held his gaze for a long moment, then asked, "And if she's not?"

Blankly he stared at Jonah, absorbing the jolt as the implications of that simple yet extraordinarily profound question sank in.

"I…"

"You need to think about this. Either way, you have a huge decision to make."

Sonya wanted him to raise her child. Lily could be his daughter regardless of biology. But what about her grandparents? They might want her and challenge Flynn for custody. Should he respect their wishes? And what about Iris?

He wanted Lily if she was his and, he admitted to himself, maybe even if she wasn't. But how would Iris feel? What was he going to do?

"I guess I'll have to discuss that with the Travers." And Iris. He needed to talk to Iris.

But first, he needed those test results. Because Jonah was right, if he was Lily's biological father, that would take the decision out of his hands.

"So, Debra, it says here that you've been working as an office manager for a shipping company in Anchorage for the last three years?" Iris looked up from the résumé Debra had submitted the week before as if she hadn't already memorized it.

Debra Zenn was twenty-three years old and had a two-year degree in office management from a community college in Seattle. Her computer skills were adequate, references were good and in her spare time she enjoyed figure skating, volunteering at an after-school program for kids and scrapbooking. She'd scored well on the test. On paper, she was perfect.

"That's correct." Debra tucked a lock of silky brown hair behind her ear and smiled at Iris—she was personable, attractive, with a pleasant voice and a nice presence, although Iris thought her skirt was a little short for an office setting, especially an interview. But, hey, maybe she liked short skirts.

Iris wanted her to be the one. Really. She did. Wanting and the reality, she'd learned after six interviews, were two very different things. It reminded her of the baby books she'd been reading, and how when she'd quizzed Janie and Emily about actual parenting versus what she'd learned, they'd laughed and laughed and laughed.

She wondered how Lily was doing.

At Hazel's insistence, Iris had left Lily with her and Margaret and went to work. Leaving the baby had been difficult but she'd scheduled the interview last week and she owed it to Tag to hire her replacement and get the person trained before she moved. Hannah and Cricket had been filling in for her at Copper Crossing the last few days.

"And your current place of employment is Anchorage Water, Sky and Ground?" Iris tacked on an encouraging smile when the distracted Debra didn't immediately respond. "Is that accurate?"

Eye contact, however, was one of the woman's biggest problems. Mainly because she kept "contacting" with Tag. Like she was doing now.

"Debra?"

"Umm, yes," she answered, swinging her gaze back to Iris. "That's correct, Anchorage Water, Sky and Ground is my current employer."

"Tell me about it."

"Okay, well, um, like Copper Crossing here…" Debra paused to gesture around the breakroom where Iris had been conducting the interviews. Her gaze zeroed in on Tag, again, and lingered.

Iris stifled a sigh. She'd encouraged Tag to sit in on the interviews and she wondered, not for the first time, if that had been a mistake.

At Tag's encouraging chin dip, Debra continued, "It's a regional shipping company based in

Anchorage. They have a fleet of trucks, three boats and two airplanes. They ship *everything* you can imagine." The entire response was directed at Tag, as if Iris wasn't the one asking the questions.

Mistake.

Leaning toward him, skirt officially hiking up into the range of inappropriate, Debra added, "Part of my job is to be the *best*."

Tag's eyebrows drifted far up onto his forehead as he subtly leaned back in his chair and away from Debra.

"And what do you mean by that, *exactly*?" Iris asked. Several seconds of dead air screamed back at her. "Debra?"

Debra tore her attention away from Tag. "You know, to identify the best type of packaging and form of transport for absolutely any object, no matter how big or small."

"Hypothermic moose?" Iris peered intently at Debra, but she could feel Tag's eyes locking onto her in surprise.

Debra's mouth formed a silent O before she stuttered, "Wh-what?"

"You said everything I can imagine. I'm imagining a cow moose who has fallen through the ice on Jasper Lake. After being stuck in the frigid water for hours, she's now freed but requires medical attention. Wildlife officials have determined that she needs to be transported two hundred miles to a wildlife rehabilitation center."

"Oh… I, uh, don't think we ever handled a live-moose transport." Swinging toward Tag and displaying her cleavage, she gushed, "Have *you*, Captain James? I'd love to hear about it sometime."

Captain James? Iris mouthed behind her back along with an eye roll. Time to wrap this up. "All right," she said flatly. "Debra, I'd like you to *imagine* that you're working here at Copper Crossing and you're about to arrange your first problematic transport. What's the first thing you do? Who do you call?"

"Um, Captain James?"

Iris couldn't tell if that was her answer or if she was passing the question off to Tag.

"Why would you do that?"

Debra hesitantly asked-answered, "Because he's the pilot?"

"Yes, he is that," Iris agreed patiently. "At AWSG did the pilots also prepare the planes for transport?"

"Where?" Debra asked, expression twisted with confusion. She was beginning to sweat. Iris felt a tinge of sympathy, but she needed someone who could handle both the office work and the high-pressure situations that sometimes arose.

"AWSG, Anchorage Water, Sky and Ground—you used the acronym in your written description of your job duties."

"Oh, of course. Um, not usually…"

Iris studied her for a few long seconds then asked patiently, "If not the pilot, then who?"

"The ground crew?" She immediately answered her own question more confidently. "Yeah, I'd call the ground crew."

"And then?"

"And then Captain James?" Another eager smile at her brother.

"Okay," Iris said, rising to her feet. "I think I have all I need." Tilting her head toward Tag, she added, "Captain James, do you have any questions for Debra?"

She could see from the twitch of her brother's lips that he was valiantly fighting off a laugh. "Uh, nope. Can't think of any."

Iris offered a smile and reached out a hand. "Thanks so much for coming in today, Debra. I'll be in touch."

A triumphant-looking Debra thanked them both, gathered up her bag, tugged on her too-short skirt and headed for the door. But not before tossing one more inviting look over her shoulder. "It was really, really wonderful to meet you, Captain James. It would be an honor to work for you."

When she'd departed, Tag gave Iris a pointed look. "A hypothermic moose? In what universe would we transport a live moose in one of my airplanes?"

"Well, *Captain*," Iris drawled. "It could happen."

At his dubious grin, she added, "It was a hypothetical to see if Debra could think on her feet."

"I take it she failed?"

Iris executed a slow incredulous shake of her head as if to say *you were here*. "Miserably."

Chuckling, Tag reached around and rubbed the back of his neck. "Iris, I know that you are aware of the fact that we're not hiring a rocket scientist here, or even a pilot. I don't expect to find another *you*."

"I know that." Iris reassured him with a pat on the shoulder. "I do. But you do need more than a…Debra. You need a multitasker, a problem solver, someone who can think under pressure and outside the box. You need…" Iris stopped in midsentence as her gaze drifted toward the recycle bin. She crossed the room toward it.

She was dumping it out when Ally came through the door.

"Hey, guys, are you—" Ally stopped short as she caught sight of Iris. "I take it the interview is over already. How did it go?"

"Don't ask," Tag said, reaching for Ally's hand.

"Good," Iris said at the same time.

"Uh-oh," Ally said. "Another one? Wasn't this the promising applicant with experience?"

"Yep," Tag said.

"You'll thank me later," Iris assured them both as she took a seat on the floor and began shuffling through the papers.

"If you say so," Tag muttered. To Ally, he added, "She literally has experience in this exact business. She works for an air-transport company based in Anchorage."

After a pointed look at Tag, Iris addressed Ally. "Unfortunately, Debra did not have the ingenuity and strategic thinking required to join the ranks here at Copper Crossing Air Transport."

Ally tipped her head like she was thinking carefully about her next words. "Iris, are you sure you're not being just a tad picky about the applicants? Tag is right that the job—"

Iris interrupted, "Did I also mention that she was ogling your husband?" Iris held up her thumb and forefinger, leaving about an inch of space between them. "And that her skirt was this long?"

Ally swiveled back toward Tag.

He scoffed. "Iris exaggerates."

"I do not. Ally, you know my track record here." Iris had been the one to accurately predict the attempt by Tag's ex to sabotage his and Ally's relationship.

Ally offered a helpless shrug. "Sorry, honey. Clearly, Debra wasn't qualified."

Tag chuckled and shook his head. "You two…"

"I know. Lucky you, right? A sister and a wife who always have your best interests at heart."

"Yeah, buddy, don't forget it," Ally teased. "But, Iris, I have to ask, what are you doing?"

Tag answered, "As far as I can tell, she's either sleep-deprived from taking care of Lily, or she's literally lost her mind and is looking for it in the recycle bin."

"Ha! Found 'em." She held up some sheets of paper and returned to her desk. It took only minutes to quickly grade the exam. "Highest score so far," she muttered, vaguely aware that Tag and Ally were watching her. Did she want to do this? Relief and satisfaction mixed with determination to stifle any doubt. Iris found herself smiling as she realized she was going to enjoy telling Ashley that she was the successful applicant.

"Found what?" Tag peered at her, curiosity stamped across his face.

"Iris, are you okay?" Ally asked.

Still grinning, she looked up at them. "I am now. I just found your new office manager."

Picking up her phone, she dialed the number near the top of the application. A few weeks ago, Iris would have lost a lot of money by betting this was a call she'd never make.

CHAPTER NINETEEN

"ASHLEY ELLER IS working for Tag now?" Seth asked, stretching one arm across the back of the sofa in an obvious attempt at nonchalance.

Hazel, on the other hand, sounded anything but. "You sure about this, Trippa?"

"Yep." Iris peeked into the bassinet where Lily was napping. "I am." And she was. It felt good to put that part of her life behind her. Strangely, it felt good to help Ashley. Iris sympathized with her—she knew what it was like to feel alone, to feel different and not quite good enough. She joined Seth on the sofa.

"Why wouldn't she be?" Seth asked.

"Because Ashley is a mean girl," Hazel snapped, somehow managing to do so quietly from her spot in the recliner. "Who was awful to Iris in school. I don't understand why you ever liked her in the first place."

Seth picked at the sofa cushion. "She's misunderstood. She couldn't have been that bad or Iris wouldn't have hired her, right, Iris?"

Her brother looked so hopeful that Iris almost agreed. But there was no way she could let Seth pursue Ashley unless he knew the truth.

"Hazel is right, Seth. She was worse than awful. I'm giving her a chance because she apologized, and besides, people can change. I want to trust her, but..." But that didn't mean she trusted her with Seth's heart. "She's trying, but she still has some things to sort out."

"In other words, stay away from her, Seth," Hazel said, leveling him with a determined glare.

This was the only topic Iris had ever known her triplet siblings to fight about. They argued, sure. Disagreements, yes. But the topic of Ashley Eller infuriated Hazel. Iris had always assumed it was because of her, but now she wondered if there might be more to it than that. Derrick Shaw, the love of Hazel's life and the man who'd left her heartbroken, was Ashley's cousin.

Seth said, "Iris is right. Ashley has changed."

"Okay, Seth, everyone knows that leopards can't change their spots. They move and contort themselves so that the spots appear to be different sometimes but that's it."

Seth shook his head. "What does that even mean?"

"It means Ashley is a leopard and you are a wildebeest. She will bring you down."

Iris cringed, her gaze bouncing from Hazel to Seth and back again.

"Hazel—"

Lily let out a small cry. Grateful for the interruption, Iris went to get her. Although, she had a feeling this subject was far from over where her siblings were concerned.

THE SAMPLE DOESN'T MATCH. You're not the father."

Flynn heard Trent's voice, but it took him too long to make sense of the words.

"Flynn, are you there, buddy?"

"Um, yeah, I'm here. Just a little surprised, to be honest." He realized now that he'd already prepared himself for the news that he was Lily's father.

"Me, too. I thought under the circumstances, since she went there seeking you out and all, that you must be the one."

And Trent didn't even know about the will. It was on the tip of Flynn's tongue to say that it didn't matter—he was still the one.

"Just so you know, it's not me, either. I went ahead and ran my DNA, too. I got a little paranoid. So, that's a relief."

Relief? Flynn should be awash with it. But instead, he didn't know how he felt. Not being Lily's dad, not acceding to Sonya's wishes, meant a way simpler life on so many levels. But what would it mean for Lily? Sonya's parents were older and likely not prepared to alter their lives so radically to raise a child.

But was he? Not really, no. There would have been no decision to make if biology linked him to Lily. And yet, Sonya had known Flynn wasn't the father and she'd still wanted him—him and Iris—to raise her child. He couldn't explain it, but in his heart, they were already linked. Bottom line, he wanted to do this. He wanted to do this with Iris. But what would he do if Iris wasn't in this with him?

"Thanks, Trent. That's good to know."

"You can always submit her DNA to one of those databases and see if any close relatives pop up."

Flynn thought about that possibility. He'd ponder it later, talk it over with Sonya's parents. First, he needed to find out where they stood regarding custody of their granddaughter.

"I really appreciate you doing this."

"Anytime. Hopefully, it's the only time, huh?"

Flynn managed a chuckle. "For sure."

They ended the call. Flynn made a quick call to Jonah and then went to tell Iris the news.

IRIS AND FLYNN left Lily sleeping in Seth's arms while they went for a walk outside. Another stunningly beautiful summer day radiated around them as they strolled across her parents' green lawn. Flowers bloomed in the beds, birds chirped in the trees. Alaska at its finest. Iris had to admit that she did see this place differently now.

She'd felt the tension in Flynn since he'd arrived nearly an hour ago. She suspected he had news, but she wasn't about to interrogate him while he'd fed Lily her bottle, changed her diaper and then rocked her to sleep. The way he sang to her and whispered sweet baby compliments made Iris's insides melt. She marveled at how fatherhood seemed to be a part of his makeup. Content and completely comfortable with the baby, it made her wonder why he'd never considered being a father.

They reached the edge of the lawn, where the ground sloped down and slender poplar trees gave way to the brushy forest below. Flynn reached out and entwined his fingers with hers.

"I have news."

Giving him a warm smile, she said, "I know,

I just can't tell if it's bad or good. I don't even know what would be bad or good at this point."

"I'm not entirely sure, either, if I'm being honest. The DNA results came back. I'm not Lily's dad."

The logical part of her brain said she should be relieved. Now she and Flynn could go on with their life, their plans, but... "What about Lily? What happens now? Do you know who the father is? Is there any way to find out?"

"Trent and I both think it would be difficult to find out. Plus, we don't even know for sure if Sonya becoming pregnant had anything to do with the lab. I believe it was, but I have no proof."

"Sonya's parents will take her, right? If you can't find the biological father?"

Iris had several other questions, but before she could get them out, Flynn said, "There's more."

She gave his hand an encouraging squeeze.

"Jonah called me yesterday and we met for lunch. I didn't want to say anything until I had the test results. Sonya went to see him before she died."

"Okay."

"Sonya made a will. She wanted me, us actually, to be Lily's guardians in the event of her death."

Once again, Iris recalled that day in the park, when Sonya had said she had an appointment and pointed in the direction of Jonah's office.

"Us?" she repeated.

"I believe so, yes. The will gives me custody, but she had Jonah add 'and his future wife.' You know, I told Sonya we were getting married. I think, like Lily's name, this was her way of letting me know that she wanted you to do this with me."

Iris nodded. The way he spoke and the words he chose—*do this with me*—made Iris's heart ache with a brand-new pang, deep and sharp.

"I thought she came here to Rankins and put my name on the birth certificate because she knew I was the father, but that wasn't it."

Flynn wasn't Lily's biological father, but Sonya had made him Lily's dad. She'd made Iris… No. She hadn't named Iris specifically, so that meant that while she approved of Iris, she trusted Flynn to find the right mom for Lily, whoever that may be.

"The will wasn't signed, so technically her parents are still her heirs. But Jonah says he is compelled to disclose the contents to the Travers. Apparently, I can ask the court to consider the will and validate it. They could dispute it."

"Are you going to do that?"

"Not sure. I don't want to fight the Travers for custody. Lily is their biological granddaughter. Jonah has a meeting with them this afternoon and he's going to explain all of this. I'll meet with them after they've made a decision. Depending on what they say, how they feel about the terms of the will, I'll go from there."

"I see." Her heart, already fragile, cracked a little more. Because she knew Flynn and she knew what he would do, even if he hadn't yet admitted it to himself. She also knew herself, and she knew what she couldn't do. She loved him so much. How she wished it was that simple. She'd do anything for him. Except this.

"Iris, I don't know what to do."

Eyes awash with tears, throat clogged with emotion, she somehow uttered, "Oh, Flynn, yes, you do. You know exactly what to do, and I love you even more for it."

Iris watched as those soulful brown eyes of his filled with tears. "I feel like I don't have a choice..."

"I know." His integrity, his empathy and compassion, were such huge parts of why she loved him. How cruelly ironic that these qualities were the very things that were going to tear them apart.

Iris wrapped her arms around him and they hugged.

Flynn loosened his hold to smile down at her. "I have to go to work. I'll let you know what happens."

JONAH HAD TWO cushy leather love seats that faced each other in his office. Flynn sat on one, with Richard and Cynthia across from him. Flynn couldn't read a thing in their somber expressions or predict how this was going to go from the few minutes of small talk they'd engaged in.

Jonah was between them in an overstuffed chair. Betty, Jonah's secretary got coffee for him, Flynn and Richard, and tea for Cynthia.

Betty closed the door behind her and Jonah got down to business. "Before we proceed, Cynthia and Richard, I want to make sure you feel like you've had plenty of time to consider this."

Flynn nodded his agreement. They'd spent many hours with their granddaughter over the last two days. They'd taken her for the entire afternoon the day before.

Cynthia and Richard exchanged meaningful

glances, then Richard said, "Before we give you our decision, we want to ask you a question, Flynn."

"Of course, anything."

"What will you do if we say we want custody? Will you submit the will to the court, anyway, or let us have her without a fight?"

Flynn had been afraid it was going to come to this. Determination and certainty overrode his apprehension. He'd made his decision and he hated to do this, but what choice did he have?

"Last week, that would have been an easy question to answer. But that was before I met Lily. I don't want to fight with you. You're her grandparents, and I want you to be a part of her life. Sonya would want that. But she also wanted me to be Lily's parent. I want to be Lily's parent. I can't explain it, but I already feel like I am. I'm sorry, but I'd have to fight."

Cynthia let out a whimper that tugged at Flynn's heartstrings. Tears rolled down her face and she pulled a tissue from her pocket. Richard nodded and swallowed heavily. He also seemed to be fighting tears.

Flynn hated this, but he didn't feel like he had any other choice. Lily belonged with him. With him and Iris.

The couple held hands and exchanged shaky smiles. Cynthia dabbed at her eyes with the tissue and then looked at him. "That's what we were hoping you'd say."

"Oh. I…"

Richard explained, "We only want what's best for our granddaughter. But we also want her raised by someone who truly wants her, someone who'll fight for her. Raising a child is difficult, as you'll soon discover. We need you to be all in."

"I am," Flynn said, trying to process their decision, trying to absorb the facts. "Thank you, both."

Richard turned toward Jonah. "Submit the will. We won't contest it. Sonya had issues. We can't begin to know what was going through her mind, but we believe that in this case she knew exactly what she was doing. And we believe she did the right thing. We're so grateful, Flynn, that you've agreed to take this on. It's beyond selfless."

Cynthia sat forward. "The only thing we want, if we can even ask for it, is visitation."

Flynn looked at Jonah. "Yes, absolutely, the more grandparents she has, the better, as far as I'm concerned."

HOPE, RELIEF AND love lightened the heaviness that had taken up residence inside of Flynn since Lily's birth. After leaving Jonah's, he texted Iris and told her he was on his way. He couldn't wait to give her the news. Part of this, he now knew, had been fear. Fear that Lily would be taken from him, that he'd have to go to court, that Iris wouldn't be on board. Her reaction when he told her about the will, her encouragement for him to pursue custody, filled him with a love so intense he could barely stand it.

In a week they'd be married. The three of them would be a family. Irony of all ironies that two people who didn't think they wanted children were coming together to parent someone else's child. And not just anyone's, but his ex-wife's.

He and Iris could do this. The logistics weren't going to be easy, but they'd manage. Exiting the car, he jogged toward the James house and then up the steps of the front porch.

Iris was out of the house before he could knock.

Wrapping her in a tight hug, he explained, "They're not going to fight me." He let her go, took her by the hand and led her to the cushy chairs, where he urged her to sit next to him.

"This probably means I won't be able to come to Washington, DC, as much as we'd planned, at least not for a while. Although, the Travers want to be a part of Lily's life so maybe they'll want to take her for an occasional weekend. Hopefully, since she's been such a good baby, we can turn her into a little traveler. I was thinking—"

"Flynn, wait." Twisting in her chair, Iris paused to capture his gaze with hers. Her voice was fraught, yet resolute, as she said, "I want you to know how thrilled I am for you and Lily. She's the luckiest baby in the world to grow up with you, and you'll be the best dad."

Flynn froze. He was pretty sure the entire world stopped. And when it started again, when his heart resumed pumping, it was like his warm blood had been replaced with ice water. He could read Iris's expression.

"You're not going to do this with me, are you?" he said.

"This isn't an easy decision for me, but I…" Head shaking, she swallowed down a sob, and continued, "No. I'm so sorry, Flynn. I wish I could. But I can't."

"What do you mean, you can't? You mean, you won't."

Silence stretched between them. Disappointment flooded through him and he tried desperately to rein in his anger. Why was he angry? That wasn't fair.

"I thought you were okay with this. When I told you about the will, you were okay with me…"

"I am okay with this. I encouraged you to follow your heart because I could see where it had already gone. I didn't—I don't—think this was a decision that you should make with me in mind. It's your decision."

"Iris, it's yours, too. It's what Sonya wanted. She wanted us to raise Lily together."

"I know. But she didn't have the facts, not at the time, and I'm not sure she had any right to ask this of us—of me. I'm not like other people, Flynn. You know what I mean. I never have been. I've come a long way in tackling my childhood, but this one issue for me is incurable. Sonya didn't know this about me, so in a way, it was partially our fault for not being honest with her. But that doesn't matter now because I also believe this was meant to be. And I know you can do this. I want you to do this. I want this for Lily. You're going to be a fantastic dad. You already are."

"But you love Lily, I know you do. I can see it. And you'll be an amazing mo—"

"I do," she interrupted and nodded. "Love her." Swallowing, she pressed a hand to her mouth and looked down for a moment. Facing him again, she appeared resolute. "Absolutely, I do. I love you both. That's why I'm doing this. You need someone who can help you, who can be a good mom for Lily. I'm not… That person isn't me."

"How can you say that? She needs us, she needs you. I need you." Flynn wanted to ask her to stay. He wanted to beg. But he also knew it wasn't fair. How could he ask Iris to raise someone else's child when she didn't want one of her own?

She stood. "I'm so sorry. I'm going to make this easier on both of us and head to DC tomorrow. My mom said she'll watch Lily as long as you need her to until you figure out what you're going to do long-term. Maybe you could ask Shay to help out, too, since she's cut back her hours at the inn. And, of course, Hazel, although I don't know how long she's going to stick around."

"Iris, I—I love you so much. I don't want to lose you."

"I know, Flynn. I love you, too. And you didn't lose me. You didn't do anything wrong.

You did everything right. In fact, I don't think I'd love you as much as I do if you hadn't made this decision. I hope you can forgive me."

CHAPTER TWENTY

HAZEL STOOD IN the bedroom next to Iris's open suitcase and pressed the heels of her hands against her forehead. "This is…unbelievable. So, all this time you thought Flynn was Lily's dad and you didn't say anything? Now you know he's not Lily's dad, but he is her legal parent, or at least Sonya wanted him to be. And you're her new mom, or you will be when you marry Flynn?"

"Yes, to most of that." Iris rolled up another T-shirt and stuffed it into the suitcase. "Except—"

"So in the blink of an eye, Lily goes from being an orphan to having the best parents ever. I mean, aside from the tragedy of Lily losing her mother and… Wait, what are you doing?" Hazel frowned. "Are you packing? That's an awfully big suitcase for three days in Vegas."

"It's not for Vegas. There isn't going to be any Vegas. Flynn is going to be her dad, but I'm not going to be her…" She couldn't say the word *mom*, it was like a knife to her heart every time she tried.

Hazel sank down across from her on the carpet. "What do you mean?"

"Hazel, I know you probably won't understand this, but I've never wanted children."

"So? Me, either, particularly. But life happens. If someone gave me one like Lily I wouldn't say no."

"I'm going to Washington, DC, tomorrow."

"Tomorrow? But you don't start work for another few weeks." Hazel's stare felt like a heat-seeking missile zeroing in on her scalding cheeks.

"You don't understand. I can't do this. So that means I can't marry Flynn. I'm leaving."

"Iris, that doesn't make any sense! That's not right."

"Hazel, please don't make this more difficult for me than it already is. It's not that I don't want to, it's that I can't. I'm not equipped for motherhood."

"All right, okay…" Head shaking, like she was searching for words, she held out both hands. "Listen, I'm going to give this to you straight because that's what we do for each other. So here goes. You've been acing motherhood for the last few days. You're a natural.

Lily already feels like your daughter to me. She feels like my niece. Mom and Shay and I were joking last night about how we wish we didn't have to give her up. I don't understand."

"I know…" Sadness and regret filled her to the brim. She needed to keep it together. This was the right thing to do, no matter how awful it felt. "I don't expect you to understand. I don't expect anyone to. I'm just asking you to support me here. I have to go. I can't stay any longer." Iris stared into her sister's eyes and willed her to understand. She didn't think she could handle it if Hazel looked at her with even a trace of the disappointment she'd seen on Flynn's face.

Then her sister did the most wonderful thing ever. She crawled around the suitcase, wrapped her arms around her and hugged her tight. "Of course I support you, Trippa. Always and in all ways." And then they cried.

IRIS SPENT HER first day in Washington, DC, staring at the TV in her motel room. If she stayed extremely still, focused on the screen and didn't move at all, it didn't hurt quite as much. At least, until that car commercial came on where the dad safely buckles the baby inside and then a series of scenes shows the little girl at stages of her life, each more tender and poignant than the last. In fact, why did nearly every commercial suddenly seem to feature a baby? And weren't they in an inordinate amount of movies and television shows, or was that just her?

Okay, so it still hurt. It really, really hurt. Like her heart and soul had been ripped out of her. She felt restless and helpless and useless.

The second day she forced herself out of bed. Feeling the need to remind herself of how she loved this city, she ventured out to visit her favorite haunts. Huge mistake. She'd taken Flynn to all of them. An adorable family consisting of a mom, dad, baby and ponytailed toddler in a stroller were buying bagels in her favorite shop. Without an ounce of embarrassment, the father made goofy faces and chattered at an infant in a front pack just the way she knew Flynn would do. The baby giggled wildly. Iris barely managed to keep it together long enough to find a bench in the park across the street, where she broke down and cried while six pigeons stared at her like she'd lost her mind. She thought they might be right.

The third day she changed tactics again and decided to shop for an apartment. The lease had expired on her place shortly after graduation, and, not knowing how long it would be before she got a job, she'd opted not to renew. Most of her belongings were in storage and she knew she'd feel better once she got settled. Apartment hunting would have been a great distraction until she found herself in the middle of a two-bedroom wondering if it had enough space for three.

Time, she told herself—she just needed to figure out a way to make it pass. Work would be the best distraction. Too bad the office was closed. Sebastien had told her to let him know when she was scouting apartments. So, after viewing yet another lovely two-bedroom, this one in his neighborhood, she decided to drop by.

A disheveled Sebastien opened the door wearing a rumpled T-shirt and basketball shorts. His normally perfectly mussed black hair was spiked up at odd angles and he'd gone at least a day without shaving. Iris regretted her bad timing, but before she could apologize, his face broke into a welcoming smile and he waved her inside.

"Iris, hi! You're here. I'm so happy to see you. Come in."

Somewhere behind him there was a noise. It sounded like a baby crying. Great, now she was hearing phantom babies to remind her of how much she missed Lily. Like she needed reminding. The ache in her heart started all over again. Maybe she was coming down with something.

"Sorry if I'm a little frazzled. Our adoption came through. Come in and meet Madison."

"Your…what, who?"

"Oh, that's right, you don't know. I didn't say anything before because Drew and I have been close a couple of times. We've had foster children and been on the cusp of adopting and it's always fallen through."

"This is the really important thing you had to be back for, isn't it?"

"It is." He added a happy nod. "Stupid probably, but I didn't want to say what was happening and jinx it."

"I understand. My sister and her husband have had a few of those experiences."

"It's brutal. But the papers are signed and we're parents now." The sparkle, the joy in his eyes was unmistakable. It reminded her of Flynn when he'd given her the news that Lily was theirs. Not theirs, she reminded herself. His. Except…

"Congratulations! How exciting." Happily, she recognized how much she meant those words. It felt good to acknowledge an emotion that wasn't sadness or longing.

Drew appeared in the doorway with a bundle of baby in his arms.

"Hey, Drew. Congratulations, Daddy."

"Hello, Iris. Thank you! Nice to see you again. Do you want to meet Madison?"

Ouch, she thought. Too soon to hold a baby?

"Sure," she said, her feet moving forward.

Drew passed her the baby. Her heart squeezed with warmth and affection.

"Hello, Miss Madison," Iris cooed. "I am so happy to meet you, little one." She swayed and gently bounced the way Lily liked.

The baby quieted. Madison smiled at Drew.

"Wow." He returned the baby's grin. "Baby whisperer."

"Not exactly. It just so happens that I've had a little practice recently. It's hard, isn't it? To know what to do?"

Sebastien came closer to gaze at his daughter. "It is, but we're so grateful for this blessing that we can't bring ourselves to complain. I mean, to finally have the opportunity to be parents, it's…" Choked up, he nodded for a few seconds. "We were beginning to believe it wouldn't happen for us. Parenthood isn't something everyone gets in this life. The fact that someone trusts us enough to care for this little life is… It's a gift. No matter how hard it might be at times, we will never take it for granted."

Iris felt something slip loose inside of her. "That sounds…perfect."

Then she looked carefully at the two men. "How long has it been since you guys slept?"

"Oh, um… We've been trying to take shifts, but it's not easy. She cries, and you just want to make it better, you know?" Sebastien half grinned.

She did know. Iris nodded as the darkness evaporated inside her once and for all and a lightness rushed in to fill the space. There was also now an urgency that made her want to run, but she knew she needed to stop and think. And she wanted to do something else while she did so.

"I do understand. But why don't you let me take a shift? You two go catch a nap."

The glances they exchanged were eager yet fraught with uncertainty.

Iris laughed and pointed toward the back of the apartment. "Hey, Dads, go get some shut-eye. I got this. I promise I know what I'm doing."

BETWEEN RESPONSIBILITIES AT the hospital and the clinic, Flynn spent nearly every second with

Lily. He didn't have the energy to try to not miss Iris. He'd tackle that later.

Janie let Flynn borrow her crib and a few pieces of furniture and he set up Lily in the second bedroom of his apartment.

He found Doc there, hovered over Lily on her changing table, stethoscope to her chest.

"I don't like this." Doc looked at him as he approached. "Take a listen."

Flynn accepted the stethoscope, held the chest piece in place and listened while concern tightened in his own.

"You hear it, too, don't you?"

Flynn nodded. "We're taking her to Anchorage."

IRIS LEFT SEBASTIEN and Drew's and realized she was hungry for the first time in two days. She picked up a pizza and went to her hotel room. She let herself in and immediately belted out a loud scream. There were people. Relief rushed in when she realized they were her people. Ones she was incredibly happy to see. Tag sat on the sofa. Hazel reclined on the bed.

"Holy cow! You guys scared me. What are you doing here? How did you get in?"

Tag said, "We're here to talk to you."

Iris set the pizza on the coffee table.

Chuckling, Hazel got up and moved to sit on the sofa next to Tag. "I pretended to be you, told the front-desk guy I forgot my key card."

"That worked?"

"Yep. I didn't actually say I was you, I said our last name and your room number, which you texted me for some reason."

Had she done that? She didn't even remember. The fog that had taken over her brain, however, was starting to clear.

Tag interrupted, "Listen, will you please sit down and hear us out?"

"Yes, but I should—"

"Wait." He motioned for her to take a seat, so she claimed the chair opposite them. "I'm simply going to ask you the same question you asked me when I couldn't find the courage to admit what I wanted where Ally was concerned."

"You're going to ask me if I want to be senator?"

"Funny," Tag replied flatly, although one side of his mouth pulled up in a smile.

"I think so."

"Who's deflecting now, little sister? It won't work, so here goes—is this really what you want? A life here in Washington, DC, without Flynn and Lily? If the answer is an unequivocal all-caps yes, then I'll shut up and leave you alone."

"Wow. Impressive. That quote was almost verbatim, and from like six months ago, too."

He shrugged a shoulder. "It was a powerful thought from an extremely insightful and intelligent woman. You have a knack for seeing through the complexities of a situation and getting to the heart of the matter—at least, where other people are concerned. For some reason, the ability seems to get a bit lost when it comes to your own life—and who you love."

"Iris, what are you afraid of?" Hazel asked. "That's the real question."

"It's complicated. What if I turn out to be a terrible mom to Lily? It terrifies me. What if I can't handle the bad stuff? The idea of having a child and watching her go through what I did…" Placing a hand on her aching chest, she gripped her shirt for a second before continuing. "I've always believed I wasn't strong like you guys. That I was fearful and cowardly. Even though…" *I'm so, so much stronger than I thought.* Was it strong enough? The answer was immediate and consuming—she was strong enough to try and that's what mattered. She might not be perfect, but nobody was, and that was no reason not to try. And no one would ever try as hard as she did.

Tag leaned forward and placed his forearms on his knees. "First of all, Iris, being afraid does not make you a coward. Every time I get on an airplane, every time I go out an emergency call, there's an element of fear. As far as my personal life goes, I don't even want to talk about how pretty much everything about having a relationship with Ally terrified me.

"My point is that life is all about risk. Almost everything worth doing involves taking a risk. And risk is scary. But I know that fear is not a reflection of who I am. There's nothing wrong with being afraid, it's healthy. It's being afraid and not trying that's the problem."

Hazel waved at them. "Okay, my turn. I know your childhood was different than ours. It must have been horrible, watching the rest of us do things that you wished you could, things that you weren't physically capable of. But guess what? You *can* do those things. You've proven that. Fishing, hiking, kayaking, flying an airplane, for crying out loud! Cricket can't stop talking about how fast you picked up on piloting. And yes, even being a mom. You're a natural. Everyone says so."

That made her smile a little. "My plans never included being a parent."

"Plans? Ha. You know what they say about life happening while you're busy making plans?" Hazel went on because clearly this astute cliché didn't call for a response. "Have you ever thought that maybe you've been focused on this plan of yours for so long that you've never taken the time to reevaluate it? That's what your work is all about, right? Watching interest rates fluctuate and wages increase, and the market goes bullish or whatever those indicators are, and you adjust your economic forecast so that people and business and government can plan accordingly."

Iris grinned and repeated, "The market goes bullish?"

"Whatever." Hazel waved a hand. "It's hard to keep up with your ramblings."

Tag's half shrug and conciliatory grin said he agreed.

"My point is that conditions change in our lives and sometimes that means we need to adjust. That's life. Which is exactly what you've been doing this whole time you've been home—working as Tag's office manager, your relationship with Flynn, learning new skills to impress your boss. Even giving Ashley a chance like you did proves that you can adjust. It also proves that you're a risk taker, too, just like the rest of us. And guess what, you also learned that some of these things weren't nearly as bad as you thought they were."

Iris smiled. "Except backpacking. That was actually worse."

"Wait a sec." Hazel's gaze narrowed in on her. "You said, What if *I'm not* a good mom, what if *I can't* handle… Like present tense. You've already made up your mind, haven't you?"

"I pretty much had, but this conversation reinforced it. Thank you, guys, for coming all this way, for caring about me this much. I have the best family in the world, and, if Flynn will still have me, I'm about to add two more members."

Hazel's smile was pure joy. "I can guarantee he'll still have you, Iris. My list does not lie."

Iris returned the smile. "I need to get home." Home? Yep, she realized, Rankins was home. And, with a little maneuvering, maybe Washington, DC, could be, too.

Removing her phone from her bag, she fired off a text to Flynn asking him to call her ASAP.

"Good." Tag sighed with relief. "Because I already bought you a ticket to Anchorage. We weren't above kidnapping you, but I'm glad we don't have to. We leave tonight."

WHEN IRIS BOARDED the plane, Flynn still hadn't answered her text. He was probably busy at the hospital, she told herself. He might not have seen it. She couldn't allow herself to consider the possibility that he might not want to talk to her.

With a stomach awash with butterflies, she turned on her phone when they landed in Anchorage. Nothing. The nervous combination of anticipation and excitement that had been fueling her settled into anxiety and disappointment. Even though it might be what she deserved after the way she'd left.

But she wasn't about to give up. She'd spend the rest of her life making this up to Flynn and Lily.

From the airport in Anchorage it was only a few miles to the private airfield that Tag used, and then a short flight to Rankins. She and Hazel were waiting while Tag prepared the plane when Hazel's phone rang.

Frowning, she answered the call. "Hello?… Yeah, in Anchorage. She's right here beside me…Oh…Okay. Yep, we'll be there as soon as we can." Ending the call, she looked at Iris, and said, "That was Flynn."

"Okay." Why was Flynn calling Hazel?

"He's here in Anchorage."

Iris felt her hopes rise, but why hadn't he called her?

Hazel answered the question before she could ask it. "He's at the hospital with Lily."

"Hospital? What's wrong with her?" Iris felt light-headed. Just when she was ready to step back into Lily's life her worst nightmare was coming true.

"He called me because he didn't want you to panic. He didn't say what's wrong, but he said she's going to be fine."

Fine? There were so many angles to that word. What did it mean? But Iris wasn't panicking. Resolve and determination fueled her now. She needed to be with them.

"We have to go there."

"I know." Hazel nodded, already backing away. "I'll go get Tag."

Flynn met them outside the pediatric unit.

Iris ran toward him. "Flynn, what's wrong with her?"

"It's just a heart murmur."

"Just a heart murmur? That meant surgery for me!"

"I know, but at this point we don't know that it will come to that. But that's why we're here. I ordered some tests and we'll know more when we get the results."

"Where is she? Is she alone right now?"

"Doc is with her. But we can see her, too."

Iris nodded impatiently. "Good, let's go."

Flynn explained that they'd just finished the echocardiogram. When they arrived at the room, Lily was crying, and Iris couldn't get to her fast enough. The nurse finished wrapping a blanket around her and passed her over to Iris, who had no intention of ever letting her go again.

"VENTRICULAR SEPTAL DEFECT," Iris said, repeating the diagnosis. "Same thing I had."

"Yes, but Lily's is small. Dr. Conway and I both feel hopeful that the hole will close on its own within a year. Approximately eighty percent of the time these go away."

"What if it doesn't?"

"There are some options now that are way less invasive than the surgery you went through."

Iris nodded confidently. They'd fix this,

one way or the other. She thought of her mom and dad and how strong they'd been for all of them. She and Flynn would do the same for Lily. Their love would help heal her. Hers and Flynn's, and Doc's and the rest of her family's.

"Iris, are you sure you're up for this?"

"I'm up for this and for whatever else she needs. And for whatever you need, Flynn, if you'll take me back."

Flynn reached for her hand, kissed it and then placed it over his heart. "In here, I never let you go."

Tears burned her eyes. "I'm so sorry I left. I just… I let the fear get to me, but I'm not afraid anymore. Not like that, I mean. I've learned so much about myself and I want to do this. I want to be Lily's mom. Can you forgive me?"

"Of course I forgive you. I knew you'd come back."

"Really?"

"I hoped." He chuckled. "It was the only way I could get through it. After everything you've gone through in the last few months, I just held on to the belief that you'd figure out there isn't anything you can't handle, no fear you can't conquer. I couldn't handle imagining a future without you. I would have broken down and our daughter needed me."

"I tried not to think about it, too. I was so lonely. I missed you guys so much. It made me see that living my life trying to avoid bad things that might happen meant missing all the good stuff, too. I've spent my life doing that and I've missed out on too much. I don't want to do that anymore."

She took a moment to look around and absorb Flynn's words, her emotions. "Let's get married, Flynn, and make it official."

"Okay. Three-day waiting period in Alaska."

"After the last three days of horrible," she said, smiling, "I think the next three will be a breeze."

EPILOGUE

One year later

"HOW DID YOU find out?" Flynn asked Iris as he steered their SUV onto the road leading to Copper Crossing Air Transport.

"Flynn, you should know by now that there are too many people in this family to keep a surprise truly under wraps."

"Who was it?"

As if they were talking to her, one-year-old Lily belted out a "Doc" from the back seat. Lily loved everyone, but it was possible her great-grandfather was her favorite person.

She and Flynn shared a quick laugh before Iris turned and told Lily, "Yes, buttercup, we'll see your Doc soon."

Iris took a moment to enjoy Lily's reaction as the baby let out a squeal and a giggle. Only her mom's cats generated a similar reaction. Lily had Sonya's electric blue eyes, a smile that lit her entire face and a sweet, affectionate disposition. She was so grateful. Facing forward again, she exchanged a grin with Flynn and her heart seemed to expand inside her chest, crowding her lungs and stealing her breath. These were the moments, the seemingly ordinary ones, that got to her the most. Sometimes the love Iris felt for her husband and daughter nearly overwhelmed her.

After a quick stop at Copper Crossing, they were heading to the Faraway Inn, where her family was throwing her and Flynn a surprise one-year anniversary party. At least it was supposed to be a surprise for Iris. Much to her family's disappointment, Iris and Flynn had opted out of a wedding reception the year before. They'd been so focused on Lily, Iris's new job and starting a life together that after marrying at the courthouse, they'd declined an official celebration. Iris kept putting it off, so it really was no surprise that her family had finally taken matters into their own hands and arranged a party without her input.

Iris thought it was an incredibly sweet gesture. But first, they needed to pick up Lily's bag, which Flynn had accidentally left behind the day before when their friend Ashley, who was also Tag's office manager, had babysat Lily for a couple of hours.

Life had finally started to settle down. Lily's heart defect had healed on its own just as they'd hoped. She was healthy and thriving. Their schedule was working out better than they'd anticipated. Iris spent two weeks in DC and two weeks in Rankins, where she worked from home. Flynn flew to DC as much as he could when Iris and Lily were there. Drew and Sebastien babysat Lily in DC, and she and Flynn helped out with Madison in return. In Rankins, Lily had more babysitters than she could use.

The timing was fun, too, because Iris and Flynn had finally found the time to take a delayed honeymoon. They had tentative plans for a trip to Iceland after Flynn finished his residency. But for now, the two of them were heading to Washington, the one on the west coast, for five days to explore Seattle and then do some fishing and kayaking in Puget Sound. With any luck they'd spot some killer whales.

Early the next morning, Iris was flying them to Anchorage where they were catching a commercial flight to Seattle. Her stomach coiled nervously at the thought, but not because of the whales or the flying or any of the other myriad fears that used to plague her. This, she recognized, was normal parental concern. It would be the longest time that Lily had been without either her or Flynn. In her heart, she knew their daughter would be fine. Spoiled even, but in all the best ways while in the care of her family.

"Was it Doc?" Flynn asked. "Did he let it slip?"

"No, actually it was Hazel."

"Hazel?" Flynn repeated in a surprised tone. "Really?"

"I know. Very unlike her to slip up secret-wise. She's been off her game lately and I think something is up with her. We were Skyping and she said, 'I'm so excited to see you.' And I was like, 'See me when? You're not supposed to be home until October.' She probably could have covered it up, but you know how we are with the melding of the minds, I was instantly suspicious. Shay had mentioned our anniversary that morning and I don't know, I just guessed about the party."

"Hmm." Flynn pulled into the parking lot and shut off the engine. "That means she didn't tell you everything then?"

"Everything? What do you mean?"

His enigmatic smile told her something was up. "We're not here to pick up Lily's things. I didn't leave her bag with Ashley. Your brother Tag wanted me to bring you here. He has something for you."

"Oh, no, he didn't?"

Before Flynn could answer, Tag was beside the vehicle, a pregnant Ally with him. They'd just learned that Ally was having twins and her brother was beside himself with happiness.

Tag opened her door. "Hey."

"Hi," Iris answered a bit tentatively.

He waved her out. Ally was already greeting a chattering Lily, unbuckling her car seat. She gathered Lily in her arms and placed a loud smooch on her cheek.

"I have something for you," Tag said, propping one hand on his hip. "Now, I don't want you to think that you're going to get a gift like this on every anniversary. In fact, this really isn't for your anniversary."

Iris shook her head because she could see the airplane sparkling on the runway behind him. He'd obviously washed and polished it for the occasion. "Tag, we talked about this."

Wrapping his arms around her, he gave her a tight hug. "You talked. I disagreed." Stepping back, he said, "Now come and take a look at your new plane."

A ball of emotion settled in her throat as they walked toward the plane.

Iris had been flying for over a year now and loving it even more than she'd thought she would. She had to admit it would be nice to have her own plane to fly her and Flynn and Lily back and forth to Anchorage and beyond at their convenience. They'd talked about exploring more of the state together as a family. After years of avoiding all things Alaska, Iris was enjoying what she'd missed out on as a kid and then overlooked as an adult.

Cricket came out of the office and joined them.

"Hey," she said.

"I couldn't miss this. It's not every day my prized student gets her own airplane."

"What in the...?" Tag's question trailed off when they reached their destination. Bewildered, Tag shook his head and pointed at the side of the plane, his former plane, sitting on the tarmac. Thick black stripes covered the spot where it used to read Copper Crossing Air Transport. Underneath it, in block letters, some words had been added—Property of Iris James.

"That is shameful." Tag glared at Cricket. "What did you use, a giant Sharpie?"

Iris snuffled out a laugh while Flynn stepped closer to inspect the handiwork. "I think it's duct tape."

Cricket slid a hand over his mouth to cover

his laughter. "It wasn't me. Unfortunately. I wish I was that clever." Pulling out his phone, he quickly snapped a couple of photos of the prank.

Laughter erupted from inside the airplane. "Got ya!" Kayleen opened the door, a roll of black duct tape in hand. Anne, Chloe and Summer were right behind her.

"Kayleen!" Iris said, hurrying forward to embrace her friend after she hopped out. "Anne, Chloe, Summer." She hugged each of them. "What are you guys doing here?"

"We're here for our annual Alaska excursion."

"But that's not for a couple more weeks."

"It was originally," Kayleen drawled, "but we had a change of plans."

"Wait," Iris said. "Did you come early for our party?"

"You know about the party?" Ally asked.

Flynn looked at Ally. "Yeah, she figured it out."

Ally huffed an amused sigh. "Sure, she did. I knew she would."

"We did," a grinning Kayleen answered Iris. "We'd planned to come next month. But Anne was chatting with Bering a couple weeks ago and he mentioned your anniversary party and that Tag was giving you your plane today. And, well, we couldn't resist a good surprise." She added a satisfied chuckle and waved a hand at the plane. "This was sort of a spur-of-the-moment thing. We got here and I saw the plane sitting here and it came to me. I confess I have no self-control."

"For which I am so, so grateful," Cricket quipped.

Kayleen looked at Tag. "You could have got-ten it painted first, you know?" she joked. "You think Iris wants to fly around giving you free advertising?"

Tag chuckled. "Stop busting my chops. I in-tend to."

Cricket was gazing at Kayleen in adoration. "Kayleen, will you marry me?"

She belted out a laugh. "You know, I might have considered it if I wasn't too young to set-tle down."

LATER THAT EVENING, after a fun-filled party that had Iris wondering why she'd waited so long to acquiesce, she sat on the deck of their apart-ment above Doc's garage and wondered how to best broach the topic on her mind with Flynn. Their bags were packed, and since they were leaving early in the morning, they'd tucked Lily in at her parents' house, where she'd be staying for the week. She heard the sliding door open behind her.

"Hey," Flynn said, stepping out to join her. "What are you doing out here?"

"Thinking."

He stepped closer, leaned in and kissed her neck. "Good things, I hope?"

"The best things." Iris glanced up and felt her heart swell with love like it always did when she looked at him. "The very best things," she reiterated. "Happy anniversary, Flynn."

He moved around to sit in the chair beside her. "I have something for you." He produced a gift bag. "It's not quite as showy as a new airplane but I think you'll like it."

Iris grinned and thought about Hazel's list. Flynn was a brilliant gift giver, thoughtful and creative. She reached inside and removed two picture frames.

"They're the digital kind." Reaching over, he tapped a button on the side and a slide show began to play. "On this one, there are photos of our life in Alaska to keep at our place in DC." Iris watched photos flash by—baby Lily cuddled in Hazel's arms in the hammock in her parents' backyard, Iris and Flynn kayaking, Lily fishing with Doc, Lily with her new cousin, Augusta, Shay and Jonah's daughter, lying on a blanket. And on it went. Flynn fired up the other frame. "And this one we'll keep here." Photos of their life in DC lit up the screen—Flynn, Iris and Lily at the bagel shop, Lily on the steps of the Lincoln Memorial with Flynn, Lily with Sebastien, Drew and Madison at the National Zoo.

Tears flooded her eyes. "Flynn, it's perfect." She leaned over and kissed him. "My turn." She reached over and picked up a folder from the ground beside her, relieved that Flynn had given her the opening she needed to start this discussion. She handed it to him. "It's not a done deal or anything. I wanted to talk to you first."

Expression a little wary, he opened it, but kept his eyes on her. "What is this?"

"The paperwork to buy Doc's practice."

"Iris, no. We already agreed on this. My residency is almost finished and we decided we'd move to DC. I don't care where we live as long as we're together."

"I know. I know you say that, and I believe you. But I see you, Flynn. I see how much this place means to you, how much you love it here. I know your dream is to be a small-town doctor."

"You love DC. You love your job. You are living your dream, Iris, and I would never take that from you."

"I know, and it just makes me love you more, if that's possible. But my dream has evolved—it's about our dreams now. And I keep thinking, what if we don't move to DC permanently? At least, not right away. I know this commuting is challenging but we're making it work, right? I'm not saying we'll do it forever. Lily might reach a point where she needs to be more settled or we'll get tired of traveling. But let's do it for as long as it works."

"Are you sure about this?" He asked the question carefully, but Iris could see the possibility, the happiness sparkling in his eyes. Flynn had done so much for her, given her so much joy, fostered her courage and given her new dreams. It felt incredible to return the favor.

"I've never been more sure of anything in my life, except for you and Lily. And honestly, I'm not ready to leave this place behind so soon. Not when I'm just learning to appreciate it. With you."

* * * * *

Get 4 FREE REWARDS!

We'll send you 2 FREE Books plus 2 FREE Mystery Gifts.

Love Inspired® books feature contemporary inspirational romances with Christian characters facing the challenges of life and love.

FREE Value Over $20

Get 4 FREE REWARDS!

We'll send you 2 FREE Books plus 2 FREE Mystery Gifts.

Love Inspired® Suspense books feature Christian characters facing challenges to their faith... and lives.

FREE Value Over **$20**

YES! Please send me 2 FREE Love Inspired® Suspense novels and my 2 FREE mystery gifts (gifts are worth about $10 retail). After receiving them, if I don't wish to receive any more books, I can return the shipping statement marked "cancel." If I don't cancel, I will receive 4 brand-new novels every month and be billed just $5.24 each for the regular-print edition or $5.74 each for the larger-print edition in the U.S., or $5.74 each for the regular-print edition or $6.24 each for the larger-print edition in Canada. That's a savings of at least 13% off the cover price. It's quite a bargain! Shipping and handling is just 50¢ per book in the U.S. and 75¢ per book in Canada.* I understand that accepting the 2 free books and gifts places me under no obligation to buy anything. I can always return a shipment and cancel at any time. The free books and gifts are mine to keep no matter what I decide.

Choose one: ☐ **Love Inspired® Suspense Regular-Print** (153/353 IDN GMY5)   ☐ **Love Inspired® Suspense Larger-Print** (107/307 IDN GMY5)

_____
Name (please print)

_____
Address   Apt. #

_____
City   State/Province   Zip/Postal Code

> Mail to the **Reader Service:**
> **IN U.S.A.:** P.O. Box 1341, Buffalo, NY 14240-8531
> **IN CANADA:** P.O. Box 603, Fort Erie, Ontario L2A 5X3

Want to try 2 free books from another series? Call 1-800-873-8635 or visit www.ReaderService.com.

MUST ♥ DOGS COLLECTION

SAVE 30% AND GET A FREE GIFT!

Finding true love can be "ruff"— but not when adorable dogs help to play matchmaker in these inspiring romantic "tails."

YES! Please send me the first shipment of four books from the **Must ♥ Dogs Collection**. If I don't cancel, I will continue to receive four books a month for two additional months, and I will be billed at the same discount price of $18.20 U.S./$20.30 CAN., plus $1.99 for shipping and handling.* That's a 30% discount off the cover prices! Plus, I'll receive a FREE adorable, hand-painted dog figurine in every shipment (approx. retail value of $4.99)! I am under no obligation to purchase anything and I may cancel at any time by marking "cancel" on the shipping statement and returning the shipment. I may keep the FREE books no matter what I decide.

☐ 256 HCN 4331   ☐ 456 HCN 4331

Name (please print)

Address   Apt. #

City   State/Province   Zip/Postal Code

Mail to the **Reader Service:**
IN U.S.A.: P.O. Box 1867, Buffalo, NY. 14240-1867
IN CANADA: P.O. Box 609, Fort Erie, Ontario L2A 5X3

Get 4 FREE REWARDS!

We'll send you 2 FREE Books plus 2 FREE Mystery Gifts.

FREE Value Over **$20**

Both the **Romance** and **Suspense** collections feature compelling novels written by many of today's best-selling authors.

YES! Please send me 2 FREE novels from the Essential Romance or Essential Suspense Collection and my 2 FREE gifts (gifts are worth about $10 retail). After receiving them, if I don't wish to receive any more books, I can return the shipping statement marked "cancel." If I don't cancel, I will receive 4 brand-new novels every month and be billed just $6.74 each in the U.S. or $7.24 each in Canada. That's a savings of at least 16% off the cover price. It's quite a bargain! Shipping and handling is just 50¢ per book in the U.S. and 75¢ per book in Canada.* I understand that accepting the 2 free books and gifts places me under no obligation to buy anything. I can always return a shipment and cancel at any time. The free books and gifts are mine to keep no matter what I decide.

Choose one: ☐ **Essential Romance**
(194/394 MDN GMY7)

☐ **Essential Suspense**
(191/391 MDN GMY7)

Name (please print)

Address   Apt. #

City   State/Province   Zip/Postal Code

Mail to the **Reader Service:**
IN U.S.A.: P.O. Box 1341, Buffalo, NY 14240-8531
IN CANADA: P.O. Box 603, Fort Erie, Ontario L2A 5X3

Want to try 2 free books from another series? Call 1-800-873-8635 or visit www.ReaderService.com.

*Terms and prices subject to change without notice. Prices do not include sales taxes, which will be charged (if applicable) based on your state or country of residence. Canadian residents will be charged applicable taxes. Offer not valid in Quebec. This offer is limited to one order per household. Books received may not be as shown. Not valid for current subscribers to the Essential Romance or Essential Suspense Collection. All orders subject to approval. Credit or debit balances in a customer's account(s) may be offset by any other outstanding balance owed by or to the customer. Please allow 4 to 6 weeks for delivery. Offer available while quantities last.

Your Privacy—The Reader Service is committed to protecting your privacy. Our Privacy Policy is available online at www.ReaderService.com or upon request from the Reader Service. We make a portion of our mailing list available to reputable third parties that offer products we believe may interest you. If you prefer that we not exchange your name with third parties, or if you wish to clarify or modify your communication preferences, please visit us at www.ReaderService.com/consumerschoice or write to us at Reader Service Preference Service, P.O. Box 9062, Buffalo, NY 14240-9062. Include your complete name and address.

STRS19R

Get 4 FREE REWARDS!

We'll send you 2 FREE Books plus 2 FREE Mystery Gifts.

Harlequin® Special Edition books feature heroines finding the balance between their work life and personal life on the way to finding true love.

FREE
Value Over
$20

YES! Please send me 2 FREE Harlequin® Special Edition novels and my 2 FREE gifts (gifts are worth about $10 retail). After receiving them, if I don't wish to receive any more books, I can return the shipping statement marked "cancel." If I don't cancel, I will receive 6 brand-new novels every month and be billed just $4.99 per book in the U.S. or $5.74 per book in Canada. That's a savings of at least 12% off the cover price! It's quite a bargain! Shipping and handling is just 50¢ per book in the U.S. and 75¢ per book in Canada.* I understand that accepting the 2 free books and gifts places me under no obligation to buy anything. I can always return a shipment and cancel at any time. The free books and gifts are mine to keep no matter what I decide.

235/335 HDN GMY2

Name (please print)

Address   Apt. #

City   State/Province   Zip/Postal Code

> **Mail to the Reader Service:**
> **IN U.S.A.:** P.O. Box 1341, Buffalo, NY 14240-8531
> **IN CANADA:** P.O. Box 603, Fort Erie, Ontario L2A 5X3

Want to try 2 free books from another series! Call 1-800-873-8635 or visit www.ReaderService.com.

HSE19R